TRAT-

ALMOST as Long
as ours,

Brotherhood

The Last Saxon Warrior

by

Frank Moran

Brotherhood: The Last Saxon Warrior
by
Frank Moran

All Rights Reserved
Copyright © 2011

ISBN: 978-0-9835729-1-6

Prologue

Two brothers; connected souls. Terry, arrogant and aggressive, is about to face a catharsis both physically and spiritually. Eric, his brother, has been confined to a wheelchair since birth. Afflicted by Cerebral Palsy he lives in a body that can do nothing. He can't speak, or move voluntarily. Only his mind can connect him with his true purpose. A prisoner in his head, his mind takes him back a thousand years to a life as a warrior destined to become a monk who would create a secret society that would remain hidden for a thousand years. He is moving both Terry and himself towards a destiny that can only be completed if they both survive.

Chapter One

The eyes blinked constantly. They were blinking in time to a noise which sounded like a shopping cart moving very fast and clashing against steel railings; steel against steel. The eyes belonged to the impassive face of a young boy, twelve years old, Eric Shepard. He was in a wheelchair that was being pushed at an alarming speed by an older boy of sixteen, Terry Shepard, his brother. Terry was banging the wheelchair into the metal rail that ran along the walls of the hospital corridor. He tilted the chair back on its wheels and yelled, "Charge!"

Eric's eyes stopped blinking. The boy was no longer in a wheelchair, but standing in a muddy battlefield facing a screaming Norman Knight on horseback. The crashing sounds of battle surrounded him. Beneath him, lying wounded was a man whom he was defending. He stood astride the body of the wounded man, an axe in one hand and a sword in the other. There were men dead and dying all around him and thundering towards him were four knights on horseback. The lead knight swung a mace toward his upraised sword. As the sword was pulled from his grasp he reached for the lead horse's bridle and twisted it fast. The horse skidded forward in the mud. The knight leapt from the charger swinging his massive broadsword. Eric ducked under it easily as he spun back to face the knight. Then he froze as the flat of the blade swung towards him. He saw in its reflection a boy in a chair who drooled and jerked like his body was broken. Then the flat of the blade hit him and lifted him off his feet.

His eyes blinked open and Nurse Scott stood in front of the chair holding the armrests firmly. He could hear his brother Terry behind him breathing heavily.

"Let go of the chair," said Nurse Scott. "How can you do this to your brother?"

"He enjoys it," answered Terry. "It's the only excitement he gets in life."

A strange disconnected moan came from the chair as Eric arched up and his body thrashed with muscular spasms.

"Now you've upset him," Terry said as he headed towards the bathroom. "Explain that to Doctor Doolittle." A powerful hand clamped around Terry's arm. "I need to pee, Doc. Let go."

Doctor Emanuel Kissen looked at Terry and spoke slowly. "This has to stop. You could have killed or seriously injured your brother."

"He's already seriously injured, and in my opinion, dead."

"Your brother has Cerebral Palsy. So obviously your opinion is wrong."

"Let go," Terry said as he pulled his arm away and disappeared into the bathroom.

Doctor Kissen followed him in. "Are you purposely being stupid?"

"That would be my brother, doc."

"He is far from stupid."

"How would you know? Does he tell you how clever he is?"

"Where is your mother?"

"She's coming. I ran ahead with blinker as she hates to keep you waiting."

"His name is Eric. Please use it."

"Or what?"

"If you treat him like that again, in this hospital, you'll need the wheelchair."

"I'm a minor, doc. Know what that means? Empty words, idle threats and broken promises. He's a drooling vegetable who can do nothing. What's your excuse?"

Kissen barely contained his anger as he said, "You won't always be a minor. So pee and get out of here before I forget that you are."

Terry brushed past him and walked down the hall. He approached the wheelchair as Eric was being comforted by Nurse Scott and his mother. "I'll be in the cafeteria," he said. "I need some money."

His mother gave him five pounds. As he walked away she threw him a coin as an afterthought. "For the coke machine," she said.

Doctor Kissen was coming down the hallway. "Easy money, Terry?"

Eric watched as the coin spun through the air. It passed his eyes as Terry caught it. Terry looked at Doctor Kissen and said, "I think so. Or is this the day you work for it and cure him?"

Anna Shepard was horrified. "How dare you, Terry!" Eric's eyes stopped blinking as Terry closed his fist around the coin.

The heat and dust stung his eyes as he landed on his back in the ancient churchyard. The eyes of the dead looked on as Eric stumbled alone to his feet to face the boys that had been goading him. Their leader, Cissa, punched him in the face. His nose was bleeding and tears stung his eyes. He punched back and saw the larger boy go down. As he brushed back his damp, straw colored hair from his eyes, he offered his hand to the boy. The boy's father was the local bailiff and lawgiver, the most powerful man in the county, not a good choice for an enemy.

The fallen boy, in his humiliation, picked up a rock from the ground and threw it at Eric screaming, "Damn Farmer!"

Blinded by the rock, Eric staggered back, his hands up in defense. The noise from the screaming boys suddenly stopped and the blood in his eyes prevented him seeing where his opponent was. He staggered back, blinded by pain and anger, more anger at the insult than his cowardly adversary's attack, he said, "Fight on then. I am waiting."

A voice he did not recognize spoke, "You are alone, warrior. Your enemy has run from you. Come to me." Eric moved in the direction of the voice. His vision cleared and he saw the two horsemen; one tall and dark, the other shorter and stockier, built like himself. It was he who had spoken. "Come warrior. Must Harold Godwinson ask a farm boy twice?"

"I am of good blood, sir, and proud to be the son of a farmer."

"Who are you?" Godwinson asked.

"Eric, Lord. My name is Eric Shepard."

"So is your father a man of peace, Eric?"

"My father's sword served King Edward when Godwin brought his armies against him. It came to nothing. The rebels were outnumbered."

"That's true. I was there," Godwinson said. "In fact, all Godwin's sons were.
I think no less of your father for going to the aid of his lord, and no less of you for defending your father."

The other rider was Harold's brother, Tostig. He was less forgiving than Harold. "Put him to the sword or one day his sword will be in your back," he hissed.

"Ride on Tostig, I will join you soon. Listen to me, lad. There are few men would tell me to my face that they support that poisoned old man against the sons of Godwin. One day you will know that Godwin was a good lord who loved England more than Edward could love anything."

"I meant no offense, Sire."

"I take none."

"My mother says that Godwin was too big for England, and King Edward is not big enough."

"Your mother, is she of Mercia?"

"No, my Lord. She was born in Danelaw and is descended from Cnut himself."

Godwinson smiled. "A Viking. I knew it by the way you fought. Listen to me, Viking," he almost whispered. "I, too, am a Northman and one day I will need men like you to fight for me. Will you?" he asked leaning from his saddle.

Eric felt strangely weak. He fell to his knees and said, "I will."

Godwinson sprung from his saddle. "Give me your hand on it, man." Eric took his hand which was strong and calloused and shook slightly. "I shall wait for you, Viking. When you are as tall as yonder cross behind you, there will be a place for you among the housecarls." He mounted his horse and rode off. He turned in his saddle and said, "Why fight in a churchyard?"

Eric called after him, "I have more supporters here."

Godwinson smiled and reached into his pouch and threw a coin to Eric. As it spun in the air he said, "You are a bought man and may not sell yourself to any other lord, agreed?" Eric tried to answer but no sound came as he looked on the face of King Edward on the coin which had been defaced by a dagger. He tried to throw it away but his hands wouldn't move.

Eric's body seemed trapped in some kind of metal chair.

Doctor Kissen said to Anna, "I understand how you feel."

"You can't possibly know how I feel. I have a father at home with Alzheimer's possibly Parkinson's, Eric with his condition and Terry who wants to be a teenager, not a caretaker. My father communicates with Eric on some deeper level and that's as much as I can hope for. So please, give him his check up so we can go home."

"Okay. Anna, will you answer some questions and then I'll examine him?" Eric began banging his head against the back of the chair. "Alright, I hear you, Eric. I'll have Nurse Scott take you to the playroom and get you a drink."

"Check him first, then we'll talk. He's been sitting without attention for too long."

"Good idea." He measured the movements of Eric's arms and legs, then his head and neck. He checked his blood pressure and eye movements. Nurse Scott came in and he asked her to take Eric while he talked to Anna.

Anna stroked his cheek and whispered in his ear, "This won't take long."

Doctor Kissen sat opposite Anna. He began tentatively using his best bedside manner. "Anna, I know you've had explanations. It's tedious, but necessary. Please bear with me. I'm trying to find a way into Eric's mind."

"How will you do that, Doctor? Eric is twelve years old. For ten of those years doctors like you have been giving us hope, but hope becomes heavy when it's obvious you don't know where to start. I know all the terms, the possibilities. Eric's brain is damaged. We don't know how badly. Each case is different, some worse than others. It could have been lack of oxygen. It could be congenital, but who knows? No one, apparently and, if they did, could they fix it? No! So let's not torture us any more than is absolutely necessary."

"Wow! That was quite an attack."

"It's been years in the making, Doctor. However, it's not really against you personally. You can't help. Just admit it and stop wasting our time. It isn't as if it's your fault. It just....."

"Coffee?"

"What?"

"Can I get you a coffee?"

"I don't drink it."

"Can I get you anything?"

"A bigger house?"

"I know you've been through this before."

"Okay," she paused. "Out of curiosity, why are we doing it again?"

"This isn't for you. It's for Eric."

"Fire away."

"Your pregnancy with Eric, was it different from your first?"

"Yes."

"In what way?"

"In a way that won't give you the answer you're looking for."

"Do you feel responsible for his condition?"

"Do you think I am here for therapy?"

"I'm sorry. I didn't mean to upset you."

"Then you should confine your questions to the relevant subject, my son." Anna got up to leave. Terry sped into the office with Eric in the wheelchair.

Doctor Kissen said, "Alright, we can continue this later." He leaned across the chair and stroked Eric's face, "See you soon, Eric."

Anna looked at him and said, "Only if you can stay on the subject, Doctor." Anna and the boys headed for the exit.

Nurse Scott walked up to Doctor Kissen. "That boy is nasty."

"Just hormones, Valerie."

"Yeah? Which hormone is responsible for cruelty, doctor?"

"The same one that's responsible for the secondary sexual characteristics."

As Anna and the boys left the hospital, a man in a priest's collar passed them. He was unusual only in that his face was hard and impassive and his eyes cold as steel. He held the door for them to leave. Eric's eyes flickered across a tattoo on the inside of his wrist that looked like a sword and a rose.

Eric heard the footfalls of a horse walking behind him. As his eyes stopped blinking he turned to look and saw a priest riding towards the village. The local boys were running towards the horseman. Eric was standing outside the churchyard and noticed he threw a larger shadow than the cross he had once fought beneath. As the priest got closer, the boys drew back. His face was scarred and his pale eyes impassive as he rode into the village. His saddle was a warrior's and under his priest's cassock was a strange shape that could only be a sword. As he rode past, looking neither left nor right, Eric fell in behind him watching him with interest. His heart jumped as the man, without turning, spoke.

"Walk ahead of me boy. Lead me to the forge." His voice was as cold as his eyes. As Eric reached for the horse's bridle the man's voice cut through him like steel. "Walk ahead. Do not touch my horse unless you wish to lose your arm. He knows only me." Eric walked ahead in silence until they reached the forge.

Gothrum, the blacksmith, was a fat, lazy, bully of a man. He had a fierce scar on his face from a burn he claimed was caused by his son, Oleg, who worked the bellows or held horses for his cruel father. Oleg had developed a limp shortly after his father's accident. The boy spoke only once of the accident, and his face was so severely bruised afterwards that he never did again.

The stranger reined his horse in front of the forge. Eric was about to speak when the smith said directly to the stranger, "Go away. I am resting."

"My horse has cast a shoe..."

"Ride on," said the smith.

"It must be replaced," said the stranger.

"Must!" screamed Gothrum as he sprang to his feet surprisingly fast for such a fat man. "No one ever tells me what I must do."

The rider, his face expressionless, said, "I will replace the shoe. My horse would kill you."

What happened next was strange to watch. Gothrum reached for the rider's ankle to throw him from the saddle. At the same instant, without any apparent movement or change of expression, the rider took Gothrum's wrist in his hand. Gothrum began to sweat, his face contorted into a mask of pain. He began to cry silent tears like a fat baby. Still the stranger held on. He whimpered and seemed to faint as the rider threw him to the ground. He then vaulted from the saddle. His cassock moved revealing his sword, mail shirt, and a strange scar on his arm like a sword or cross. It looked bloody.

"You're bleeding" said Eric.

"A scratch, nothing compared to the bleeding that will come" said the stranger.

Gothrum' son, Oleg, came limping out of the forge carrying bellows. He saw his father glaring at him. He limped away, dropping the bellows as he passed Eric. Eric reached down and picked them up as the stranger said, "Can you fire the forge boy?" Eric smiled and within minutes they were working together.

The man worked like he had done it all his life, the metal taking perfect form in his hands. Eric was red faced and sweaty, as much fascinated by the tattooed and scarred arms of the warrior as his ability as a blacksmith. As the man shod the horse he glanced at Eric. "You have strong arms, boy. Better you carry a sword than push a plough."

"Is there wealth in carrying a sword?"

"There is gold to be had," said the stranger. He stared at Eric with his stern, pale eyes. "True warriors fight because that is what they want, not the spoils of war, but war itself."

He went to his saddle which he had placed on the ground in front of the forge and withdrew from it a leather pouch. He leaned against it and beckoned Eric to join him. "Drink with me, boy. You worked hard for me." They sat together leaning against the saddle. He opened the pouch and shared his cheese, bread, and from around his neck, a flagon of wine with Eric. "The wine is rough. It's Welsh fare."

"Are you Welsh, sire?"

The stranger laughed, "No, boy, I am not. But I ride from Wales. Godwinson has taken the head of Griffith of Llewellyn. Actually, his own men took it and gave it to Godwinson to save themselves, spoils of war for Holy Edward. He resisted Edward's power like this one resisted my horse's need for a shoe." As he spoke Gothrum appeared and demanded his payment from the stranger.

"I am a King's messenger. Would you like the same fee as the Welshman? He was paid in steel, but lost his head. Come closer."

Gothrum withdrew saying, "No charge for the messenger of King Edward."

The stranger's face and body became ominous and he stood up without seeming to move. "Smith," he said, "I am Saxon. Remember my face for should we meet again it will be the last day you walk the Earth."

Gothrum scurried away head down in the hope his face would not be remembered. The warrior priest turned to Eric and reached into his pouch as if to pay. Eric said, "Sir, I was glad to help you. I ask no fee. I once shook the hand of Earl Godwinson."

"You should have told him you wished to be a warrior."

Eric took the coin from his pouch and showed the defaced coin to the stranger. "I did tell him." The man laughed and pulled a gold chain from within his shirt showing a matching coin. "Who are you, sir?" asked Eric.

"I am a housecarl, and by the coin you hold, a brother Saxon in allegiance to the true King. My name is never spoken. I am known by my stallion, Midnight." At the sound of his name, the stallion reared causing Eric's heart to pound at the sheer physical power. The man rose from the ground and carried the saddle which he placed and adjusted on his horse. "I must go now. Show no one

12

your coin. It could cost you your head." The stranger mounted his horse.

Eric said, "Take me with you so I may serve Earl Godwinson."

The horse reared and twisted in anticipation. The rider spoke almost as if to himself, "I don't know, taking you with me could be a mistake. However, I could take you to Wallingford."

"I will tell my mother I go to seek my fortune."

"I will wait until I have watered my horse. If you do not return, I will ride on."

Eric returned as the rider rode through the gate. "Midnight," Eric yelled and the horse turned. The housecarl pulled Eric up behind him as Midnight reared.

As he crashed to the ground the wheelchair was pulled up by the priest who said to Terry, "You push too hard. Stop!"

Terry replied, "Okay. I've stopped."

"Is this your brother?" asked the priest.

"Yeah, can't you see the resemblance?"

Just then Anna drove up in their van. "Come on Terry. Hurry Up!"

The priest looked into Terry's angry, dark eyes and replied, "Not really, he is brave and you are not." As the priest turned on his heel and walked into the hospital, Terry wanted to say he was as brave as anyone, but watching the priest walk away, he didn't feel it.

Chapter Two

Nurse Scott looked up from behind the nurses' station and almost jumped. Standing before her was a priest and she had no idea how he got there. He had walked the hospital corridor and made no sound. She wasn't even sure he was breathing. "Yes" she stammered.

He smiled. "Thank you," he replied. "But perhaps I should ask a question first."

"I meant how can I help you?" she said.

"I'm here to see Doctor Michael Armstrong, the head of the Oncology Department. May I? That was the question. Now you should say 'yes'."

"You're very funny for a priest."

"You're very nervous for a nurse."

"It's just that you don't look like a priest."

"I know. I look like a boxer because I was, and actually much better than you would think by looking at me. And by the way, you look like a nurse. Maybe it's the uniform and the stethoscope."

"I'll call Dr. Armstrong," she said just as Michael Armstrong appeared from the elevator. "Doctor Armstrong, thank God," she said. "I mean I....."

"Wolf," said the priest. "The Reverend Stan Wolf."

The doctor smiled and reached for the Reverend's out stretched hand. "I saw you from upstairs lifting the boy in the wheelchair."

"Ah, yes. It wasn't really him that needed lifting. It was the other one."

"You mean the older brother," said Nurse Scott. "Yes, that one. You should pray more often, Valerie," said the priest as he scanned her nametag. "You're blushing. He must have been listening."

"Well Father Wolf, let's get up to my office and we can talk about why you are here. Shall we?"

Terry looked back as he pushed the wheelchair into the van. Within minutes they were at the front door of the Shepards' small, semi-detached house. Terry raced to his room to get changed for his soccer practice. Anna took Eric into the living room where her father, Sid Shepard, sat facing the television which wasn't on. He rolled his forefinger against his thumb and hummed as his head shook slightly. Eric began to hum in unison with his grandfather.

"Dad," said Anna. "Let's have some tea. Tea, Dad, alright?"

He seemed to come back from the abyss in his mind and got up to help Anna make the tea. As he passed Eric he said, "And how is my brave boy?" Eric gently rocked back and forth to the sound of the chair squeaking.

He turned for one last look at his village as he sat behind the nameless warrior on a stallion named Midnight. As they approached Wallingford, the housecarl reined in the horse by the banks of a small stream allowing the horse to drink. They sat by the stream and he spoke to Eric about the days to come. He said, "This will be our last talk before we enter Wallingford." Then, almost as an afterthought, "No one would know if you turned back."

"Will I see you?" said Eric.

"Probably not," said the housecarl. "I attend to affairs of State. You will hear of me but it is unlikely we will talk like this or meet unless it is on the battlefield."

Eric felt suddenly alone. His face must have shown it as the housecarl said more gently, "Listen to me. I travel abroad and often alone. You are a new recruit. So we will share a memory of this day, and should destiny decree it, we will meet again."

They left the stream and half a mile outside of the gates the housecarl lifted Eric down from behind him and said, "From here you walk."

As they approached the gates Eric was awed by how formidable the fortress was. The main house was taller than anything in his village and surrounded by a stockade that enclosed many smaller buildings. The stockade had spikes sticking out from different angles more like a place to keep you in rather than keep you out.

The guard opened the gate as they approached. Eric was stunned by the look of the guard. He wore a burnished steel helmet, a chain mail shirt over a muscular body covered by scars and tattoos, by his side he carried a broadsword and dagger and in his right hand a javelin. Eric's thoughts were broken by the voice of the housecarl.

"Judge a man not by what you see. The true man is the spirit, not what he carries, but how he carries himself. It is important to take care of our weapons, they are the tools of our trade, but it is just as important to take care of the men you stand beside, as our trade is war."

"Is that always true, Sire?" asked Eric.

"Nothing is always true," he replied.

As they moved through the gate and it closed behind them, Eric felt his stomach tighten with anticipation. They passed through another inner gate and the noise and activity increased one hundred fold. It was like entering a gladiatorial arena. Men were standing talking bare chested and sunburned. Some were demonstrating axe attacks with willow staves. Others lay against the walls talking. Many were practicing wrestling and axe moves together. Eric felt like he had entered Vallhalla, the Great Hall where Viking warriors who had died bravely were taken. The moment of death was acknowledged by the Valkeries who rode out of Vallhalla to bring back their souls.

"The blacksmith seems no threat now!" said the housecarl.

"I would gladly go back and fight him," said Eric.

"There is no going back," said the warrior. "That chance has passed. You will become a housecarl if they want you."

Eric looked directly at him and said, "They will want me. I'll become one of them or die."

The older man looked at the fiery youth and smiled. "You may do both. These men are wild animals. Dogs of war, they will gain glory, wealth and ultimately what they live for, death on the field of battle. Even now many of them have wealth beyond your wildest dreams, but their wildest dream is a warrior's death."

As Eric looked at his friend's earnest face he once more became aware of the many scars. "Does fate decide which men will die and which will have riches?" asked Eric.

"Riches you will come by easily, death inevitably," he said. As the housecarl looked at him they passed a group of warriors prancing on their toes and moving around each other fast without touching each other. One of the warriors hailed Eric's companion.

"Midnight looks well, my Lord." Eric smiled at the prancing warrior.

"Does that amuse you, boy? Do it hour upon hour after an hour you will wish you could die. They do it all day, then plunge into the river and swim a mile in their chain mail and armor. It hardens their feet, makes their legs strong and their spirit indomitable. It will not amuse you when you have to do it."

"I'm sorry, Sire."

"A housecarl never says he is sorry, so never say it again."

"I don't understand."

"If you make a mistake, find a way to make up for it, even if you must die for it. When a man says he is sorry it is usually a lie. He is afraid and a housecarl must never be afraid. Never refuse battle to anyone. Never walk away until you have won or are dead, in which case you will be carried away."

"I understand, Sire."

"Do you? Our lives are defined by killing and dying. We must meet death as an equal with courage not fear, weakness, or sadness. It is our destiny. I have one last thing to say to you, so listen well. Find a friend and stick with him. Be at his back in battle, or have him at yours. Be beside him in the hall and at his side when you sleep. Death seeks out a single warrior quickly. Only in this way will you survive your chosen path. You will be tested sorely here, just as they might test an axe. They will try to make you weep. You must not. To make you afraid and you cannot be afraid. It is their way of knowing they are taking a man into their company. Their lives depend on it, as will yours." He wheeled his horse and looked back at Eric. "I must attend the King."

"Which king?" Eric joked.

The warrior stared at him. "There is only one king. Remember that once you walk through that door or you will never walk out." Wulfstan hammered on the oak door and Eric trembled as it swung open.

He gazed into his grandfather's face who said, "Come back, sleepy head. We've made tea and I've got you a special straw."

Eric blinked at his grandfather and arched in his chair emitting a sound between a laugh and a sage sounding, "aaha," as if to say, "ah, yes, the special straw."

Sid sat beside him as Anna returned with the tea and biscuits for afternoon tea in the Shepard household. She placed the tea between her and her father on the coffee table. Sid reached for the special straw and cup for Eric and managed to connect the two with a little difficulty.

"Here we are," he said as he held the cup to Eric's lips. "Did you notice how the straw fought before it would fit in the cup, and the cup was shaking? I told you it's a special straw, so hold on tight with your lips. No telling what might happen next."

"It would make no difference to him what happens next," said Terry as he crossed the room in his soccer outfit. "He knows nothing about what goes on in the world."

"Maybe he knows a lot about what goes on in his own world," said Sid.

Terry crunched on a biscuit and picked up his teacup. Anna came in from the kitchen as Terry stood up. "Come on, Mum. I'll be late."

"Is it just a practice match?" said Anna.

"Do you think that makes it okay for me to be late?"

"No, Terry. Meet me outside and I'll have you there in minutes."

"Okay. Don't be long talking to Granddad. See you," he said as he kicked the soccer ball against the door. It slammed against the wood.

Eric stopped blinking and gazed in wonder at the Great Hall.

"Come boy," the sentry said as he marched Eric into the Great Hall. "There are two other halls just like this one," said his escort. It was big enough to seat five or six hundred warriors. There was a huge hearth that a man could walk into easily. Although by the look of the intense fire, it would not necessarily be wise to do so. The walls were covered with rich tapestries and weapons and armor of all types. As he gazed in awe the hall fell silent. A voice suddenly roared.

"Farmer, have you come to feed the pigs?" The Great Hall erupted into laughter. Eric stood still and let the anger he felt wash over him, and in the silence that followed he answered the warrior.

"I fear you must feed yourself. Perhaps when you are ready for market I can help with the butchering." The giant that leapt across the table moved like lightening and in his hand flashed a gleaming war axe that Eric knew was going to end his life. It whooshed past his ear like a tree felled in a storm as it jarred into the central post behind him.

The silence that followed made him think it had cut off his ear and he was deaf. He stood his ground, unsure if the earth was shaking or his legs from fear. The silence was broken by the warrior's raucous laughter as he clapped him on the back driving his already palpitating heart into his mouth.

"Come eat," said the warrior. "You have more heart than muscle, but soon that will change."

The talking, jesting and laughter resumed and Eric had met his axe friend, Grimm, a name he wore easily. Time went by slowly at first and Eric would find himself sitting by the stockade ready to climb it and escape to his home to see his mother and father. As the days and challenges became greater, he found that time began to move faster. Endless days of practice with the axe, sword, stave, wrestling, lifting and running with logs, swimming a mile in full armor until they challenged each other to swim farther and fight harder.

Eric sat by his friend Grimm who said, "Come, eat more. You slow down."

"Soon you will be ready for market," laughed Eric. He looked at his friend and remembered his first night eating in the Great Hall as one of the old warriors bid him bring the spit from the flames with a half-eaten hog on it. He did not look to Grimm then, as he knew all eyes were on him.

He had walked the length of the Hall feeling the warriors watch him. As he stood before the massive fireplace the heat seared his eyelashes. He reached in and gripped the spit and lifted it off the rack. Immediately his hands blistered. The pain sent spasms through his arm muscles as he turned to walk back the length of the Hall. The smell of the roasted pork and his burning flesh assaulted his senses. He walked towards the old warrior resisting the urge to run or drop the spit. Sweat was running down his face and dripping into his eyes. The warriors were silent as he passed and laid the spit in front of the old warrior. A wave of admiration passed through the hall like a wind.

The old man said, "I had a son, he died in battle. If you wish, I will take you as my son."

"I have a father, sir. He awaits me in Mercia, but I thank you. I am honored."

The old man said nothing and walked away. Grimm put his arm around his shoulders and said, "Come with me, young friend." Eric followed obediently as his hands had swollen to twice their size. Grimm took him to the river and told him to hold his hands under the water. He then put hog fat on the wounds and bound them tight. Eric felt sick. "Two days and you'll have your hands back."

"I don't think I'll ever get my hands back but who cares, as long as they work."

"C'mon," said Grimm. "Let's get some rest." They entered the Great Hall as the warriors were beginning to prepare for sleep. Grimm slammed the door.

Eric opened his eyes. "I'm sorry," said Sid. "I tripped."

Eric could feel the intense cold. Anna had icepacks on both his hands as Sid had tripped spilling his hot tea on Eric's left hand and knocking Eric's cup from the holder onto his right hand.

"It's okay, Dad," said Anna. "The ice will help and I'll call and ask the doctor to see him tomorrow. There now, Eric, is that better?"

Eric just moaned and twisted except it sounded like he said, "Oh, God."

"Dad, why don't you just watch some T.V.? I'll take Terry to his game and be back in a couple of hours."

Sid smiled his guileless smile and said, "Okay." He stroked Eric's hair. Anna gave him the remote for the T.V. and the remote for his comfy, electric easy chair and left. She got into the van as Terry kicked the ball against the door.

"I'll be late thanks to you. I may even be stuck on the bench for the whole game. Thanks for nothing!"

"Terry, I don't know why you are always so angry. I'll explain to your coach. Granddad spilled tea on Eric's hands. I had to see to that first."

"Is it serious, I mean bad burns?" said Terry.

"I don't think so. I'll call Dr. Kissen when I get back."

"Doctor God," said Terry. "Thinks he knows everything, but can tell you nothing."

"That's enough, Terry."

"It might be for you, but my geriatric grandfather and imprisoned brother may need a little more."

Anna braked and began to cry silently as they arrived at the soccer field and Terry leaped from the van to join in the game. She sat for a moment to compose herself, then got out of the van and walked over to the coach. "Hi, Bob, sorry we're late. Little problem at home."

"It's okay, Anna. It's only a practice. Everything okay with Eric?"

"Oh, yes, he's fine. My dad spilled his tea. His hands shake and he forgets what he's doing."

"Well, don't worry, Anna. Your hands have been full for a very long time. Maybe next week I can pick Terry up and save you some running around."

"Thanks, Bob." As the game began, Anna watched Terry play. She was concerned by the intensity of his aggression. Everything he did seemed driven by anger. When he stopped he was almost always ready to collapse into an exhausted sleep. As they drove home, Terry slept beside her. Anna decided she would ask Doctor Kissen his opinion of Terry's increasingly strange behavior.

As they entered the living room, Sid sat in front of the T.V. He was pressing the remote for the chair which was going up and down in an even frequency. "T.V. is broken," he said to no one in particular. Eric moaned quietly in his wheelchair.

Anna said, "Wrong remote, Dad," and in one simultaneous action switched the remotes.

"Oh! It's okay now," said Sid. "Chair feels funny, though."

She went into the kitchen and called to Terry, "Are you hungry?"

"No," he replied, "Tired. I'm going to bed." As he walked away he switched the remotes back. The T.V. went off and the chair began its rhythmic ascent and descent. Sid said, "TV's off, but the chair feels okay."

Chapter Three

Anna put Eric to bed. She sat him upright and she talked to him about the soccer game and Terry, how well he played, and his increasing anger at everything. Eric shook his head and moaned gently. She looked in on Terry before going to bed. She was shocked by a giant bruise on his shoulder. She closed the door and called to speak to Doctor Kissen.

"I'm sorry to call so late, but we had an accident with Eric. His hands were burned by hot tea and I wondered if..."

"Bring him in. Wait, is he comfortable now or do I need to see him?"

"No, Doctor, he's resting. I have iced his hands and he seems to be sleeping normally."

"Bring him in first thing tomorrow. I'll be here by 8:oo a.m., or page me if you need me earlier. You have my number. Now you go and get some rest."

"One other thing, Doctor. I wanted to ask you about Terry."

"Ah, yes, Terry. What about him?"

"After his soccer game tonight he had a very severe bruise and seemed exhausted. Not in the normal way. I mean..."

"Oh, Anna, I don't think you need worry about that. I'm sure he gives as good as he gets. Soccer is a rough game and quite frankly, he's quite a rough boy."

"That's what I mean. He wasn't always like that. Now he is very angry and seems very violent when he plays. It's not just the game. It's everything he does. Even at home if he isn't sleeping he is always mad at something.

He bruised himself and it seems worse than a normal bruise."

"Alright, Anna, bring him in. I'm sure that will delight him, but if he won't let me see him, I'm sure I can get him checked out. He's probably run down. By the way, how is your father?"

"To tell the truth, he seems to be deteriorating fast. He accidentally spilled the tea on Eric's hands."

"Well, it must be about time for his check up. I can call Don Goldberg and we'll see everyone tomorrow."

"Let me think about it, Dr. Kissen. I don't know if I can manage all the boys on the same day."

"I think the question is whether I can manage them all on the same day. Bring Eric, anyway, and if possible Terry and Sid. See you in the morning. But get some rest."

"It's Midnight!" Eric yelled. As he turned, the stallion came crashing through the gates carrying its nameless rider. As Eric ran towards Midnight Grimm tripped him. Eric rolled and got to his feet in a killing rage. He spoke menacingly to Grimm, "You'll pay for that, Dane."

"Move," said a voice from above.

Eric was again knocked off his feet as Midnight and his rider almost rode over him. As he got to his feet for the second time he looked first at the horseman who had ignored him, then at his axe friend who spoke just one sentence, "He's not your friend."

Eric picked a quarter staff from the rack that lined the wall of the stockade and moved to the center of the practice area. He had a bruise on his cheek and blood on his nose from one or both of his falls. Grimm looked at him, picked up a quarter staff and said, "Oh, you don't wish to talk right now."

26

Eric lunged at him with the weapon. Grimm blocked the blow and moved away easily bouncing on the balls of his feet. Eric held the staff in the center gripping it tight with anger, his feet planted firmly on the ground. "Stand and fight you coward," he yelled in anger. Now all the housecarls in the compound closed in to watch. No one had ever called Grimm a coward, at least no one still living.

"Perhaps if you think before you act or speak we could end this without you having a headache."

"I won't listen to you ever again!" yelled Eric.

"Then again," said Grimm, "perhaps not."

Eric charged forward attacking high to the left, changed direction, aimed low at Grimm's legs. Grimm continued to parry, then suddenly swung at Eric's head. Eric ducked under the staff and lunged forward. Grimm, who seemed off balance, stopped, pulled his staff back fast and hit Eric a glancing blow on the forehead with the end of the staff.

Eric opened his eyes slowly, his head pounding. Grimm had placed cool, linen rags on his head and cleaned his battered face. As he sat looking at Eric he spoke. "Now that you have the headache will you listen?"

"What," said Eric.

"He is Earl Wulfstan. His father wanted him to enter the priesthood and sent him to the monastery at St. Albans and then to Rome to study Latin and Greek. After his father died, he gave up his title and his name and became a housecarl in the service of the King. I mean, Harold Godwinson, he recognizes no other. He is the only one who could challenge Godwinson if he chose. Like his allegiance to the King, such things are said in whispers. Otherwise it is treason to Edward."

"He said his name is never spoken," said Eric.

"It isn't, but that doesn't mean we don't know what it is or who he is."

"I wish you had just told me that," said Eric nursing his head.

"I tried, right up until you called me a coward in front of the King's men and the second most powerful man in England."

Eric smiled, "That was stupid."

"I think you are coming to your senses," said Grimm. He smiled, "Remember, you must never approach the King or his earls. They will approach you. Rest, I'll bring you some bread, cheese and wine."

"No wine," said Eric, "water, but first I must sleep."

"Come on, sleepy head. Let's go. Doctor Kissen is waiting for us." Eric's eyes shot open as he looked for a friend named Grimm but was unable to tell anyone because he couldn't talk, walk, move or look happy or sad. All he could do was think.

As Anna pushed him along the hospital hallway he watched the lights flicker past and wished that Terry were pushing him so he could descend into that other life of ancient soldiering and maybe never come back to this body which imprisoned his soul and mind so that all he could do was watch life while other people lived it. Terry always angry, Mom always sad and tired. Even Granddad lived it more than he did, he could move.

"Where are we going?" quipped Sid from his hospital wheelchair that was being propelled by Terry towards Doctor Kissen's office.

"To see Doctor Death," answered Terry.

Anna Turned to Terry imploring, "Please, Terry, don't do this. It's already difficult and I can't take much more."

"Okay, Mom. I'm sorry. I just can't help it sometimes. My life makes me angry."

"Mine, too", thought Eric as Nurse Scott came out from behind her station to help Anna.

"Well," said Nurse Scott, "you've brought the troops. Mrs. Shepard, let me take Eric in first. I'm sure Doctor Kissen is waiting for him."

"Well, now at least he has a reason," said Terry. Anna looked at Terry and told him to take Sid to the cafeteria until she came to get them. "Fine," said Terry speeding away with his grandfather in the wheelchair.

Sid yelled, "Ho, ho," but his face looked like he was in the path of a locomotive.

Doctor Kissen gently unwrapped Eric's hands. "You did a great job, Anna. The burns are superficial. We'll wrap them for a couple of days and give him a little liquid analgesic for the pain."

"How bad is the pain, Doctor Kissen?"

"I imagine it's the same for him as it would be for you or me. The worst is over, Anna. The ice was the right thing to do. Just keep an eye on him and keep me posted. Okay, let's see Terry." Doctor Kissen ruffled Eric's hair and walked across and called Nurse Scott from the doorway. "Valerie, could you go to the cafeteria and get Terry and Sid? Send Terry in and you take care of Sid until Doctor Goldberg arrives."

Within a few minutes Nurse Scott ushered Terry into the room.

"Have a seat, Terry. Tell me what's been going on."

"Nothing, really. I get tired a lot, bruised a lot, and I'm angry a lot of the time." "Any idea why?" asked Doctor Kissen.

"No, have you?"

"Well, not yet," said Doctor Kissen

29

"I think it's the Internet," said Terry.

Doctor Kissen looked at Terry expecting trouble and got it. "What do you mean?"

"Terry, please be polite," Anna interjected.

"Its fine, Anna, I want to hear what Terry has to say."

"All the information I could possibly need is on the Internet. As a result, doctors like you don't answer questions, you ask them. Isn't that true?"

"Part of what you say is true. A doctor's entire career from student to physician is all about asking questions. Sometimes the questions a patient asks, the doctor can't answer but if the patient can answer the questions the doctor asks, it may provide a clue as to what the problem might be."

"That sounds like more double talk to me. Before the Internet you were all little gods with the power of life or death over humanity. Now your secrets are out in the open and when you can't provide an answer, or provide the wrong answer, Internet research can do what all you money grubbing demi-gods can't."

Anna turned white and tried to speak. Doctor Kissen raised his hand. "Please Anna, let him finish."

"I'm finished," said Terry.

"Alright, may I speak now?"

"Yes," Terry said as he stood up.

Doctor Kissen looked at Terry. "You know there is a frightening power in being able to heal the sick, but it is more frightening to know that sometimes we can't. I can say for myself I have never felt godlike, but have often been grateful to Him for allowing me the grace to do what I do. It seems to be the only place where God and I communicate. I don't have all the answers and neither does the Internet; like a scalpel or stethoscope it is merely a tool. I can't honestly say what is wrong with you, but I would like you to see a friend of mine whose expertise is another branch of medicine."

"Is he an oncologist?" said Terry.

"Why do you ask?"

"Because I have leukemia. I spent most of last night on the Internet."

Anna stood up and fainted. Doctor Kissen called in Nurse Scott and asked Terry to sit down. "Valerie, get Anna some air." Nurse Scott helped Anna outside. Doctor Kissen turned to Terry. "I don't know for sure, but you could be right. My colleague is the best in his field, and you have many of the symptoms. It can be cured, but we must work together. Can we have a truce?"

"A truce for the truth doc, I don't want to be treated like Eric."

"On my oath as a physician, Terry, I am doing my best for Eric, and Doctor Armstrong will do his best for you." Doctor Kissen called Doctor Armstrong, "Mike, I have a young man in my office I'd like you to see as soon as possible. Right now would be great. I'll send him up. He's on the tenth floor, Terry, ten twenty." Anna returned with Nurse Scott. "Terry, would you get the elevator while I talk to your mom?" Terry headed for the door kissing Anna on the cheek as he passed her.

"Where is he going?"

"He is going to see a colleague of mine and you're going with him." Terry waited by the door. "I'll take your father along to see Doctor Goldberg and Eric can stay with us until you come down. Mike Armstrong is a good man. He will answer your questions better than I can. Come back here when you are finished upstairs and don't worry, I won't lose your father."

"He can do that without your help," said Terry.

Anna went to the elevator with Terry. As the metal doors opened the priest Terry had spoken with yesterday stepped out past them. The elevator doors closed and the priest smiled at Nurse Scott as he leaned over and spoke to Eric.

"Well, Sir Knight, can you hear me?" whispered the priest into Eric's ear.

The great hall was silent and Eric answered, "I hear and will obey you". All of the housecarls stood in silence as he swore his oath of allegiance to the King. The captain bade him place his hands on the blade of his sword.

"I am the King's man until death," he said and a roar went up from the warriors as his armor, sword and axe were placed on his body. Each man gave him some valuable gift, a goblet encrusted with precious stones, a priceless dagger, the gifts and gold were piled high. Eric was overcome with emotion.

Grimm smiled and said, "This is your fortune. Guard it well for such riches come once in man's lifetime." He raised his drinking horn and called out loudly, "Eric, the last of the King's first housecarls!"

There was a great cheer rose from the Hall with much thumping and banging on the tables as the great oak door smashed open and a warrior fell from his horse and stumbled to the fire in the Great Hall. "Godwinson has betrayed us and taken the oath of William, Duke of Normandy. He is backing the Norman's claim to the Throne of England."

Eric awoke the next morning with Grimm's hand shaking his shoulder. "Get up. Pack your treasure chest and send it to your father. War is coming and we must be ready."

Eric spoke to the warrior that had brought the message of Godwinson's betrayal. His name was Gareth and he was a London housecarl fiercely loyal to King Edward, with little regard for the sons of Godwin.

"I hear you travel to Mercia," said Eric.

"I do," he replied.

Eric explained that his family was of Mercia and he asked if Gareth would deliver his personal chest to his father.

"I will," said Gareth. "I will guard it as I would guard the King's gold. I travel with twelve of the King's men to Edwin, Earl of Mercia, to deliver the news of Godwinson's actions."

"A good choice of words, Captain," said Eric.

"I know Godwinson's man when I see him. Load the chest. Your father will have it in two days." Eric offered him a beautiful dagger of burnished steel. The grip was inlaid with a gold and leather. "Keep it," said Gareth. "War is coming and I may have to return it to you blade first." He smiled at Eric and called out to his men, "Ride out, Edwin awaits us."

Grimm put his arm around his shoulder and said, "Rich yesterday, poor today. You made and lost a fortune faster than any man I know."

Eric smiled and said, "My father will have more use for it than I will."

Eric opened his eyes and heard his mother sobbing next to his bed. What can be wrong he wondered. Anna wiped her eyes and said, "Good morning. Your hands look much better this morning. I have to see Terry and Doctor Armstrong this morning, but Granddad and Aunt Jennifer will be with you until I get back." She kissed him on the forehead and went into the kitchen.

Eric could hear the sounds of Anna making breakfast and Granddad sitting in his chair humming. "What's wrong with Terry" he thought, "and why is he with a doctor? What happened? The priest seemed to know something, but what? How can I tell them I'm in here and alone, and more afraid of this being real than dying on a battlefield."

The front door of the house opened, then closed and Eric could hear his Aunt Jennifer talking in hushed tones to his mother. Suddenly she swept into the room and hugged him, sat him up and proceeded to wash his face and comb his hair. Eric loved when his aunt got him ready for the day, although he was never sure why. Just a strong feeling with no way of knowing why he had it. As she dressed him and sat him in his wheelchair, he breathed in that fresh clean scent that reminded him of something else, but he couldn't remember what it was.

"Come on, handsome, time for breakfast," she said as she wheeled him to the kitchen table and he smelled all the food he had never tasted. Eric sat at the table in his wheelchair swallowing the kind of food that had been fed to him since he was a baby. He knew it was because he was unable to chew. In his mind he could chew. He had tried and awakened in that other time and place.

Anna kissed Eric and Sid then left the house, the door slamming behind her. Suddenly the door opened again and she was standing there. "Sorry, Jen, I am so used to rushing I forgot about you. If you need me, call me. I'll be with Doctor Armstrong and Terry. Thanks for the help."

"It's okay," said Jennifer, "we're on the same wavelength. See you later."

Anna closed the door and left. Eric could still smell the faint lemon and peppermint scent of Jennifer as she moved about the house talking to Sid and then to him as if either of them could answer. Sid tried but gave up as the words he searched for eluded him.

"Alzheimer's and Parkinson's are an interesting combination, Dad, like Cerebral Palsy. Interesting means sorry, we don't know what to do," said Jennifer as she chattered on assuming only she was listening.

Chapter Four

"Are you deaf?" a feminine voice asked.

"Answer," said Grimm.

"No, your Highness, I did not see you alight from the litter."

"Who are you?" she said.

"Eric Shepard, your Majesty, housecarl at your service."

"Which house?" said a thin voice.

Eric looked into the face of King Edward and was shocked. He looked both ancient and strange. Standing beside him his queen, Edith of Wessex, Harold Godwinson's younger sister, was as youthful and beautiful as Edward was ancient and dried up. The king sat in an elaborate chair that had been brought for him. His queen stood at his side, vibrant and sensuous. Eric was in love. As she moved he could smell lemon and peppermint. "I am of Mercia, but a Wallingford Carl, Sire."

Edward looked into his eyes. It was a strange feeling. Eric thought he looked like he was already dead, those pink, pale eyes and thin, wispy hair. The King looked away and continued to speak. "My most loyal subjects, I came to you personally to allay your fears. Duke William means us no harm. There will be no war. Normandy is our friend."

Grimm said in a loud, clear voice, "He is no friend of ours, Edward, but we judge friendship differently from kings."

The King's housecarls of London moved forward. The captain next to Grimm loosened his war axe. Eric did the same and there was an ominous silence that followed the distinct sound of weapons unbuckled for combat.

Edward broke the tension by looking at Grimm and saying, "Duke William will not bring an army to these shores."

"Do you give us your word as King?" asked Grimm. The London carls prepared to move forward.

Edward raised his hand and beckoned Grimm forward. "Fear not, my friend," he said. "Step forward." The Wallingford carls laughed at the thought that Grimm would fear anything. As he stepped forward Eric stepped with him.

The King looked at Eric and said, "If he dies, will you die with him?"

"He won't die today, Sire, nor will I."

Edward stared at him with that strange, vacant look and said, "I need men like you closer to me. Will you come to London?"

Grimm and Eric spoke as one, "No, Sire, we are happy here."

"Happiness is but a moment of respite in a world of turmoil," said Edward.

"What of my question, Sire?"

"I answered once, that should be enough," he said waving his hand in dismissal.

Grimm and Eric withdrew to the parade ground as food was brought for the royal party. They passed within a few feet of the Queen. Eric glanced up quickly and caught her gaze as she looked directly at him. As he turned away the scent of lemon and mint permeated the air. Within the hour the Royal Party had gone. The King commanded the housecarls to fast from dawn until dusk, from Ash Wednesday to Easter Sunday, and pray henceforth from dusk until dawn for the safety of England. It was late in the year 1064. Ash Wednesday was six weeks away. It promised to be an austere winter and lean new year.

"By Ash Wednesday we'll have a new king," said Grimm, "so don't worry about fasting. Praying, on the other hand, is our duty, especially if it speeds up the coronation of the new king."

The carls gathered together at sunset to pray as the King had commanded. Eric closed his eyes as the tension of the day slipped away from him and he joined in the murmur of prayer. The smell of the hard packed earth was replaced by that strange feeling again.

He opened his eyes as his Aunt Jennifer kissed his forehead and said, "I think we'll go inside. It's getting chilly." She pushed his wheelchair up the ramp into the kitchen and took him into the living room where Sid sat watching Oprah clicking his remote as his chair moved back and forth in an easy rhythm.

Anna came in a little later, she walked into the living room and automatically exchanged the chair remote for the T.V. remote and the channels clicked by as Sid surfed for a picture to catch his attention. She smiled halfheartedly at Jennifer who said, "I'll make some tea, you talk. Sit down, Anna."

Anna sat down and said, "It's Leukemia, but it's complicated, of course. I spent the day with Doctor Armstrong and the priest, Father Wolf. He is coming over tonight to talk to me. If you can, Jen, would you stay and listen?"

"Of course I will. I want to know as much as you do."

Anna paused then began to speak, "Terry has a combination of two types of Leukemia. It rarely happens that someone would get such an odd combination, Acute Myeloid Leukemia and Acute Lymphoblastic Leukemia. What's worse is now that he knows he has it he seems worse, less energetic, less angry, more damaged and less Terry. It's karma. I must be paying for something I did in a former life."

Jennifer smiled and said, "Hold on a minute. You are not ill, Terry is. Therefore, if you believe that twaddle, then it's him that's paying, and if you ask me it has nothing to do with a former life."

"Meaning what?" asked Anna.

"Meaning he has been quite a handful in this life. Maybe this will allow him time to change."

"He could die!" yelled Anna.

"He could also live," said Jennifer.

"He isn't like the kids you teach," said Anna. "They have learning disabilities and behavioral problems. Terry isn't like that. He's bright."

Now it was Jennifer's turn to pause. "Anna, I am not arguing with you. Terry is bright, but like many of my kids his behavior may be linked to his illness."

"Is that true?"

"According to what I've read it's possible."

Continuous knocking in the background caused them to turn and look towards the front door. Jennifer walked to open the door which was already open. Standing there knocking very theatrically was the Reverend Stan Wolf.

"Good evening. Is this the home of Anna Shepard?"

"It is," said Jennifer. "I'm her sister. You must be Father Wolf."

"That sounds like something out of Red Riding Hood."

"The Shepard or the wolf?" said Jennifer.

"Amusing, the wolf, of course. Call me Stan." He smiled and said, "I'd prefer it to Father."

"I can see why you would," said Jennifer. "Come in or rather close the door as you appear to already be in."

"Thanks. Nice to meet you, too," he said.

"This way to the kitchen. Anna is expecting you."

"Do you have a name or should I just call you sister?"

"Jennifer, although sister is a name I'm sure you've used frequently."

"Only with nuns. You're not a nun are you?"

"Stan, thanks for coming. No, she's not a nun. She teaches children with learning and emotional disabilities, which is interesting because I know she comes across as having similar problems."

"Anna thinks I talk too much and ask too many questions."

Stan smiled and said, "Maybe I can help with some of the answers. It's why I'm here."

"How are you involved?" asked Jennifer.

"Jennifer, if you don't mind...."

"It's fine, Anna. I'd like to explain," said Stan. "I'm from Sheffield. I used to have a parish close to a steelworks factory. People in my congregation began to fall ill, children developed Leukemia. I began to pursue the disease and it became," he paused, "my obsession I suppose. I'm connected with many expert physicians in the field and I find myself a bit of a latter day crusader in a cause that I believe in."

"I still don't see how you are involved in Terry's case."

"In Sheffield fourteen of my parishioners had Leukemia. Ten of them were under sixteen years of age. The other four were adults. The children are all in remission, three of the adults died. I'm involved because I think I can help. There are many steps to be taken and I'd like to make sure Anna doesn't miss any."

"Is part of your solution the power of prayer," Jennifer said staring into his cold, uncompromising eyes.

"Only for me," he replied. "The other part is finding the type of Leukemia, environmental or other factors, and the right physician and facility for the job." He stood up, looked at Anna and said, "I will be in Mike Armstrong's office this week. Call me if you would like me to help with Terry." He said to Jennifer, "Nice talking to you." As he turned to leave he saw Eric sitting and rocking in his wheelchair. Sid was watching something historical on T.V.

The voice over said, "Harold Godwinson, King for ten months…" and Eric stopped rocking and was silent.

"Look," said Grimm, "Godwinson."

He came riding into the stockade with his brothers and his men. The four earls were a little tipsy from wine. Tostig, Harold's brother, was the first to see the kneeling housecarls. He began to laugh with such gusto that it caught the others like an infection. He was laughing so hard that he fell from his horse and was unable to get up. As he knelt with tears streaming down his face he bellowed, "Alright, where is he?" and he fell back roaring anew with laughter,

"Who?" asked Grimm.

"Edward, you great ox. Why else would you be praying?" The brothers raised him to his feet and ordered a goblet of wine, which they literally poured down his throat to end his laughing fit. The housecarls were now all on their feet embarrassed by his laughter.

"We pray for England," said Grimm.

"As ordered by whom?" said Harold.

"Edward," said Grimm to which Tostig began his laughter anew.

Harold looked to his younger brothers, Gyrth and Leofwine. They immediately took their axes to a barrel of wine. As it sprayed across Tostig he picked it up and drank. The wine poured down his throat, his beard and his chest. He dropped the barrel with a loud, "Ahh," and promptly passed out. The brothers carried him to the long house.

Godwinson turned back to his housecarls. "I'll give you a prayer," he said. "William the Tanner will not raise his banner in English air as long as the sons of Godwin breathe it."

A mighty roar rose from the throats of the housecarls as they thumped their spears and war axes, dying for Harold Godwinson would be easier than living without him as their king.

In the Great Hall that night there was much drinking and feasting. Eric watched as Godwinson shared his drinking horn with his warriors and they shared theirs with him. Eric stood up and walked to where Godwinson sat joking, drinking and telling tales. He was about to speak of a time long past when Earl Godwinson had given him the defaced coin, when an older housecarl stood up and spoke. It was Thorfinn, the old housecarl who had sent him to pick up the spit from the fire.

Thorfinn said, "I have a question. You may see it as a complaint. Either way I will have it answered."

"Well," said Godwinson, "ask, or have you forgotten?" A loud round of laughter followed Godwinson's comment.

"Laugh on, Harold, I can wait. I saw your father teach you humility as a boy, maybe you still have some as a man."

"Ask your question, carl."

"Why did we carls of Wallingford not fight at your side in Wales against Griffith of Llywellen? You took Edward's men. Look around you. We are your men, not sheep who await the whim of the butcher."

Tostig, who sat bleary eyed, said to the old carl, "That's exactly what you are."

Harold threw a menacing glance which silenced Tostig and the laughter of his brothers, Gyrth and Leofwine. He stood and faced the old housecarl. "Thorfinn," he said smiling, "You and the men of Wallingford are my battleaxe. Should I use you to cleave wood? No, my old friend, the men I took to Wales were Edward's men. I took them for a reason." Thorfinn smiled pleased and surprised that Godwinson would even know his name.

"The reason I used Edward's men is simple. I used my enemies against Edward's enemies. When the men of Wallingford ride to war, it will be to gain a kingdom. When we ride to war together we will ride back victorious or lie together on the field of Battle." The carls stood and cheered on the edge of frenzy. Eric had walked up to Godwinson, but now there was so much cheering and singing of battle hymns he turned to walk away. A voice spoke gently behind him.

"Eric Shepard, do you still carry a coin for a King?"

He turned to look on the face of Harold Godwinson. "I do, my Lord, but even without it my pledge to you is written on my heart."

Godwinson smiled at Eric and reached for his drinking horn. "And mine to you," he said as he emptied the draught with his head back. The hall erupted into cheers and singing and Grimm looked at Eric and raised his horn. When Eric looked back at Godwinson he was gone. He went back and sat beside Grimm.

"He remembered me," Eric said.

"He has an uncanny way about him," said Grimm.

"What will happen next?" said Eric.

"Drink," said Grimm, "and sleep will happen next."

Chapter Five

Eric's eyes opened to the flickering of the overhead hospital lights and Anna pushing him along the corridor humming quietly to herself. Eric sensed a positive mood but didn't know why.

"So you're awake at last. Doctor Kissen is waiting to see us. He has a surprise and the Reverend Wolf is there, too. They seem excited. I know its good news. I just don't know what. Anyway, we'll find out, that's why we're here. Hello, Valerie"

"Hello, Mrs. Shepard. Go right in. Doctor Kissen is waiting for you."

Doctor Kissen and the Reverend Wolf were deep in conversation as Anna entered with Eric. "Anna," said Doctor Kissen, "Stan has some interesting news. I wonder if we might talk privately, without Eric, for a moment."

"Why?" said Anna. "Do you expect him to respond to our conversation?"

This time it was the Reverend Wolf that answered. "No, Anna, we don't. However, we would like to assume at this point that if he could, he would." Eric moaned and began to shake.

"Alright," said Doctor Kissen. "Eric, we have something to discuss with your mother. If she approves, when Nurse Scott brings you back in we'll discuss it with you." Nurse Scott entered the room and took Eric out with her.

"It's nice that you talk to him, Doctor, but in over twelve years he hasn't responded to anyone."

"I understand, Anna, but I think we may have a way of finding out if he can respond. There is a device which has been used in the United States, New York to be precise."

"What kind of device to be precise, Doctor?"

"Well, it's fairly new and actually Stan is the one that did the research, although I just talked to the senior neuroscientist there. He is actually British, Sir Charles Paul. Apparently he attended Oxford thirty-five years ago with Stan."

Anna looked at Stan and he smiled. "E.J., may I explain from this point?"

Doctor Kissen said, "Yes, I think you'll do a much better job."

"Okay, it's very twenty first century, so do me a favor and let me explain first then ask us questions. Agreed?"

"Yes," Anna said. "I think I need coffee."

"This device," began Stan, "is amazing. It's been used successfully on four people so far."

"Four people?" said Anna.

"Later, please, as I said four people. It monitors electricity that radiates from the brain. There is special software to translate those reflections of thought into action. In essence, if Eric thinks about moving the cursor on the computer it will move. Through the electric impulses in his brain, he can learn to read and write and therefore communicate. Okay. Now," said Stan.

"Are you saying this machine will allow him to talk?"

"Yes, I am. We'll teach him the alphabet, how to read and write."

"Whoa, Stan," said Doctor Kissen. "That will only work if he is, as we think or assume, locked in."

"Locked in," said Anna.

"Right," said Doctor Kissen, "it means a person, and there are many, whose mind is functioning normally within a body that isn't. That is to say, nothing physically works from speech to leg or arm movement. Yet the mind within this person is alive and can think and feel."

"How horrible," said Anna.

"Are you willing to try this?"

"Will it hurt him?"

"No," said Doctor Kissen, "the only down side is that he may be, in fact, brain damaged to a degree that it will serve no useful purpose."

"How expensive is it?"

"Very. However, Stan has offered to on take the financial responsibility."

"How can you do that?" said Anna.

"Your sister asked if part of my solution is the power of prayer," he said. "You may tell her it is and I accept her challenge."

"You're a priest," said Anna.

"Exactly," said Stan.

"He's a Rosicrucian," said Kissen

"What's that?"

Stan looked at Kissen reproachfully and replied, "It's an ancient order. However, I am still a priest. As for your sister, the challenge will be to change her thinking, nothing more."

"Doctor Kissen," said Anna, "do you think I should do this?"

"We both do," said Stan, "however, I must go. We'll talk later. I told Doctor Armstrong I would get there a little ahead of you."

"Anna," said Doctor Kissen, "I know what this will do for you, and I'm hopeful of what it might do for Eric."

"What will it do for you, Doctor Kissen?"

"If he can talk to me, I can't begin to imagine."

"Maybe this will be the beginning of some positive things happening for Eric and Terry."

"My sentiments exactly. You still want that coffee?"

"Yes, now I need it."

"Come on, I'm buying."

"What about Eric?"

"He can buy next time."

"A sense of humor, who would have guessed?"

"It's the first time I've had something to joke about with you and Eric. I'm so excited I feel drunk."

"Are you married?"

"No, are you asking?"

"Okay, let's get Eric. I think we should talk to him."

Valerie Scott was at the nurses' station having ice cream with Eric when Anna and Doctor Kissen came out of the office. She looked at Doctor Kissen and said, "We're under stress. We need this."

"Okay," he said, "bring him in and you come too. By the way, we need coffee."

"Doctor Kissen, you don't drink coffee," she said bringing Eric into the office. Doctor Kissen gave her a scathing look. "Okay," she said. Ten minutes later she returned tray in hand. "This should do it."

"Alright," said Kissen as Valerie poured coffee. He explained to Eric that soon he hoped to teach him to communicate.

Eric closed his eyes and said, "Wulfstan is in trouble I tell you."

Grimm sat up and said, "It is midnight, the Hall sleeps. It is a nightmare, no more."

"I must go to the gate," said Eric.

"Go back to sleep. I am your axe friend. If you go, I must go." He sighed, rolled over out of his blanket and said, "Come, I'm no longer tired anyway."

They crept into the courtyard. There on the ground lay Earl Wulfstan bleeding from a wound in his side. "I'll get him into the barn," said Eric. "Bring hot water and ointments so we may repair his wounds."

Grimm ran off to bring the medicines that would be required to help the most important housecarl in England. Eric was about to lift Wulfstan, when out of the shadows came a housecarl swinging his axe. Eric rolled under the carl's axe arm. As he turned he saw that the carl had lifted the axe to strike off the head of Wulfstan. Eric hurled himself bodily at the carl knocking the axe from his hand. As they grappled, the carl pulled out a short stabbing sword which Eric turned on him and drove into his chest. He rose in silence.

Grimm stood looking at him. "First blood," he said. "You could not have picked a better opponent or a more worthy cause."

"What does this mean?"

"It means you must hide me outside Wallingford," said Wulfstan. "There are other carls in the service of Edward that will come to finish me. Leave me a dagger."

"We'll hide you till you are stronger. You will not die like a hunted dog as long as we live."

"That is a noble thought, young friend."

"No more talk," said Eric. "Help me move him and tend his wounds."

By this time Wallingford was awake. The captain sent men to find a farm close by where they could hide Wulfstan and still be close enough to protect him.

"Do you remember me?" Eric said. Wulfstan's eyes opened and stared at him.

"I do, but you must not show that you know me. I am no longer protected by my title."

"Then I should know you as you are known by the Carls of Wallingford and you shall be protected by mine."

Wulstan laughed causing him no little pain. "You have a title?"

"I do. I am a housecarl of Harold Godwinson and my oath to him is your protection."

"I thank you. Bring the captain and the men you trust and I will tell you how I come to be here now."

Eric stood up and said to Grimm, "Get the captain and the men." He looked back at Wulstan and said, "All the men of Wallingford can be trusted. We are Harold's men."

Wulfstan began to talk to the men of Wallingford and they settled down around him to listen. Ten housecarls disappeared into the night to check the walls for unwelcome guests. "I was in Normandy. I traveled as a beggar commissioned to help the tanner into the next world. The wily William is as fast as a snake. He pulled a serving girl in front of himself and she lies dead in his place. All hell broke loose and pursued me with the intention of taking me back. I escaped on a ship captained by a Dane. I was not in the best of condition as I had a running fight from Bayeux to Carusburc. When in sight of England I went overboard and swam to shore with my lungs filled with seawater. Edward's men were waiting for me and pursued me to the gates of Wallingford. I killed six on the way here, the seventh was dispatched by Eric Shepard. The London Carls will want revenge for you harboring me."

"You are one of us," said Eric. "Let them come. Revenge is a poison that serves only itself."

"No," said Wulfstan. "I must find Godwinson and Wallingford must find a way to appease the King."

"Quarter staves," said Grimm. "We'll challenge them to a battle of sticks."

Wulfstan smiled, "It is a good idea. You men will have to prepare for the battle that will surely come. Edward will not last long and William the Bastard will not wait long. I must go north and find Godwinson. The wind changes direction and William already has a fleet of ships built for his attempt to steal the crown of England."

As dawn broke the next day, Wulfstan and three housecarls were already sailing north up the River Thames in search of Harold Godwinson. The thundering hooves of horses approached the Gates of Wallingford. About thirty of Edward's London housecarls sat on horseback outside the gates as their captain hammered on the gates to be admitted. The gates swung open and the riders entered in a flurry of dust, cloaks and the clanking of swords and axes against chain mail. The captains faced each other, the London captain demanding to see Earl Wulfstan.

The Wallingford captain, Thorkell, said, "We have had no visitors except you and your men. Look around if you wish."

The London captain, realizing that he had come too late, sent some of his men to have a cursory look around. They came back shaking their heads. They mounted their horses in preparation to leave.

Thorkell said, "Brothers, as you see we suffer the rigors of the King's fast for lent. It seems the London household has no such imposition. Will you honor us and meet us the Monday after Easter for a jousting of the sticks?"

The London captain knew this would be no friendly joust. The growing hatred between Edward and Godwinson was reflected in the men. The London captain bowed then mounted his horse. "How many men, one thousand? Unless that is too many for you."

"We agree," said Thorkell.

"Wodensfield near St Albans," said the captain, "or is that too close to London for you?"

"Not even London is too close to London for us!" yelled Grimm. All the Wallingford carls joined in cheering and yelling. The London housecarls rode back through the gates as fast as they had ridden in.

As the dust cleared Eric looked into the face of Doctor Kissen who was saying, "I believe you can hear me. We just have to prove it by getting an answer." He turned back to look at the group of people who stood behind him, Doctor Armstrong, Anna and Nurse Scott.

"Mike," said Doctor Kissen, "I didn't hear you come in. You've heard the news, then?"

"Yes, E.J., I have," said Doctor Armstrong. "I know how excited you all must be. However, I need some time with Mrs. Shepard to talk about Terry. I'd like you to come up to my office first then we'll go over to the observation room to see Terry and talk with him, okay?"

"Yes, of course," Anna said. She had once more taken on the white pallor of sick fear.

"Anna, leave Eric with us and when you come down we'll work out the details of our plans for him."

She kissed Eric on the cheek and proceeded to the elevator with Mike Armstrong to face whatever new challenge he had in store for her.

Chapter Six

Terry sat up in bed in the observation ward willing his eyes to stay open. It had been an ongoing battle for the last three weeks. He looked across the ward into the window of Doctor Armstong's office as his mother and the doctor engaged in what looked like a very serious conversation. He dozed intermittently. When his eyes opened, his mother and Doctor Armstrong stood beside his bed wearing masks and gloves. He smiled and said, "Sorry, I left my money at home."

"Very funny, but I brought you something anyway," said Anna. She pulled an Easter egg from her pocket.

"Sorry, Anna, he can't have that."

"Oh, I didn't think," said Anna.

Mike Armstrong smiled at Terry, "Well, it's good to see you haven't lost your sense of humor."

Terry smiled. "I just found it since I've been lying here with nothing to do except converse with the fighting priest, Stan Wolf."

Anna held his hand in hers and smiled, "He's been a saint. In fact, it seems he never sleeps."

"Well, since the joy of chemotherapy it seems I do nothing but sleep."

Doctor Armstrong smiled at him. "The good news is you can go home next week."

Terry looked at him and said, "And the bad news?"

"You get to come back and visit every other week."

"That doesn't sound so bad."

"That's because I haven't told you everything yet."

"Am I going to die?"

"There you go again," said the Reverend Wolf as he walked into the room masked and gloved like Anna and Doctor Armstrong. "Looking for an easy way out?"

Terry smiled and said, "Okay, give me the rest of the bad news."

The three masked grownups stood around the bed and Mike Armstrong began to explain some of the changes the boy would have to deal with. "Alright, every other week you'll receive chemotherapy much like you've been having. That means your immune system will be weak, you'll be open to infection. You'll take Septrin, which is a strong antibiotic, to fight infections like pneumonia. Your soccer career for the present is over. Your platelet count was very low which is part of the reason for the severe bruising.

"What you have is a rare combination of leukemia; Acute Mylocytic and Acute Lymphocytic. The hard lump we found in your abdomen was a collection of fast growing leukemia cells which, thanks to the chemo and your own fast action in deciding to deal with it, is going down which means the cancerous cells are being destroyed."

"So am I getting better?"

"This is the first battle. It's too soon to say it's over, but you are getting better. We have to continue to see what happens next."

"Okay, how's Eric?"

"He's been asking for you."

"Is that a joke?"

"No, no, we have lots to tell you; partly about you and partly about Eric."

"Granddad?"

"He's fine, just about the same as when you last saw him."

"Have you found a treatment for Eric?"

"Not exactly. However, we are in the very early stages of teaching him to communicate through the use of electronics and a computer."

"We, I mean I broke the computer."

"Actually," said the Reverend Wolf, "you have a new computer. So does your brother. However, as you mother has said, rather a lot has been going on. We are all in the very early stages of several challenges. We'll talk during the week and I'll help you with any questions you have. In the meantime, I must go. I have an appointment with Eric."

Anna got up and almost kissed Terry on the cheek.

"Sorry Anna" said Mike, "No kisses or Easter Eggs for a couple of weeks."

"I forgot" she said. "I'll be back tomorrow."

"Let's get some tea" said Stan as he guided Anna to the door.

Doctor Armstrong moved his chair round the bed to examine Terry. He placed his hand on Terry's abdomen and Terry said, "What's a Rosicrucian?"

Doctor Armstrong stopped his examination and said to Terry, "Isn't that a question for the Reverend Wolf?"

"Do you know?"

"Vaguely, but I think you should ask him."

"I will," said Terry. "I think it's interesting how grown up people continually pass the buck."

"You might find it less interesting once you become one of us."

"Do you think I will?"

"Will what?"

"Make it to become one of you."

"Yes, I do. Now lie down and rest. You have another round of chemo in about two hours."

"I know and a round of throwing up in about four. Anyway, as my mom often says, 'that which doesn't kill you will make you stronger'."

"She says that?"

"Yes, she does. I'll tell you, though, if she had the chemo she wouldn't believe it." Terry closed his eyes. Doctor Armstrong sat by his bed for a moment unsure as to why he wasn't leaving. Suddenly he started to speak.

"I can tell you what little I know of the Rosicrucians." Terry's eyes remained closed as Mike continued. "Their symbol is the Rose and the Cross. They are associated with the Free Masons who in turn are the modern version of the Knights Templar. I think they believe in rebirth or reincarnation. They are, after all, a secret society. What I know from my own experience is that since Stan Wolf entered my life, and the lives of my patients, only good things have happened as a result. Your brother is a living human being trapped, no not trapped, imprisoned in a body that doesn't work and the Reverend is working tirelessly to allow him a way to communicate with the world. Anyway, that's a brief synopsis." As he stood up to leave Terry's eyes opened.

"Thanks, Doc," he said and closed his eyes. Doctor Armstrong smiled and left.

It seemed only moments later that he opened his eyes and steely blue eyes stared back at him from behind a white mask. "How do you feel?" said Stan Wolf.

"Scared," replied Terry.

"That's normal," said the priest.

"I'm not brave like my brother. You're right."

"That's how you were then, not how you are now."

"So now I'm brave? I just told you. I'm very scared."

"To be brave is to conquer fear and you, my young friend, are doing a fine job."

"The truth is I'm going to die and no one wants to tell me."

"We all die. However, the time and place is out of our hands. At this time you have a fight on your hands, so don't lie down and submit. Fight. You have the courage."

"How's Eric?"

"He's learning the alphabet and can already, through his computer, say 'Terry'."

"So is he clever?"

"He appears to be."

"When can I see him?"

"Next week. Tuesday, in fact, when we take you home."

"Why are you helping us so much?"

"I think you are improving rapidly. Asking so many questions requires strength."

"What does it require to answer them?"

"Strength."

"Why?"

"Because I know where you are going with your questions, so I have a proposition; leave the big questions until next week when you get home and I'll have time to reflect on my answers, okay?'

"Okay," said Terry smiling at the priest.

"Your mother asked me to let you know that she will be in to see you later today. We'll talk as arranged next week. I have some other people to see before I leave so hands up and remember the old one two punch." He winked and walked out the door. Terry waved, turned to the bowl by his bed and threw up.

Chapter Seven

Eric sat in his wheelchair and stared at the computer screen. Suddenly it came to life as the cursor moved across the screen. The alphabet blinked back at Eric. The cursor began to pull letters from what looked like typewriter keys on the screen. First the T, then the E, R, R, Y, pause, I, S, M,Y, B, R, U, T, E, R. The word "Bruter" is cancelled and replaced by "Broter" which is cancelled and replaced by "Brother" and a strange high pitched moan from Eric. Anna, Jennifer and Stan Wolf gathered round the chair. Anna was in tears.

The Reverend Wolf said, "Eric, you're moving along very quickly. I think Doctor Kissen will be a very happy man."

Jennifer took Stan Wolf by the arm and maneuvered him into the kitchen. "I think you may be a little premature. He wrote three words. In fact, the computer wrote them. I don't think you can just jump in and assume that after twelve years Eric is communicating."

"Would you like to look and see if he has holes in his hands?"

"I don't find you very amusing."

"I'm glad because I wasn't trying to be. It seems you don't approve of me or my efforts on behalf of Eric and Terry."

"I'd like to know what you get out of this, or what you want from my sister and her family."

"Perhaps you should ask yourself what you want? Maybe reassurance that this technology will never enter your world and give the people you're responsible for some of the freedom Eric is about to experience. Imagine if it could improve learning disabilities and behavioral problems. Would you be less valuable? I don't think so. I'm sure your job would remain intact."

Before she realized what she was doing, Jennifer raised her hand and slapped the priest across the face. Anna stood in the kitchen doorway about to wheel Eric in for lunch as the sound of the slap cracked the air like a whip.

Eric looked up as the branch cracked. "C'mon," said Grimm as he pulled the thick branch from the oak tree. "Give me your axe and we'll dress this staff to be fit for the dance at St. Albans."

Eric passed the short woodman's axe to Grimm who expertly trimmed and shaped the quarter staff that would be Eric's at the jousting of the sticks on the following day. "Will the Queen be there?" he asked.

Grimm looked at him, "Don't be a fool, boy. She is the Queen of England and Godwinson's sister."

"No one knows how this game will end. I just want to know where she is when it does."

"Maybe you should concern yourself where you will be."

"I will be her shadow if I can be nothing else."

"If Edward or Godwinson hear of this you won't even be a shadow. We go to war to see who will wear Edward's Crown. She is the present king's queen and the next king's sister. Even if both men die it will bring you no nearer to her."

"I know. I don't want to be near the queen, I want to be near the woman."

"Prepare yourself for tomorrow. Edward's men will not be any gentler with us than we will be with them."

Eric picked up the newly made quarter staff and went inside to sleep.

The next day as they stood side by side in Wodensfield, Grimm smiled at Eric and said, "Stay close to me. As you can see we are all dressed alike, leather tunics, leggings and boots. Once we don our helmets we'll all look the same so do not get in front of our line as we move forward. It will be friends behind us and enemies in front. There will be little time for mistakes. When it begins move with me, no faster or slower. If you go faster we cannot protect each other, slower and the men behind will run over you."

Suddenly a blast from a horn sent two thousand warriors trotting towards each other on the day after Easter Sunday to begin a joust that would leave many lying on the field near St. Albans, never to return home again.

A London carl closed on Eric. Eric side stepped and swung at his head. The carl ducked under his staff and came up smiling. Eric dropped the angle of his staff and thrust at his legs. As the carl side stepped, Grimm pole axed him from the side and said, "Three down. Would you like to help? Pick one, anyone you like. Even a small one would be better than nothing."

Eric smiled, drove his staff into the ribs of one man and hit the side of his head. As he dropped, he brought the staff across his body smashing it into the face of two of the London carls who were fighting as a team. He lifted it like a spear and drove it into the jaw of a carl who had forced Grimm to his knees.

"Four," said Eric as his eyes lit up with the fury of battle.

Grimm stood up and the sounds of clicking sticks were everywhere. He watched as Eric faced another of the London carls. He was fast and clever. They met each other blow for blow. Suddenly the London carl spun away from him and back very fast. On the return spin Eric ducked and swept his legs from underneath him. He fell heavily, his head cracked against the earth and he lay still. The horn sounded and the carls stopped and drew back. A five minute rest period was called so they could remove the fallen from the field. The London carls took some refreshment while the men of Wallingford observed their fast.

Grimm began beating his staff against Eric's and started a chant that the Wallingford carls picked up. Soon Wodensfield was filled with a sound of impending doom. As the men of London came back on the field it became clear this would be a fight to the finish. Grimm ran into the fight forsaking his own advice. Within seconds he was surrounded by the men of London. He gave a good account of himself before a quarter staff hit him so hard it broke on his head.

Eric ran into the London men screaming and swinging left and right. An older housecarl of Edward's elite force stepped forward and cracked him across the head. He fell forward to his knees. He reached for the fallen staff to protect Grimm. Just as he passed out he saw a Wallingford carl step across his body and fight furiously, driving the Londoners back, and for a brief moment looked into the eyes of Harold Godwinson.

He opened his eyes and took in his surroundings and realized he was in a strange place. His body had been bathed and a cool, damp, linen bandage was around his head. Sitting on a chair across from the bed was England's young Queen Edith. He tried to rise from the bed, but the cool blue eyes and a voice he had only heard once, but that came to him often in his dreams, said, "Stay where you are."

"Your Highness, I should not be here."

"I had you and the friend you lay across on Wodensfield brought here to St. Albans Monastery. The black monks are friends to the children of Godwin."

"How many men died?"

"Over two hundred."

"How many from Wallingford?"

"There were one hundred men dead from each house. You are fortunate the numbers are equal. It will make the King's punishment less severe."

"What is the punishment?"

"Wallingford is to be burned to the ground and the Wallingford carls will be joined to the London House of his majesty, King Edward."

"Godwinson will never accept that."

"No, my brother is head strong. I don't suppose he will."

"Why did you bring me here?"

"I wanted to talk with someone my own age who isn't Norman, a waiting woman or a scheming princess. In other words, a man," she paused, "you."

"I wish I knew what to say to a queen. I'm the son of a farmer."

"I'm the daughter of a man who, like you, was a warrior. We are both Saxon and of a similar age."

"You are the Queen of Edward the Confessor."

62

"Soon I will enter a convent and become a nun."

"Why would he do that to you?"

"It really has nothing to do with me. He is the King. I am merely a pawn in the game of kings. He dislikes women, me no more or less than others, but he has never known physical love of any kind. He is disgusted by the thought of it." She paused as Eric took in this information. He looked into her eyes unable to think of what to say next.

"Do you like me a little?" she said.

"I....I, you're the Queen," he stammered.

"I am a virgin," she said staring into his eyes.

"So am I," said Eric immediately wishing he'd said something else. She smiled at him, as her dress fell at her feet and she moved towards the bed.

As Eric watched her, he heard himself say, "We could be killed for this."

"You could have been killed yesterday." As she pressed her lips to his ear, she whispered, "Now at least if we die we can say we tasted the sweetness of life before we are returned to the earth."

Eric's eyes opened and the computer screen stared back at him with one word flashing back at him. "Edith."

"I want out of here!" flashed across the screen. Eric moaned and twisted in the chair. Jennifer walked across to Eric and tried to calm him down. She reached down and turned off the computer. Eric thrashed about, his muscles locked in spasms. Anna came into the room and, with Jennifer, attempted to soothe him. After half an hour of Eric thrashing about in distress Anna called Doctor Kissen.

He answered the phone himself. "Hello," he said as the words tumbled out of Anna's mouth.

"Eric is having some kind of fit. It seems to be caused by the computer."

"I can't leave just yet, but I will call the pharmacy and have them get him some muscle relaxant medication."

"What can I do in the meantime?"

"Is the computer still on?"

"No, Jennifer turned it off."

"Okay, turn it back on and see what happens. I'll remain on the line."

Anna turned the computer back on and as the screen flashed, "welcome," Eric stopped thrashing around. "He's stopped."

"Okay, I'll get you the medication anyway. Bring him in if he starts acting like he is in any kind of trauma. Also, I want to see how he's progressing with the Cyberthink Program so if not today, tomorrow."

"He seems to be doing well with it except that there was a strange collection of words on the screen when we switched the computer on."

"What were they? Actually, let me log on from here. It might be more useful to me to do it that way. Pick up the medication, Anna, and I'll see you tomorrow. How about eleven o'clock?"

"Fine, we'll see you then."

Doctor Kissen walked across the corridor to the elaborate electronic computer room that had been set up by the Reverend Wolf. He sat in front of the computer and accessed Eric's computer to check the words on the screen. The screen lit up with the words "Edith I want out of here," then suddenly went blank.

A voice behind him asked, "What was that?"

"Hello Stan. Those were Eric's latest words. I think he just erased them."

"What were they?"

"Edith. I want out of here."

"Do we know an Edith?"

"No, I don't think so."

"Maybe I can talk to him tonight. I'm taking Terry home."

"How's he doing?"

"Better. It's still an uphill battle."

"I don't know how Anna gets through her days."

"With difficulty I imagine."

"What about you, Stan? What keeps you going, God?"

"He keeps us all going, even you."

"Not me. I gave up on that a long time ago."

"Well, I have to get Terry home. However, I'd like to hear about that sometime."

"Hear about what?"

"The whatever it was that stole your faith."

"Another time."

"Alright."

"Tell Terry to come visit me if he feels like it."

"Change is always good, is it not? Good night."

"Change?" thought Kissen as he left, "What changed?" and a voice within him said "you have".

"What's a Rosicrucian?" Terry said as he stood up dressed and ready to go, a little thinner, no hair and looking vulnerable.

"Hello to you, too," Stan paused.

"Oh, hello," said Terry.

"Thank you," said Stan. "It's a secret society which appears not to be very secret."

"Is it only for priests?"

"No, it's not. The name comes up occasionally, but usually 'secret society' ends the conversation. I can see that won't be the case with you."

"Will you explain it to me?"

"No, I'll give you an overview. It's like a private club for knights, the kind that carry swords."

"Do you?"

"No, listen. They are the descendants of the Knights Templar who were tortured in Italy and France in the Thirteenth Century. They were the Brotherhood of the Knights of the Order of the Temple of Solomon, the Freemasons, and the Brotherhood of the Rosy Cross who are the Rosicrucians."

"I've heard of them," said Terry.

"As I said, a secret society which appears not to be very secret."

"Tell me more."

"I can't really. It's a long complicated story. The rose and cross is a symbol for the heart of Christ in the care of the Rosicrucian order."

They drove home in silence. When they arrived at the Shepard's front door Terry said, "So why is it secret?"

"Do you know of the Knights of the Round Table?"

"Yes. King Arthur? Of course I've heard of them."

"What about Charlemagne and his twelve paladins?"

"No, never heard of them."

"Jesus Christ and the twelve apostles?"

"What's your point?"

"It's part of the answer to your question. Let's go in. We can pick this up later. It's a long story with a lot of information."

"Okay," said Terry as the front door opened and Anna and Jennifer came racing out to meet them.

"Terry!" cried Anna. "I'm so happy you're home. How do you feel?"

"A little tired," said Terry, "but not too bad."

"I'm glad you're here."

"I missed you."

"I know. We all missed you. Wait until you see Eric."

"I've heard he talks. At last I have my brother."

Anna began to cry. Jennifer said, "Okay, let's all go in. Come on Terry, I'm sure you're desperate to see Eric. Reverend Wolf, I owe you an apology."

"Thanks, and I you," he replied. "Let's call it even, shall we?"

Jennifer stared at him as Anna and Terry walked through the front door.

"We must talk, Jennifer, and resolve the issues you have with me."

"Believe me it's a lot more than issues, Father."

"Will you have dinner with me one night? And please, call me Stan."

"No, I will not have dinner, but I will call you Stan."

"In that case, call me and we'll discuss the development of Eric and the recovery of Terry."

"And if I don't?"

"Then you don't, I suppose. Look, I don't want to play games. Call me before the end of the week. It would serve no purpose for you to undermine the work I am doing with Eric. Regarding Terry, you should talk to Michael Armstrong. Dr. Kissen is still Eric's primary physician. They will keep you informed of the progress we are making with the boys. After Friday I will no longer be accessible to debate with you. Now if you'll excuse me I must see Eric."

"For the moment, but I don't trust your motives," said Jennifer to no one in particular. Stan was already talking to Eric.

"So who is Edith?" said Stan

Eric awoke. She lay beside him smiling and looking into his eyes. "I must go," she said. She slid a ring from her finger. "Don't forget me."

"You are the Queen of England, how could I?"

She pressed the ring into his hand, closing his fingers about it.

Eric looked from the ring into the Queen's eyes and said "I have nothing
to give you in return."

"It is a gift, not an exchange."

"The gift was given before the ring. Accept my heart in exchange."

Edith took Eric's face in her hands. "To barter love for love is the only gift.
Take the ring as a token of mine"

"Thank you, Your Majesty. I hope you will not forget me"

Edith kissed Eric gently and replied, "To you, Eric, I am Edith. As long as
the sun rises I will carry you in my heart."

She stood and said, "The men of Wallingford will come for you and your friend."

With that she was gone, only the smell of lemon and mint remained.

The Benedictine came into the cell and smiled, "Come you must bathe. Then you and your friend must leave."

"I don't need to bathe."

The monk smiled, "I would advise it. It will protect you and your friend."

Eric realized the smell of lemon and mint was on him. He entered the bath house. The monks had left his clothes and fresh linen for him and Grimm to dry their bodies after they had bathed. A large piece of soap the size of a cheese flew past Eric's ear. He turned in time to see Grimm leap into the large communal bath beside him. Grimm laughed.

"We won," he said.

"I think the numbers were equal," said Eric.

"They lost two more than we did."

"That's not much of a win for the price."

"They paid more than us."

"Wallingford is to be destroyed by fire and we will be taken into Edward's House as London carls."

"Never!" boomed Grimm.

"I know," said Eric.

"Maybe war will come first, or Edward will die. Godwinson will never leave us to that fate. What's that smell?"

"I don't know."

"It's coming from you. Lemon and....what have you done?"

"Nothing you need to know about."

"Are you seeking death?"

"No, I am seeking life."

"You are Godwinson's man. He'll kill you himself."

"Maybe. I have a feeling we will all be facing death on the battlefield before that happens."

"You are a fool."

"I am a man and sometimes a fool."

Grimm pushed his head under the water. When he came up Grimm said, "Come get dressed. We must all get back to Wallingford. If Edward intends to burn us out it will be soon and he may see it as an opportunity to reduce our number further." They leapt out of the water, dried, dressed and walked outside to the waiting Benedictine monks and two of the housecarls of Wallingford who sat on horseback holding the reins of two horses.

"Brothers, we thank you."

The Benedictines bowed. Thor and Thorfinn said nothing but dropped the reins as Grimm leapt into the saddle. Eric stood dumbfounded as the other horse stamped and whinnied. "It's Midnight," he stammered.

"Mount up, it's a gift. And close your mouth."

Eric mounted Midnight and within seconds left the monastery behind in a cloud of dust.

Chapter Eight

As the four riders approached Wallingford they could see much activity. The men were gathering their weapons and belongings, saddling horses. A London housecarl rode out through the gates. "What news?" said Thorkill.

"The King has rescinded his order, Wallingford stands. There is a rebellion in Northumbria against Earl Tostig. The King has asked Godwinson to stand against the rebels."

"This is to be expected," said Grimm. "Tostig fed on his people as a wolf feeds on sheep."

"They have chosen a new Earl, Morcar, brother of Edwin of Mercia," said the Londoner. "They are marching south." With that the London carl spurred his horse. He called over his shoulder, "Tomorrow the King comes. Be ready to march."

"What about Tostig?" asked Eric.

Thorkill smiled, "As always as far from the fight as possible. I heard he was in London with the King trying to gain the upper hand on his brother."

"Always traitorous," said Grimm.

"At least we know him to be an enemy," smiled Thorkill. "He'll bring himself down."

The next morning the King arrived with two thousand housecarls. Wallingford stood ready, two thousand men under the command of their captain. Thorkill rode out to meet them.

"Where is Godwinson?" said Eric.

"He rides beside you," replied Harold Godwinson as he rode to the forefront of his men. Their cheers shook the earth. He approached Edward and bowed before him.

Edward looked into his eyes and knew it would not be long before all men, and indeed the country, would be bowing before this man. His power was as raw and physical as Edward's was ecclesiastical.

Edward smiled at Harold Godwinson and said, "Your brother has left for Calais. Apparently the Northumbrian air is not good for his health."

"It won't be good for anyone's health if we don't douse the fire." Harold wheeled his horse and called to Thorkill. "Fall in behind the King."

The two thousand carls of Wallingford surrounded Edward's entourage. The captain of the London carls rode up to Godwinson and said, "Pull your men back. We are the King's escort."

Godwinson looked into his eyes and said, "Now is not the time to test me."

"Captain," said the King, "bring twelve men as my retinue. The rest will ride behind Wallingford." The moment passed and the London captain knew the King had saved his life.

Godwinson turned to Thorkill. "We ride to Oxford. As we approach, fan out in case diplomacy doesn't work." Harold's brothers, Leofwine and Gyrth, rode close behind him. When they reached the outskirts of Oxford, the rebel army had already set up camp.

"It looks like they out number us ten to one," said Eric.

"That just means that a lot of farmers will die today, if it comes to that," said Grimm.

"My father is a farmer," said Eric. "It's a pity they must die for the greed of their lords."

"It's the way of the world," said Grimm, "close up to the King."

The main pavilion had a table set in front of it and there, sitting on the edge of the table, were the rebel brothers Edwin of Mercia and Morcar who now held Northumbria. No one spoke as the King's army approached. The only sound was that of two thousand housecarls dropping from their saddles, axes gleaming in the sunlight. The rebels backed away almost as one.

"Stand still," hissed their commander.

Grimm spoke to Eric quietly, "If they move against Godwinson, kill Morcar. I'll kill Edwin."

Thorkill smiled, "If they move against Godwinson they will be butchered by two thousand men."

Edward's Archbishop, Stigand, supported him while the Archbishop of York, Aeldred, helped seat him on a chair. Godwinson strode forward to the table and two of Morcar's men ran forward carrying a chair for him. Eric took it from them in one hand.

"My Lord, please sit by the King."

Godwinson growled and prowled back to where Eric had placed the seat. Edwin spoke first.

"Sire, the people do not want Tostig Godwinson. He is cruel and no better than a pirate."

"Watch your tongue. He is an Earl," said Godwinson.

"So am I, but I don't pillage my own lands, raping and butchering where I may."

"Only the King may take or give an earldom."

Morcar looked straight at Godwinson. "Is that how your father got his? With the King's permission?"

Godwinson stood up and kicked his chair away, "You call my father a thief?"

"I call him a man strong enough to hold what he took," said Morcar. Godwinson's army swayed forward on the wind of war. Suddenly Edwin spoke.

"My brother speaks in anger. Let not that be the path we take. Your Majesty, the people want Morcar. What say you?"

Edward sat up as if just awakened from sleep, "It is the will of the people. So be it."

Edwin stepped forward, "So says the King. My brother Mocar is the Earl of Northumbria. What of the pirate, Tostig, an outlaw?"

Godwinson was stunned at how quickly and cleverly Edwin had orchestrated the meeting. The King turned and whispered to Archbishop Stigand.

Stigand spoke slowly. "The will of the people outlaws Tostig Godwinson," The rebels stood cheering. Harold knew he was trapped.

"What say you, Harold?" said Edwin.

"I say the King has spoken. So be it."

"Earl Morcar," said Godwinson, "remember this day, for I will not forget it."

The King asked the Archbishops to address the rebel earls and order them to return home in the name of God, and offer no more violence to the town of Oxford or England. The men of Wallingford returned to their hall and the King and his retinue to London.

Eric was in the stable grooming Midnight who had taken to him as if he were Wulfstan. "Godwinson has asked for you," said Grimm from behind him.

Eric turned and Terry was smiling at him.

"Wake up dreamer," he said, "I want to talk to you."

Eric's wheelchair sat in front of the computer and Terry was fitting the cap on his head that allowed him to move the cursor. The screen came to life and Eric's words formed on the screen. "Are you feeling better?" Terry reached for the mouse and Eric said, "I can hear you, you don't need to write it. I do"

"I'm sorry," said Terry, "I wasn't thinking."

"It's kind of a surprise that I do, isn't it"

"Yes," said Terry, "I'm sorry...."

"Don't," said Eric, "that's all past. You didn't know I was in here."

"You write fast," said Terry.

"Are you better, I mean cured?"

"Not yet. I am better than I was but I throw up a lot and I miss my hair."

"I miss your hair, too. It used to tickle my face when you leaned over me."

"Well, well," said the Reverend Wolf as he entered the room, "the brothers in conversation, how does it feel to meet each other?"

"Great," said Terry. "Why does Aunt Jennifer dislike you, Stan?"

"I don't think it's me she dislikes," said Stan.

"It's great," typed Eric. "Then who does she dislike?"

"Ha, ha, it must be genetic, choosing the same words", said Stan Wolf.

"We have different fathers," typed Eric. "Is it me?"

"But the same mother," said Terry. "No, don't be daft."

"I wasn't trying to start a discussion on your family genetics," said Stan Wolf.

"Probably just as well," typed Eric. "So what about Aunt Jennifer?"

"I can't answer that question. Besides, we have work to do. Terry, I am here to work a little with Eric. Your mother is going to drive you to see Doctor Armstrong."

"Oh, good," said Terry, "more pills and throw up."

"What are the pills?" flashed the screen.

"You're funny," said Terry. "I never thought to ask that question."

"Alright, off you go, Terry. I'll tell him."

"I want to go," flashed the screen.

"No, wait till I come back, it's no fun." He walked out of the room, stopped at the door and said, "Don't tire out the Wolf, he has a great story to tell us when I get back." Then the front door closed and he was gone.

"What are the pills that make him sick?"

"They are part of the chemotherapy drugs to prevent the Leukemia cells growing. The one that makes him feel sick is called Mercaptopurine."

"Spell it."

"M, E, R, C, A, P, T, O, P, U, R, I, N, E."

The screen lit up and Eric said, "I'll know about it by tonight."

The front door opened and the click of women's shoes could be heard crossing the hallway to Eric's room. Stan Wolf stood up as Jennifer entered the room.

"Well, gentlemen, it's Friday. And I've changed my mind. How about dinner tonight, Stan, my place?"

"Alright," said Stan, "what time?"

"Eight o'clock. It will give you time to finish your work with Eric and me time to formulate my questions." She leaned over and kissed Eric.

"You smell like Edith," lit up the screen.

"Who is Edith?" she said.

"Someone I dream about."

"I'm flattered."

"She's young."

"Now I'm insulted."

"Don't be. You're not old, just old compared to me, Aunt Jennifer."

She smiled, kissed him again and said to Stan, "I'll let you get back to work."

"We haven't started yet, but are just about to. Before you go would you tell me where you live?"

"Bellevue Street, number sixteen. My number is in the book."

As the front door closed behind her Stan said to Eric, "I thought I'd read to you a little, then you can ask questions."

The screen lit up and Eric said, "Can you tell me about dreams?"

"Dreams," said the Reverend Wolf, "are in the realm of the unknown; what is, what was, or what might be."

Eric backed Midnight gently into his stall as he dropped a bail of hay in front of him. "Godwinson asks for me?"

Chapter Nine

Godwinson sat at the head of the great oak table. Eric and Grimm entered the hall and moved forward with caution. "I sent for you. Why do you approach me like whipped dogs? Are you afraid?"

"No, Sire," said Eric, "we await your pleasure."

"When I say I want your presence, that's what I want."

"Yes, Sire," said Grimm.

"You are both a little presumptuous. I am not yet the King."

"You were King from the day I took your coin, Sire."

Godwinson smiled at Eric. "How well I could see the man in the boy you once were. Take this," he said as he removed a short battleaxe from his belt and slid it across the table. It was burnished steel, the handle inlaid with bronze and gold. He stood up and walked towards Grimm. "You will need something bigger," he said as he stood in front of the giant. As the carls began to laugh Grimm became red faced and Godwinson took a giant spear from the wall. "This was my father's, now it is yours." Grimm stood stunned as he held the mighty spear of Earl Godwin in his hand. "I have work for both of you, but the spear must stay here," he said, "You are going to London and will be there for the consecration of the new abbey at Christmas. I require an elite bodyguard of twelve men. You will choose them and they must travel separately and in secret."

"We are your men of Wessex. Why must we hide?" said Grimm.

"So you can do the job I need done. I have many enemies, the King's men, those of Morcar, Edwin, William, even my brother Tostig. It won't be easy because you must fit into the city as if invisible but be close enough to me to see and hear the enemies I cannot. Come, eat and drink. You leave tomorrow."

"It is more than a month till Christmas," said Grimm.

"You leave tomorrow," replied Godwinson.

The next morning the twelve carls were ready to depart. They left half an hour apart, two groups of three and three groups of two, all entering the city from different directions. Godwinson's spies in London would take them to the two inns they would stay in which were close enough for them to follow him without being seen. Eric and Grimm were fascinated by the new Westminster Abbey which Edward was having built by Norman masons that he had brought from France.

The weather was turning cold and the icy fingers of winter were reaching for the city. By mid December the Abbey was almost complete. Christmas passed uneventfully.

Three days later the crowds gathered for the consecration of what was to become England's most famous church. Eric, Grimm and the other ten men of Harold's bodyguard spread out at the front of the crowd in an arc invisible to all but themselves.

As the day wore on it began to snow heavily and the Bishop Aeldred of York appeared with Godwinson and many of the earls and noblemen. Towards dusk the storm increased in intensity and Archbishop Stigand appeared to announce that the King was too ill to be there but the consecration would continue and Earl Godwinson would stand in place of the King. The Archbishop, as the senior churchman, led the service. When the service ended the

Archbishop came out followed by Godwinson, his brothers, Leofwin and Gyrth, the Bishop Aeldred and the rest of the Witan.

The Witan consisted of the various lords and noblemen who were in fact the early British parliament. They stood before the crowd in front of the newly appointed Abbey that they might acknowledge each other, the people and their princes. Suddenly there was a surge from the front of the crowd. One man broke free while several in the crowd engaged the Wallingford Carls. Grimm beat the men aside with his axe as Eric ran through the space he created. The Lords drew back in terror. Godwinson stood his ground as his assailant raced towards him short sword in hand. Harold was unarmed and without armor. The would be assassin raised his sword to strike as Eric seemed to run up his body taking off the sword arm and head in one blow. He landed in front of Godwinson, Grimm dragged the body aside, and Godwinson led the procession away from the Abbey.

"Now it's consecrated," said Grimm as Eric and he melted back into the crowd.

That night Eric and Grimm both received a purse filled with gold and a message. It said, 'return to Wallingford with your men. You are now known. Send twelve in your place, Captain.'

"Captain," said Grimm.

"I'm sure you're also a Captain," said Eric as he fell asleep. In his dream Edith stood before him and reached down and kissed him on the cheek.

He tried to sit up and his Aunt Jennifer said, "Good morning. I hope you slept well." She went into the kitchen and for a moment Eric felt happy. He looked at the screen

80

and the cap lying in front of it and thought, "I can't be here now, it's too important".

Jennifer came back in from the kitchen and said, "Are you hungry?" Eric moved spastically and moaned. She looked at the cap and said, "I suppose you need this?" She hesitated, then picked up the cap, placed it on his head and the screen came to life.

His words raced across the screen, "Where is Wulfstan and Terry? And I need the cap when you talk to me. In fact, I need it every moment I'm conscious."

"Calm down," she said, "it's the Reverend Wolf to you and you spelled it wrong in your rush to speak. He went to the hospital yesterday to see Terry after you fell asleep."

"Before or after you had dinner?" flashed across the screen.

"The Reverend cancelled and your mother met him at the hospital. Terry isn't doing well."

"Is he dying?"

"I don't know."

"I have to see him."

"No one can see him right now. He's in a kind of coma."

"What do you mean?"

"He's unconscious. The treatment seems to be hard on him."

"Please take me to see him. I don't need to be in the room."

"Alright, I'll take you this afternoon."

He clicked off the computer and willed himself to see Edith, but the chair kept him a prisoner.

"We're here," said Jennifer.

Eric opened his eyes and looked through the window of the hospital room as Terry lay in a state of hibernation unfamiliar to both of them. Anna stood with Doctor Armstrong deep in discussion. Jennifer stood beside Eric holding his hand and for the first time in his life he was glad he couldn't talk.

Chapter Ten

Doctor Armstrong took Anna into the privacy of his office. She stood on the other side of his desk white with fear and anger. "Is he going to die?"

"I hope not."

"You hope not! That's what I'm thinking, not what you should be telling me. You're supposed to be an expert. You are all the same. Practice medicine on someone else's son. I want someone who knows what they're doing."

"I understand, Mrs. Shepard. I'm following the clues of his illness. Another doctor will do the same thing. I can recommend someone else if you really have lost faith in me."

A cough from the other side of the door and a loud knock let them know Stan Wolf was outside.

"We need a moment, Stan," said Doctor Armstrong.

"No, let him come in," said Anna. "Come in Stan."

Stan Wolf entered. His face showed both strength and concern. He put his arms around Anna as she collapsed in tears. Anna struggled to compose herself. She looked at Stan and said, "I don't want to hear it's in God's hands."

"I've never said that to you. However, it is in God's hands but He isn't working alone. That's why Mike and I are here. If you come to the cafeteria with me after we talk to Mike, you'll find the rest of the support team there. Eric and Jennifer came to shore up our anxieties."

"What about Dad?" said Anna as Jennifer came along the hall pushing Eric in his wheelchair.

"Oh, I forgot. I left him in front of the T.V. I'll go home and you bring Eric. I'm sorry," she said, "I wasn't thinking."

As she turned to leave, Stan smiled and said, "Human after all." She smiled back at him sarcastically and left.

"Doctor Kissen said he would like to see Eric, Anna, and probably you, too. So if you take him downstairs I'll finish talking to Mike and we'll catch up later this evening."

Anna kissed Stan on the cheek and said to Doctor Armstrong, "I'll call tomorrow."

Mike Armstrong stood up and took both Anna's hands and said, "I know it's difficult, but it's not impossible." Anna tried to answer but couldn't. She turned and left with Eric.

Mike closed the door and Stan said, "Alright, Mike, so what's happening and how do we fix it?"

"The first question is easier than the second. He has developed Encephalomyelitis which as you know is inflammation of the brain and spinal cord as the result of Intrathecal Methotrexate Therapy. It's unusual but not unheard of. All that can be done is being done. I've withdrawn the therapy. We will begin again in two weeks with other drugs and radiation if he makes it."

"Why wouldn't he make it?"

"He's in a coma. He'll have to be carefully monitored for the next seventy two hours."

"You're saying the Chemo created the coma?"

"Yes, there are always side effects. You know that. This one is just more unusual."

"And potentially lethal," said Stan.

"We don't know that yet."

"Mike, we have to take another direction."

"I know that, Stan. In two weeks we'll see where he is and review our options."

"How unusual is this, Mike?"

"Very, I haven't seen it before."

"What are his chances?"

"I don't know. In seventy two hours I'll have a better idea. The drug and radiation therapy have been stopped. Now it's just a case of watching and waiting to see how long it takes him to recover."

Chapter Eleven

Sid sat in front of the T.V. pressing the remote continuously as the chair moved forward and back rhythmically. "Sorry, Dad," said Jennifer as she automatically changed the chair remote for the T.V. remote.

"T.V.'s back on," said Sid. "Who are you?"

"Oh, I'm the new housekeeper," said Jennifer.

"Thought I knew you," said Sid. "What happened to the chair?"

"It's resting right now."

"Okay dokee," said Sid as he slid back into oblivion. Jennifer sat down for a moment and watched sadly the man who had been her father quietly disappear. The sound of the front door broke her from her reverie.

"Is he okay?" said Anna as she entered pushing Eric up beside Sid in his now stationary chair.

"No, not really," said Jennifer as she stood up. "I have to go to work. I'll call later to see how Terry is doing."

"What's wrong?"

"Father is almost nonexistent, Eric is locked in a world we know nothing about and Terry is in a coma. Oh, and we are being financially carried by some renegade priest. What's wrong? Choose something, anything, and you'll be right about what's wrong. I have to go." Jennifer stormed out the door on the edge of tears. Anna pushed Eric into his room and put him in front of the computer but forgot to put the cap on his head.

"Wake up," said Grimm. "The King won't last the night."

Eric's eyes shot open and he stood up. The carls were on the move getting armor on and weapons ready. Thorkell, already dressed in his armor, came up to Eric and said, "We leave within the hour to join with the London carls. Burn this place. We shall not return."

Grimm smiled, "So the King gets his way after all. Wallingford burns."

"Orders from the next king no doubt," said Eric. "He wants us in London to protect his back."

Within the hour the men of Wallingford marched to London, the flames of the Great Hall of Wallingford leaping skyward ahead of the sun. As they entered the city of London on January 5th, in the year 1066, the great bells of the newly consecrated Westminster Abbey sounded the death knell of the King, Edward the Confessor. A London carl rode into their camp in the early hours of the following morning proclaiming that the Great Council had named Harold Godwinson as the next King of England. Eric and Grimm sat side by side as dawn broke, each lost in their own thoughts, Grimm anticipating the war to come and Eric wondering if he could stay awake long enough to prevent him returning to that other place and time that held him prisoner. His mind had connected him across a thousand years of time and space.

Eric and Grimm rode at the head of Harold's elite bodyguard and stopped in a semicircle outside the great Abbey. The doors opened and Harold emerged as the new King of England followed by the Archbishops Stigand and Aeldred, his brothers Leofwine and Gyrth by his side. Only Tostig was conspicuously absent and, of course, Edith who would be mourning the death of the King. As the thought crossed his mind Eric looked up at the upper window in the abbey into the eyes of Edith and he knew the loss she was mourning was not that of the King. The housecarls led the entourage away from the abbey towards the King's residence at Westminster and as Eric looked back he felt something on his head.

The computer came to life saying, 'Welcome Eric' and he wrote, "damn."

"A new word for you," said Stan.

"What's a Rosicrucian?" flashed across the screen.

"A difficult question," answered Stan.

"Will you answer it, please?"

"I talked about that very question with Terry. Kind of an overview, if you will. As a result of that conversation I had a talk with Terry's doctor, Mike Armstrong, and also our friend and doctor, Emmanuel Kissen. I'll also give the same talk to your mother and Aunt Jennifer, however it doesn't really answer the question, as the answer is yet unfolding."

"So do I get the overview?" clicked Eric's computer.

"This mark on my arm is a birthmark, and not as everyone supposes a tattoo."

"What does that have to do with my question?"

"It looks like a rose and a cross, which is the symbol of the Rosicrucians. Your question is the first of many and I want you to know why the answer you receive is different and more detailed than the explanation the others will have to accept."

"So who gets the truth then" asked Eric "them or me?"

"Everyone, but for you it is the beginning of a thread that will unravel the truth of who you are and why I am here."

"I don't understand" clicked Eric.

"You know more than anyone else involved in your life, including the secret you carry within you."

"What secret?"

"The one that ties us to another time and place."

"How do you know that?" clicked Eric.

"I've always known that I have lived before. Your aunt told me that "Wulfstan" was written across your computer screen."

"What does that mean to you?"

"It is an ancient name. He was an earl in the service of the Saxon King, Harold Godwinson."

"Is" Eric wrote.

Stan looked at the one word on the screen and said, "Our destinies are intertwined and yours is bigger than mine. Because of what I believe is happening in your other life, I will tell you what I can about the Rosicrucians, but ultimately they will still remain a secret."

"Because I'm locked in here?"

"No, because what I tell you will not compromise the Order. It's a story that covers centuries so I would like you not to interrupt. You will, of course, have questions, but wait until I have finished. The beginning is cloaked in secrecy and legend, a tale of eleven men escaping the wrath of William the Conqueror. They were traced to Bavaria where they seemed to splinter off into groups and disappear throughout Europe and the Middle East. Ten of them were Benedictine monks. The eleventh man was like a ghost. No one knew anything about him. He was as the proverbial Phoenix."

"What do you mean?" clicked the computer.

"In Southern France there are Pine groves that from time to time are ravaged by fire. Often they grow back. Sometimes, however, the fire is so fierce the groves remain dry and barren for years. Then one day, like a Phoenix from the ashes, rises a solitary tree to bear witness to the forest that once lived there. Likewise, out of the great Albigensian Forest region which was razed to ashes, there survived but one man who was to perpetuate the perennial philosophy of all men by transforming it. Like the solitary pine plunged its roots into the earth to give sustenance to its soul, he plunged his thoughts deep into the soil of humanity to give life to the universal soul of man. From the Albigenses there sprang in the middle of the thirteenth century a man with the symbolic name of Christian Rosenkreutz, a force for good in a time of evil, the last descendant of the family of Germelshausen."

"What's an Albigensian? Was he the eleventh man?" flashed across the screen.

"I don't have time..."

"It's just a reminder for my questions. Ignore them until you finish speaking."

"The desire to suppress the heresy that grew up around this peaceful man was so intense that his followers were killed, their homes destroyed, everything that would show that their thinking was different was obliterated. They had to become as shadows to survive. Historically they cannot be traced except as an esoteric legend. However, the mark he left on the world is so deep that even a life of obscurity could not erase it".

"The Albigensian doctrines spread north through France, then to the Low Countries and into Germany. Those ideas or new thoughts seemed to be carried on the wind like a seed and it flowered in the Rhean District on the border of Hesse and Thuringia in the Castle of the Germelshausen family. The men of this family were warriors, unconvinced Christians unwilling to leave paganism behind them. Germany was in the grip of Conrad of Marburg, envoy of Pope Gregory IX. His philosophy was simple, a good Christian was Catholic, heretics were everyone else. By the time the castle fell to the Catholic inquisitors years later the family all followed the teachings of the mystical Albigensian doctrine, believed in reincarnation and, as a result, were put to death as heretics".

"As the castle was put to the torch, a monk carried a child from the inferno. This was the youngest son of the Germelshausen family and the last of the line. The monk was an Albigensian Adept from an area in France called Languedoc who had instructed the family in the Hermetic disciplines. He took the boy with him to a monastery and became his first teacher. The monk was impressed by the boy's intellect. He learned Greek, Latin and had an insatiable appetite for knowledge. He was known as Christian Rosenkreutz who by the age of fifteen had devoted himself to a search we all begin but few finish, the search for truth. He traveled to Damascus and studied with the mystics and wise men of the East. He studied the Arabic literature and philosophy. He embraced the Muslim world and it embraced him, feeding his mind and spirit".

"After many years of traveling and living in the Arabic world, he returned first to Spain and then to Germany to impart his knowledge and correct misconceptions. The world, for example, is not flat. That's a very crude example. He soon realized that only slowly can wisdom enter the human heart. It took the black plague to convince people that it wasn't the wrath of God that destroyed everyone from kings to servants, it was a flea carried on the back of a rat. It became clear he could only change man's thinking very slowly. He did then what he probably couldn't do today. He laid foundations for a secret group bound by an oath that was so strong that they continued their work for three centuries without their existence being known".

"In Thuringia, he and three monks who had been his companions in the monastery formed the first brotherhood which would soon increase to eight members. He taught them the secret writing and symbols by which Adepts corresponded with each other. He wrote a book outlining his philosophy, medical, and scientific knowledge. If the Rosicrucians had attained their aims, science instead of being a source for material gain, may have been the source for unlimited development of the spirit".

"Rosenkreutz created rules for his disciples to live by. The first of these is the most difficult, unselfishness. We can all be unselfish to a degree, but complete unselfishness is as elusive as truth. Absence of pride was the second rule. In today's society this does not exist. A Rosicrucian must remain anonymous, be knowledgeable without pride or boastfulness. The third rule was chastity. Sages have always attached importance to chastity. It may be that this is suggested as a way to avoid the excesses that sometimes are associated with sex. It is said that sex with someone who one truly loves can be a spiritual experience. However, the prudishness as old as time itself has silenced all voices that would imply that sex was anything more than a dirty little secret".

"It is not known how or when he died but legend says he was over a hundred years old. At the beginning of the seventeenth century there was a rise in the public awareness of who the Rosicrucians were. Everyone claimed to know who they were, or be a member of a sect of Rosicrucianism. The Fama Fraternitatis was published anonymously. This was a loose interpretation of Christian Rosenkreutz's 'Brotherhood of the Rosy Cross".

"The only true Rosicrucians are the eight Adepts that have followed one another in unbroken succession of the Albegensian Christian von Germelshausen. They have worked in secret for seven hundred years and will probably continue that way for as long as it is necessary. When some act of kindness is done absent mindedly, that is the time you might meet one of the eight wandering wise men. Pay attention, do not be mean spirited, or you may miss the wisdom that is placed in your heart".

"I can't get my questions down fast enough!"

"Wait, I'm not finished. The symbol of the Rosicrucians is the rose and the cross. The rose is nature's masterpiece. It represents love, perfection and beauty. The cross is the oldest symbol of all. It represents the four cardinal points of the spirit. Together they represent love and knowledge. Both elements are required so the seeker of truth may ask the right questions on the nature of good and evil. When love enters the human heart, it gives unselfishly to the universe, God, or even to some creature as simple as a dog. That heart is on the path of the rose, embraced by its perfection. If man sets aside ignorance and allows his mind to stretch a little further in knowledge, he is embraced by the four spiritual branches of the cross. This is the message of Christian Rosenkreutz, who after journeying for more than a century to tell his truth, left no trace of his passing but a rose at the center of a cross and that, Eric, in answer to your question, is the meaning of the Rosicrucians."

"Are you one of the eight?" flashed across the screen.

"If I were, I couldn't tell you. You know that. So why don't you take some time to think about the questions I can answer."

"I want to see my brother," Eric said.

"I never knew you had a brother," said Grimm.

"He's a little older than me. He'll be running the farm in Mercia by now."

"So go, but be quick," said Grimm. "We don't know when God...I mean the King will send for us."

Eric sprang up off his pallet and threw some clothing in a saddlebag. "Cover for me. I'll be back in two days."

He raced down stairs crashing through the front door of the inn they were housed in and across the street to the stables. As he entered the darkness of the stable, dust motes hung in the air and danced on the breath of Midnight who stood saddled pawing the earth impatiently. The rider, who held his bridle, sat astride an equally powerful stallion as if waiting for this exact moment.

Eric's jaw dropped as Wulfstan said, "Call Grimm. The King is waiting for you both."

Grimm's horse, already saddled, stood on the other side of the warrior earl. He looked like the apocalyptic horseman awaiting the call to war, and Eric screamed "Grimm!" sure that it had come.

They rode into Westminster and the grooms attempted to take the horses but had second thoughts as the three riders all but rode them down on the way to stabling their own mounts. As they entered the chamber, Godwinson was pacing back and forth. His brothers, Gyrth and Leofwine, were standing against the walls with several other housecarls. He stopped and looked at Eric and Grimm.

"Glad you could grace us with your presence. I hope I did not upset any plans you might have had to be elsewhere." Eric looked at Grimm and Godwinson said, "Look to me, ploughboy, when I speak to you."

Wulfstan laid his hand on Godwinson's shoulder, "Sire, remember you are the King. We will all bleed for you, not because we must but because we choose to. He could have been a ploughboy. Someone wanted it otherwise. No man destroys the power of his weapon just to prove he can."

"Forgive me, Eric," said Godwinson. "Wulfstan is right. My anger is a result of a certain situation and I asked you here to help me resolve it." He looked at the faces in the room, all men he could trust. "Tostig has returned from exile. He plans to raid the coast from the Isle of Wight to Sandwich."

Grimm spoke quietly but everyone could hear. "He may face William the Tanner before we do."

"He may join him," said Eric.

"He cannot distinguish his friends from his enemies," said Harold.

"He has no friends," said Eric.

"He has me," Harold said.

"And, of course, the Pirate Copsi," voiced Wulfstan. "We all know what he is doing, Sire. What do you ask of us?"

A voice from the back of the room spoke, "Do you ask us to kill him?"

"Never!" screamed Godwinson. "Who said that?" Gyrth stepped forward.

"We are brothers," Godwinson said. "You would commit the crime of Cain on our family?"

"Brother, who among us can stop him and live," said Leofwine.

"All of you will leave at dawn disguised as seamen. You will make for his ships which will be arriving soon at Sandwich. Leofwine and Gyrth, you will stay here for the obvious reasons. Eric and Grimm will ride to my manor at Hereford. Clean the mess. Take my sister, Edith, to the Benedictines then ride on to Sandwich and join the others. You must get aboard unrecognized and bind and capture Tostig and bring him to me."

"Alive?" said Eric.

"Alive! Now go."

"The Lady Edith, Sire, why the Benedictines?"

"She will join the convent and take holy orders."

Eric was about to speak when Grimm slapped him on the back so hard he bowed forward as did Grimm who said, "We leave immediately, Sire."

Everyone seemed to be moving at once. Then the room was empty and silent. Only Godwinson remained in the silence, like the eye of the impending storm.

Wulfstan materialized from against the hanging tapestries. "It has begun, Sire, as was inevitable. Fear not, he'll be brought back."

"I know," said Godwinson. "I also know it would be better if he were not brought back. Follow Eric. Don't let him make a mistake. He's too experienced for me to accept or forgive mistakes."

As Eric and Grimm rode out from the stable Wulfstan stood at the gate already mounted. "What mess?" asked Eric.

"You'll see, one that only a madman could create. Let's ride we must be in Hereford by nightfall and Sandwich by dawn, time for questions later."

They rode hard and fast. As they crested the hill above Harold's manor all seemed peaceful and pastoral. "All quiet," said Wulfstan. "Let us approach to the rear of the stable Grimm. Eric, you ride up to the main gate."

Eric rode up to the manor. He stopped at the gate and listened. He nudged Midnight with his knees as two horsemen galloped through the gate towards him weapons in hand. A sword swung towards his head. He lay back in the saddle as the sword passed over him at the same time he reached out with his left hand yanking the rider's foot out of the stirrup. He vaulted off Midnight's back, axe in hand. He turned the cloaked figure over. The eyes shot open and a dagger flashed towards his throat. He caught the wrist and gazed hopelessly into the eyes of England's recently bereaved Queen.

"Edith, it's you," he said lamely.

"Pick me up you oaf!"

He lifted her to her feet as Wulfstan and Grimm joined the party. "Well met, axe friend," said Grimm.

"What happened..." before Wulfstan could finish his question a screaming banshee came galloping out of the tree line sword in one hand, axe in the other.

"What's that?" said Grimm staring at the ancient apparition.

"She has been my nurse since childhood and don't you dare hurt her," said Edith.

"Bring her inside," said Wulfstan.

"Not the house," said Edith, "Take us to the barn."

"Take them to the barn, Grimm. Eric and I will go to the house."

Grimm turned to face the Vengeful Grand Dam who did not appear to be running out of energy. She attacked Grimm first with the sword. She made her first pass and he ducked easily underneath the blade taking the sword away from her as she passed. She turned for her second attack. Eric looked back at Grimm who was standing hands on hips waiting.

"She must be fifty years old," he said.

"Older than that I think," said Wulfstan not bothering to look back.

She charged forward swinging the huge axe overhead. As the weapon reached the height of its arc its weight seemed to lift her off the horse as the beast moved forward. Eric could only tell she had landed by the painful look on Grimm's face. They dismounted in front of the kitchen. As Eric looked back he could see Grimm holding the horse and moving side to side trying to avoid the running attacks of Edith's very small, volatile, ancient nurse. As they entered the kitchen the first thing that assaulted their senses was the smell.

"What's that?"

"That's death and not an easy one," said Wulfstan. "Don't move. Wait until your eyes adjust to the darkness and your nose and stomach to the smell."

"Tostig did this?" said Eric as he looked at the carnage and felt his stomach retch.

"Do not!" said Wulfstan. "Stand still. Get hold of yourself. You will have to stand and fight in much worse than this."

"I think that will be different from this," said Eric.

"Not much. Remove your cloak and let us clean this up."

Grimm appeared in the doorway behind them. "This is the work of a mad man," he said.

Wulfstan looked at them and spoke quietly, "This does not require your judgment or opinions so listen. The King's brother has butchered, as far as I can tell, five maybe six men and left their body parts in the wine casks.

The message on the floor, in blood, is in Latin. It says 'Salted meat for a temporary king. England will fall at your feet and this is what it will look like'. So we must find him, but first clean the mess. Grimm, begin digging a ditch. Eric, turn over the wine casks onto the floor."

Eric moved quickly, spilling out the contents of the wine casks onto the floor. A collection of arms, legs, torsos and heads rolled out with the wine and blood.

"Build a fire. We'll burn the bodies and bury the ashes."

Eric quickly had a fire raging outside. The body parts were thrown onto the flames. As Eric and Grimm threw buckets of water onto the floor, cleaning away the blood and wine, Eric said quietly to Grimm, "One of the men was a monk. I remember the scar on his arm. He's from Saint Albans, but his head wasn't there."

Grimm looked at Eric, but it was Wulfstan who said quietly, "Take the pot from the fire and empty it."

Eric lifted the pot from the flames and the monk's dead eye sockets stared at him in anguish. He almost dropped the pot, but Grimm took it from him and threw its contents on the flames.

"Why?" asked Eric.

Grimm said nothing and Wulfstan said, "Finish cleaning up. I'll prepare the Queen. We leave within the hour."

As Wulfstan left, Eric pulled Grimm away from the light and asked, "Do you think he talked before he died?"

"Only if Tostig asked the right question. You said Tostig hated you from the first time he saw you. Well now he has a reason. You'll have to kill him."

"He's a prince of the royal line," said Eric.

Grimm smiled, "He bleeds just the same, fortunately." He stepped outside to collect and saddle the horses.

Wulfstan returned to the kitchen and looked around. "Good," he said. "When the horses are ready throw all that is left of the fire in the ditch and bury it."

Eric moved to obey, then stopped. He turned to Wulfstan. "I wish to ask you something, my Lord," he said.

"It's a question I can't answer. It is always safer to close the barn door before the horse bolts," Wulfstan replied and then paused, "I think you may be too late for that, so remember all you have learned because we are all going to war, but yours has already begun".

Chapter Twelve

Edith and her nurse, Agatha, sat astride their horses just as the warriors did. Eric and Grimm followed behind them and Wulfstan led the party. They rode hard through the night reaching the Monastery of St. Albans in the early hours of the morning. Wulfstan and Eric rode through the gates. Grimm stayed outside watching for any sign they might have been followed. Wulfstan stayed in the saddle as the Abbot and several monks gathered around the Queen.

He said to the Abbot, "My man will see the Queen to her quarters. He has a message from the King he must give her in private."

"I take it you mean the new king, my Lord," said the Abbot.

"The old king is dead, who else would it be, My Lord Abbot?"

"Of course, My Lord, how stupid of me. The hour is late and I...."

In mid sentence Wulfstan stopped him by raising his hand. He looked at Eric and said, "Be quick, there is no time to lose," and with that he wheeled his horse and rode back through the gate to Grimm. "Tostig has spies just as we do. That old Abbot I wouldn't trust even if Godwinson vouched for him."

"Should I kill him?" said Grimm.

"No, that would not help us now. Besides, the King's sister has chosen this place to take holy orders now that she is no longer the Queen."

"What delays Eric?"

"What indeed," said Wulfstan. "He'll follow, and the dawn will not wait for us," he said as he spurred his horse forward.

As Eric walked Edith to her sparsely furnished quarters Agatha spoke constantly of how things would be different now that Lady Edith was no longer Queen but she, Agatha, would never leave her. Even after death she swore she would protect her from above.

"Please go to your quarters, Agatha," said Edith. "I must speak with the King's man." Agatha scurried away looking menacingly at Eric as she left.

Edith looked at Eric and smiled sadly. "From a queen to a servant just like that," she said.

"I'll come back for you when I can," said Eric.

"If you do," she said, "England had better have another king because this one will kill you." She kissed Eric gently on the lips and smiled. "Is it different now that I'm no longer a queen?"

"You will always be a queen and as long as I live it will never be different. I must go now but I promise I will come back for you."

"I'll be here until you do."

He turned and ran through the doors to the courtyard.

The brightness of the lights surprised him as they flashed by and suddenly he stopped as Anna turned his wheelchair round and Nurse Scott took him while Anna practically ran along the hallway to the elevator. Nurse Scott smiled at him.

"So how are we doing today, young Eric? You look rested and, of course, I know you understand everything I say even though you can't respond at the present time."

Eric sat and listened to Nurse Scott chatter on for what seemed like hours when suddenly the elevator doors opened and Anna practically fell out into the hallway. Eric tried to spring to his feet but the body he was in was a shell compared to the one he'd left in the hallway of St. Albans. Mike Armstrong came out of the elevator and reached for Anna just as the Reverend Wolf crossed the hallway in front of Eric and caught her as she fell.

"He's not responding," she said. "He looks awful."

"Let's go into E.J.'s office," said Mike.

E.J. Kissen got up from his desk as they entered. "Good morning."

Mike looked at him and replied, "We have a setback, E.J. I'd like you to listen in. I have some suggestions and I may need your input. Alright, Terry is no longer responding to the chemo. There are several complications. He has two different types of Leukemia which, as I said before, is unusual but not unknown. The inflammation in and around the brain tissue has gone down. He has come out of the coma, but he is weak and the Leukemia is not in remission."

"What does all of that mean?" said Anna.

"Let me continue and I'll explain. I have a plan and suggestions. That's why we are all here. I want to perform stem cell transplantation. In this procedure very intensive radiation and chemo will probably be used. The chemotherapy and radiation are designed to destroy all Leukemia cells in Terry's body. However, they will also destroy the blood forming system in his bone marrow. Healthy stem cells, the cells in bone marrow that enable long term formation of blood, must then be infused to replenish the blood forming system."

"So why don't you just do it?" said Anna.

"I can't just do it, Anna. I need your permission and a suitable donor."

"You have my permission. Who would be a suitable donor?"

"There are three immediate possibilities; you, Terry's father, or Eric."

"Terry's father is not a possibility as I don't know where he is. I haven't seen him in fifteen years."

"Okay, well let's test you first, then Eric."

"Eric can't do this," said Anna.

"If you are not compatible then Eric is the next best choice."

"I don't want Eric tested," said Anna.

Nurse Scott opened the door to the office. "Eric seems to be having some kind of fit. He is moaning and banging his head against his wheelchair."

Stan Wolf went outside to where Eric sat at the nurses' station. "Alright," said Stan, "Let's get your helmet on."

They entered the computer room and put the helmet on Eric. The screen immediately lit up and Eric's words raced across it. "He's my brother. Test me first."

Anna came over to him and said, "Your body is weak. This could weaken you further."

"Don't be stupid," said Eric. "My body is useless. If it can save my brother at least I have a reason for being here. Test Me Now!"

"No, Eric," said Anna.

"If I am not tested before we leave here and Terry dies I will never forgive you and I'll find a way to die."

Anna began to cry hysterically. Both Mike Armstrong and E.J. Kissen sat her down and Kissen tried to reason with her. Armstrong slammed his fist on the desk. The moment of impact gave him the silence he needed.

"You have one boy dying and one threatening to kill himself. You have no time and no choice. Let me test Eric. I need to do the H.L.A. Test, Human Leukocyte Test, to see if he's compatible. If he is, and E.J. agrees, let's do it and no more histrionics. There isn't the time."

"Eric isn't mine. He's Jennifer's."

"Isn't this information a little late?" asked Mike angrily.

"Mike, I don't think you should be shouting at the mother of my patient."

"If we don't move on this, you won't have a patient and neither will I, and she will no longer be anyone's mother. And I believe she just said she is not Eric's mother."

"Could he still be compatible?" asked Anna.

"'Yes," said Mike.

"Alright," said Anna, "test him. I'm fine".

"Let's get moving. There are a hundred things that can go wrong so let's all get on the same side of the fence. Meet me upstairs. Bring Eric. You, too, E.J."

Stan Wolf was standing by the elevator as the entourage left Kissen's office. "What can I do?" he said.

"Not much right now," said Mike, "but come up. I want you to see what's going on as you are as involved as the rest of us."

Anna, Kissen and Eric took the first elevator.

Stan said, "Mike, you realize, of course, the boys have different fathers?"

"I do, different mothers, too. Even so it is still possible they are compatible."

"I don't think I understand," said Stan.

"I think you do," said Mike.

"Oh, you mean?"

"I do. The mothers are sisters."

"Right. In that case shouldn't you test Anna first?"

"I intend to test both Eric and Anna, and you too if you don't mind."

"Oh, of course. I thought I might be too old."

"Only if you're dead. Let's go"

The elevator door opened and they entered. They arrived on the tenth floor just as Anna and Doctor Kissen walked out of the other elevator pushing Eric whose eyes seemed to be blazing. Mike Armstrong and Stan followed a few seconds behind them.

"Anna," said Mike, "I want you all in my office right now so I can explain the game plan." Eric began to moan and bang his head. "No more," said Armstrong. "I know you are intelligent and can understand me so listen. Your brother is in need of immediate help. I am in charge and expect everyone's cooperation. That includes you."
Eric became suddenly silent. "Alright," said Mike, "in my office. Everyone find a seat because you will all have a job to do and the first one is to listen as I'll be doing the talking."

They entered Mike Armstrong's office and sat on whatever chairs they could find. Mike sat on his desk directly in front of Eric who had somehow become the centerpiece of the now overcrowded room.

I'll explain this as quickly as I can. Eric, Anna and Stan will be tested as potential donors for stem cell transplantation to Terry. This means an immediate blood test. Then whoever is the most suitable choice will be admitted for a couple of days. There are two ways we can obtain stem cells. Number one, they are extracted from the bone marrow with multiple aspirations. They are then given to the patient like a blood transfusion. This is called a bone marrow transplant. The alternative is to harvest them from the blood. This is called a stem cell transplant. Terry will receive those healthy stem cells in the same way, that is to say intravenously, directly into the bloodstream".

"A common complication after stem cell transplantation, or bone marrow transplantation, is a rejection reaction which can be fatal. However, a recent discovery of a 'suicide gene' can prevent this by suppressing the immune reaction that would reject the transplant. At the same time the donors' immune cells attack the Leukemia cells in the receiver. Once most of the Leukemia cells are destroyed, the suicide gene is introduced into Terry's system to prevent the donor's cells attacking Terry's healthy cells. This allows the receiver, that is to say Terry's immune system, to restore itself more quickly. I know this sounds dangerous and complicated. It is. It is also our only option. There will be more radiation and chemo. So let's get started, shall we?"

Stan stood up. "Hang on, Mike, I need to clear up the question of the suicide gene."

"Okay," said Mike.

"As I understand it, you introduce it first to Terry to kill his immune response to the donor's stem cells."

"That's right."

"Then you introduce it into the donor's immune cells to stop the attack, presumably after it has destroyed the Leukemia cells, and prevent it from attacking healthy cells."

"Yes, that's correct. Now let's get started. E.J., I would like you here to monitor Eric if he is compatible. Anna and Stan, one of you will stay with the patients, which will be Terry and the donor. Whoever is left will return home to keep the rest of the family calm as I'm sure they are all concerned."

Anna pulled Mike and E.J. outside the office. "What should I tell Eric about Jennifer?"

"Nothing," they said in unison.

"That is a conversation for another time", said E.J.

They went back into the office and Mike said, "Okay, we have a plan. Let's get started."

Stan and Anna both had their hands unconsciously resting on Eric's hands. Nobody moved or spoke. E.J. Kissen broke the silence by saying, "Mike, I'll be in my office. Keep me posted. I'll come back as soon as you need me." He ran his hands through Eric's hair and left.

Terry opened his eyes and looked across at the patient next to him. Eric was wriggling and trying to stop from sliding down the bed. Stan Wolf got up from the chair between the beds and helped prop him up. He placed Eric's helmet on his head and switched on his new laptop.

"Good evening, Terry. We're glad to see you're awake. Oh, by the way, you'll need this so you can see what Eric has to say," he said as he switched on Terry's laptop.

"Thanks," said Eric as his words spilled across the screen without punctuation. "I'm the donor I'm sharing some blood bone marrow or both with you now we'll be blood like brothers I mean like blood brothers."

"Alright," said Stan, "let's not get Terry as excited as you are. How do you feel, Terry?"

"I'm okay, tired. I feel like I'm invisible."

"Me, too," lit up the screen.

"Let me explain what's going on," said Stan. "We all three had blood tests, Eric, your mother and me. Eric is the most compatible so he will be the donor, but Doctor Armstrong will be here shortly to explain it to you."

"Where's Mom?"

"Someone had to go home to check on Jennifer and your grandfather so I asked your mother if I might be the one to stay with you boys."

"That's nice," said Terry. "Thanks."

Anna drove home in despair. Jennifer would feel betrayed she thought. She felt she had been disloyal to her sister and both her sons. Since the day of his birth Eric had been her son and to admit even to herself that it was Jennifer who bore him was painful.

She opened the front door and walked through the house to the living room where her father and sister sat watching T.V. "I'm sorry, Jen. Terry needs a bone marrow transplant and I had to tell the doctors about Eric."

"What about Eric?' asked Jennifer. As Anna was about to speak Jennifer said, "Not here, outside. We'll be right back, Dad."

"Okay," said Sid smiling.

Jennifer opened her BMW and motioned Anna inside. "The priest, I suppose he knows, too?"

"Yes, he is involved in helping us and may also be a donor."

"What a circus. Do you realize you could ruin my career if this gets out?"

"It won't," said Anna. "Besides, times have changed. Society is more forgiving. It would be nice if you were. You are a very successful professional in a very prestigious organization."

"I am about to be promoted in the next six months. A decision like this should be discussed with me first. My future is involved."

"Unfortunately I don't have time to discuss your future Right now it's Terry's future I'm concerned with, if indeed he has one. I had to let them know the truth."

"I have to leave. I'm sick of your ineptitude as a sister. If this affects my life, be assured it will affect yours."

"What do you mean?" asked Anna.

"You know exactly what I mean. Eric was a problem you took on. I told you I couldn't love him. If you put the spotlight on me you'll need another donor. Get out of my car now."

Anna stood in the driveway as Jennifer raced away. The soccer coach pulled up in a fog of exhaust fumes. "Hi, Anna, just thought I'd drop by and see what's doing. Who's the race car driver?"

"It's a long story, Bob. Come inside. Terry is in the hospital. He has Leukemia," she said as the tears began rolling down her cheeks.

"What can I do to help you, Anna?"

She wiped her tears and said, "Any chance you could stay for an hour and baby sit Dad so I can slip back to the hospital? I know it's an imposition."

"Of course I'll stay. Off you go. I'll introduce myself to your dad. See you in an hour.

Chapter Thirteen

Anna crossed the ward with Mike Armstrong. Everyone was wearing masks and gloves.

"By the way," Terry said, "I still want to know about the secret society, or is this it?"

"Well, you're definitely brothers in humor," said Stan as he stood up. "Mike, I was about to call you."

"Anna just got back so we came to see what's happening."

"How's Granddad?" said Terry.

"He's fine. Aunt Jennifer is helping me with him for a few days. Your aunt and grandfather want you both home as soon as possible."

"Which is why I'm here really," said Mike. "Let me explain what we're going to do. Eric, we'll take the stem cells from the bone marrow in your chest, that is to say, through the sternum. The reason being your chest is much stronger than your hips as your legs have been immobile for so long. You won't feel any pain and the procedure takes about one hour. You will be under general anesthetic. Doctor Kissen and several members of my team will be there to make sure all goes smoothly. Any questions?"

The screen answered, "When do we begin?"

"In about one hour. Terry, for the next two or three days you will have more chemo and probably radiation therapy. This is to kill any remaining cancer cells. The transplant will be by I.V. and can take one to five hours. Questions?"

"Yes, is this safe for my brother?"

"We have a medical team supervising the procedure. At most he'll feel tired and a little stiff for a few days."

Eric's screen spilled out his thoughts. "Oh, gee, a few days of stiffness and soreness before I get back to my usual feeling of stiffness and soreness. Let's get on with it, please."

"You're right, let's get on with it. This will be nothing compared to what you live with. I admire your courage," said Mike.

"It's not courage. I have no choice about how I live. I'm glad I can help my brother." The screen went blank.

Terry smiled, "You sound like me when I thought you were sick."

Eric burst into a high moaning squeak which was definitely a laugh.

The operating room was crowded. Eric was in a sitting position on the raised operating table. Kissen was beside him suited up in mask, gloves, headgear and looked more sterile than Eric had ever seen him. The anesthesiologist stood behind him in the same attire. There were three nurses, a technician and Doctor Armstrong. As they lowered the operating table Eric felt nervous. The anesthesiologist put a plastic mask over his face and said, "Count backwards from one hundred." He reached ninety-two when he felt a powerful thud in his chest.

He was lifted clean off the back of Midnight and landed on his back on the forest floor. The arrow had gone through his cloak, pinned it to a tree, and thrown him to the ground. He scrambled to his feet to hear the dull thud of another body landing on the ground somewhere ahead of where he stood, and then a gurgling cry as someone else exhaled for the last time.

"Mount up," said Grimm. "Wulfstan sent me back. He thought we might be followed. Hurry, we must meet him at dawn, he won't wait."

"He's been saying that to me since the day I met him," said Eric as he sprang into the saddle and they rode out onto the road towards Sandwich. "Where do we meet him?"

"He told me to bring you and said he would find us. First we must stable the horses and change clothes. We're supposed to be seamen."

"How pleasant," said Eric, "a sea voyage in the company of the madman, Tostig, and his equally vicious dog, Copsi."

"What do you know of Copsi?"

"He's a pirate, a Pict who paints himself blue and his best friend is a butcher whose brother is the King of England. Did I miss anything?"

"Aye," said Grimm, "capturing them alive while we empty the contents of our stomachs on deck."

"Oh, yes, that. I did forget about that."

They laughed together as their horses galloped towards the approaching dawn closing the distance between yesterday's carnage and the smell of death which was always behind them or before them. Eric's thoughts drifted for a moment and he wondered what life would be like as a ploughman. "Too late now," he said into the wind.

They entered the town of Sandwich at a walk so as not to draw attention to themselves. Although the town was small it was one of the Cinque Ports designated by Edward the Confessor whereby for fifteen days free service of men and ships per year the portmen and town received many privileges. They walked their horses into the stables. An old seamen sat outside between the stables and the inn. His clothes were filthy and he stank of vomit and ale.

As they entered the stable Eric said to Grimm, "Two days at sea and we'll smell like that."

A voice behind them said, "You had better get used to it then."

Grimm spun around with his dagger in his hand.

"Wait," said Eric.

The drunken seaman stood before them in the darkness no less smelly, but a lot less drunk. "Earl Wulf...."

"Quiet," said the voice. "Get dressed. The sun is up and our ships are waiting. Hurry!"

They quickly dressed and followed Wulfstan, although in a crowd they would not know him or each other except for Grimm's height. The man looked like a tree in seaman's clothing.

They boarded the ship and Eric said, "This is the last place I want to be."

"Do not make it so obvious or this will be the last place you will be," said Grimm.

There were six ships fully supplied with men and provisions, men of Godwinson's housecarls and seamen all together waiting on the elusive Tostig. He had raided up and down the coast stealing ships and provisions to add to his fleet, but so far had avoided Sandwich. It seemed he may have known there was a trap. Two weeks passed without incident, then one night Eric and Grimm awoke among strangers whose swords and axes were drawn and ready to be used against any man who resisted them. Tostig's men had arrived.

"I wonder...."

"Don't wonder," said Grimm. "Look."

Tostig's ship was drawing alongside them. He stood at the prow bare chested, eyes blazing. He wore a black leather helmet with the wings of a hawk blowing in the wind like he was about to take flight. He had the look of a madman. Standing next to him was a tall, lean warrior, his hair red and tied back in a pony tail. He had one blue eye, where the other eye had been was a fierce scar that spread upwards from the eyelid like a claw raising the eyebrow. The lower part was a jagged line that ran down his cheek and stopped beside his hawk-like nose which was pushed at an odd angle across his face.

"That is Copsi," said Grimm.

"Not much of a face left to paint blue," said Eric.

"I imagine the man that gave him that face is the one that made him famous."

A weathered seaman standing behind them said, "That's right. His name was Gerd. Copsi cut off his arms while his own face was hanging off, then had the stumps burned to stop the bleeding. He hung his body from the stern. It took him hours to die while his body was being eaten by sea creatures. Copsi watched in silence as I stitched his face back on."

"Nice job," said Grimm.

"You should have seen it before my needlework. As I said, he sat in silence. The ship and everyone on it was silent except Gerd. He wasn't silent."

"What did Gerd use on him," Eric said.

"The boss in the center of his shield. It consisted of five spikes, one in the center and four surrounding that one. Watch when he comes on board. He carries it high on his left arm to remind him of Gerd."

"I think his face might do that," said Eric.

"How many ships do they have?" asked Grimm.

"Sixty. Some of them belong to Godwinson. Copsi brought about twelve or fifteen."

"Isn't Copsi from Orkney?" said Eric.

"That he is."

"Then he is subject to Harald Hardrada, the Norwegian King."

"That's right," said the seaman.

"He defies his King?" said Eric.

"He's cruel, not stupid, housecarl."

Grimm moved close to the seaman and placed his dagger under his heart. "What did you say?"

"You are among friends. There is not a man on board who would betray Godwinson for those mad dogs. Listen, Copsi is here because Harald Hardrada sent him to help Tostig and then Hardrada will help himself. Godwinson isn't the only warrior king. Hardarada is a man who knows how to profit from the mistakes and the weaknesses of others, even if it's only betrayal."

"Betrayal seems to be something you're familiar with friend," said Eric.

"It's something we're all familiar with, friend," said the seaman.

"Well, now we know why Copsi is here. Why are you here?"

"To make sure you get what you came for and remind you that it must be delivered as requested and not as you would like."

Grimm was about to speak and the seaman said, "That is all. No more talk. We must not be seen together. If Tostig recognizes you as men of Harold Godwinson you will die here and believe me there will be no glory in it." With that he walked to the port side of the ship and watched as Tostig's ship pulled alongside them.

Tostig and Copsi stepped easily over the side of the ship. As they landed on deck Tostig seemed to stumble although there was no object that might trip him. Copsi reached to help him up but he brushed him away saying, "I need the help of no man."

He walked across the deck towards where the ship's men had gathered. Part of one of the sails had come loose. As it whipped across the deck Copsi ducked under it easily whereas Tostig seemed not to see it and it lashed across his face like a whip. His head spun with the force of the blow. Some men moved as if to steady him. He laughed.

"Just the kiss of the wind," he said. He and Copsi walked the deck of the ship looking the men over. He stopped before Eric and looked at him. "You remind me of someone. The long hair and painted face are different. Are you a Pict?"

"No, Sire," replied Eric as he looked into the strange eyes of Tostig Godwinson. He seemed to stare without looking. The expression was that of a man in constant and severe pain.

He passed on, looked at Grimm and laughed, "You I would remember."

Copsi stepped in front of Eric and said, "Your face, did it hurt when they pricked it with blue dye and mixed it with your blood?"

"I don't remember."

"I also have little memory of my painted face, but look closely at it now. I've seen men faint under its onslaught."

"In battle it would not be your face that concerns me, but the shield you wear on your arm and the axe you constantly stroke."

"You use your eyes well."

"They say your one eye sees more than any man's two."

Copsi stared at Eric intensely and smiled a feral smile. "You are a warrior alright, but no seaman. You stand on deck like a drunk and beneath the blue dye your face is green. You grit your teeth to hold your gorge."

"No," said Eric. "I grit my teeth because you are so pretty and I'm mindful of my manners."

Anger flashed in that one steely blue eye for a brief moment. "Fearless is good," he said, "but only until you taste fear."

"All men taste fear. We don't all swallow it."

"We shall see," replied Copsi.

Tostig signaled Copsi to board their ship. As he stood on the deck his eye never left Eric. "Now you have two enemies," said Grimm. "Slow down or we'll have to fight to get into the war."

Tostig stood at the helm of his ship as it bucked across the waves. He seemed less intent on sailing than fighting the elements or some other unseen enemy. "Even the sea rebels against those two messengers from Hell," said Eric.

"If you can keep control of your tongue long enough we can send them back there," smiled Grimm.

That night the ships anchored off the coast of Norfolk and Tostig ordered a raid for provisions and men.

Eric said to Grimm, "Now is our chance to kill him."

Grimm looked at Eric and said, "We gave our word to take him alive."

The old seaman had been listening to the exchange. "Our ship will not go on this raid but you should both know that on the King's orders the man that kills Tostig Godwinson is to be dispatched with him." He moved silently away into the darkness of the ship.

In the early hours of the morning, they heard the pillaging ships return with supplies and men of fighting age who had been offered the choice to fight for Tostig or instant death. 'Not such a difficult choice really', thought Eric. The ships did not set sail again until the late morning. They sailed north then turned into the estuary of the Humber.

"He seems to be heading for his old Earldom," said Grimm. "This truly is madness. Even if we take Northumbria there is not a man in the county that won't try to kill him."

"I think he knows that," said Eric. "He is courting death and challenging it to take him."

He no sooner had spoken when the Northern shore lit up with fires one after the other, the flames carried by some invisible force as a call to war. A call that Tostig heard because he screamed out before he turned his ships to the South shore, "I am coming back to destroy you all. Keep the fires burning. I will use them." His voice echoed across the water like an eerie portent of death.

The old seaman came back to sit with Eric and Grimm. "I thought you did not wish to be seen with us," said Eric.

"Makes no difference now," he said. "We're shipmates in the service of Tostig."

"You have a way of rubbing me the wrong way, old man," said Eric.

"Quiet," said Grimm. "We're heading for Lindsey."

"It won't be easy pillaging against the men of the old Danelaw," said the seaman.

Grimm said, "That's true. I've fought alongside them. They don't surrender."

"None of this sounds very promising for what we must do," said Eric.

The old seaman got up and said, "See you on the other side," and left.

The ships grounded close to the shore. All was silent. Eric began to move and Grimm said, "Wait, can you hear anything?"

"No," said Eric. "Let's go and get this done."

"This is not right," said Grimm.

"What?"

"Not to hear anything," he said.

Just then Tostig jumped into the slimy shallows of the water axe in hand. Copsi and the others immediately followed. Eric and Grimm leapt over the side together, carrying only their daggers. They began running through the darkness guided by the sound of Tostig's voice telling his men to keep up. The ground was wet and marshy but Eric and Grimm passed most of the men and were running alongside Tostig. Ahead of them was a small, marshy brook and a little further on a small sleeping village. As Eric and Grimm leapt across the brook they heard a thud. Tostig stumbled, his axe left his hand and he lay sprawled on his back, his face illuminated by the moon. Eric saw his chance and picked up Tostig's axe and raised it to strike.

The voice of the old seaman changed as he said, "Look at him, Eric. He's blind."

Eric dropped the axe and looked at Wulfstan. "It's you," he said. "Why did I not know you?"

Wulfstan replied, "In our work a disguise must often be changed."

"Harold's ploughboy," said Tostig. "I should have known that voice. We are betrayed!" he screamed.

Eric, Grimm and Wulfstan turned to face the onslaught of Tostig's men. The first three men came running out of the trees screaming. As Wulfstan and the two housecarls drew their weapons the whistle and dull thud of the arrows striking Tostig's men dropped them into the brook on top of their leader.

"Get out," yelled Wulfstan and he was gone.

"You're right," said Eric. "The men of the old Danelaw don't surrender." He turned to Grimm and saw him go down. His dagger was knocked from his hand and his head exploded.

Eric opened his eyes and E.J. Kissen, Mike Armstrong and Anna were all at his bedside.

"How do you feel," said Mike. "You look okay," he said answering his own question. "You can have your cap and computer in about an hour. Terry is doing okay. Other questions will have to wait. Rest! One hour."

Eric opened his eyes and his laptop was in front of him, his cap was on his head and he began to ask questions. "Is Terry okay?"

Anna was by his bed. "Yes, he seems to be okay."

"Good," flashed across the screen, "because I have a headache, feel like I've been punched in the chest and, of course, I can't move my arms or legs. Could we sue?"

"That's not funny, Eric."

"No it isn't," he replied.

"I'm sorry," said Anna. "I know you must be tired."

"Actually, I'm not sure what I am."

"Eric, please, I'm tired and I can't think straight."

"That I can do," flashed across the screen. "I can't do anything else straight like stand, walk, talk or even lie down."

Chapter Fourteen

Anna drove home from the hospital alone. The van moved through the quiet streets and for the first time in many years she was aware of how lonely silence could be. She pulled into the driveway surprised to see Jennifer's car was already there.

The front door opened and Jennifer said, "I'm sorry about last week, I mean the things I said. I've made tea and Dad is having a day of lucidity. It's like he woke up from the nap he took ten years ago. Look, try and forgive me. I know you helped me with Eric. I just didn't think it would ever be discussed again."

"Neither did I," said Anna. She went into the kitchen. Sid was sitting drinking tea.

"Hello, dear," he said, "How are the boys?"

"It's a little early to say how Terry is but the bone marrow transplant seems to have helped. We should know in about two weeks, I think."

"What about Eric?"

"He seems very unhappy. In fact, when he couldn't communicate it was easier to handle him because I never knew how unhappy he was or how he must feel to have a mind and spirit trapped in a body that at best is a small prison cell."

"When he comes home I'll make a point of spending more time with him," said Sid. "I can learn to use the computer, too."

"No need," said Jennifer. "Just talk, he can hear you and answer as fast as you can make a comment. Oh, I don't just mean you, Dad, I mean anyone."

"That's okay, Jen, I know I'm a little slow, but I don't foresee a problem unless I stop."

"Now, Dad, please don't talk like that," said Anna. "Both boys love you very much and I couldn't run the house without you so no talk about stopping. I need you full throttle as always,"

"Right," said Sid. "In that case I'm off to the kitchen to start the dishwasher."

"I'm sorry, Anna," said Jennifer. "I wasn't thinking."

"You're always thinking. That's the problem. Be a little more selective. He is our dad."

"I know. I know," said Jennifer. "I've worked with kids and adults with learning disabilities and behavioral problems for over ten years and I've watched you with Dad, Terry, and Eric and you're so much better at it than I am and I don't know why."

"Oh, I'm sure I couldn't do your job."

"You just did. That's what I'm telling you. I have to go." Jennifer got up and left, slamming the door. Within thirty seconds the door opened and she said, "Can you move your car?"

"No," said Anna. "The key is on the counter. You move it."

"Why can't you just pull it out so I don't have to dance back and forth moving both cars?"

"This is what you do, Jennifer. Why don't we all make things easier for you? Alright, let's go. I'll move my car."

Anna went out to the car. Jennifer got into her BMW and slammed the door. As Anna backed out Jennifer screamed out of the driveway in reverse and raced down the street. Anna went back into the kitchen and sat down. Sid had filled the dishwasher and smiled at Anna.

"It looks like I'm not the only one that works at full throttle."

"I think we're at a high stress level right now. You and I handle it better."

The door bell rang. As Anna was about to stand up Sid said, "Sit. I'll get it." He opened the door and standing there looking a little sheepish was Bob Anderson, Terry's soccer coach. "Good evening," said Sid. "Have we met?"

"Evening, I'm Terry's coach. I wondered if Anna was at home."

"She is, come in."

Bob came in holding a soccer ball. "Evening, Anna, this if for Terry. The whole team signed and wrote messages to him."

"How kind," said Anna. "Sit down. Have some tea."

"Well, I don't want...."

"Please," she said. "Sit. Let me read it."

All the boys' names were on the ball. One boy had written, *'we can't win until you win, get well soon, Kevin'.* Another had written, *'bend it like Beckham, then break it, get well, Alex'.* Then in large black letters someone had written, *'**if you need our blood there are twelve of us**'.* It was signed Horace.

Anna had tears running down her face. "Who is Horace?"

"He is the fat boy who is usually on the bench, but sometimes is the goalie."

"Bob, thank you so much. I'll take it to Terry tomorrow. I'm sure it will cheer him up."

Bob got up to leave, "Remember, Anna, those boys are serious. They all have parental approval, except Horace. He lives in a group home. It was Horace who organized it. Tell Terry we'll be in to see him as soon as we are given the okay."

Anna kissed him on the cheek and thanked him again. Sid got up and saw him to the door. "Thanks coach. It looks like you taught your boys more than soccer."

"I wish I could take credit but my pupils have become my teachers. Good night," he said and turned and walked down the driveway.

Two days later Anna sat beside Terry with the soccer ball. He couldn't touch it, but Anna held it for him to read. He smiled as he read it and said, "Look at Horace, a knight after all and I was never very nice to him."

"Well, when you get back to the team you can change that."

Terry looked over at the glass window and outside smiling at him was a fat, ruddy faced boy. He raised his hand weakly and waved in recognition. Anna turned and standing in the window was the Reverend Stan Wolf who just waved back.

"He was there," said Terry.

"He still is," said Anna as Terry's laptop clicked into life.

"Is he one of the eight?" flashed onto the screen. Eric was moaning quietly. Anna slid her chair over to him.

"So, how do you feel? You can come home today."

"I feel fine," flashed across the screen...."on the inside anyway".

Anna stood up and said to Terry, "I'm going to talk to Doctor Armstrong and Doctor Kissen. I'll be back as quick as I can. She leaned over and kissed Eric, then left for Doctor Armstrong's office.

"Is who one of the eight what?" flashed across Eric's screen.

"Wise men, Adepts, the Chosen of Rosenkreutz," clicked across Terry's screen.

"You mean Horace? He's sixteen, dufi," flashed back to Eric.

"What does that have to do with anything. He's a messenger. He has given you a message of strength and courage. All you have to do is read it Terry"

"He was at the window. He disappeared," flashed back.

"Maybe it was just your imagination....Smokey."

"I think I liked you better before I knew you could think, especially in old Motown hits"

"Well, I didn't like you better before you could think, but then that's only been about two weeks."

"Okay, I'm sorry. So I was a lousy big brother."

"No, you were a lousy human being. The brother part was the least of your worries. Maybe lying on your back out of control taught you something."

"What?"

"To think."

"Are you always going to be like this?"

"I hope not," replied Eric. "I have things to do and places to go."

Terry coughed and said, "You're a great brother. I'm glad I found you. Try and remember I'm the oldest," he laughed.

Eric moaned quietly as his answer crossed the screen, "You're not even close." Then the screen went blank and he appeared to be sleeping.

Terry looked at the message and thought, "I suppose he's right. I have been a little immature." He closed his eyes to rest for a moment. When he opened them he discovered Eric had gone home. Standing beside the bed was Horace. Terry heard him say, "It will be a hard fight but you must honor your brother and do it."

"What do you mean, Horace?" There was no answer as Horace was no longer there. Stan Wolf sat down beside Terry. His eyes opened again.

"I think I'm hallucinating," said Terry. "I keep seeing Horace Rose and he talks to me, but I hear him in my mind. There isn't any sound."

"It may be that you were dreaming about him," said Stan.

"Eric said he was one of the eight, a chosen messenger or something like it. What did he mean?"

"Ah," said Stan, "that's a good question. Sometimes help and support come from the place you least expect it."

"I treated him like crap."

"Interesting, and still he wants to help you."

"What does it mean?"

"He's chosen you. Sleep. You must get well."

"I am a little tired. Stan, you know I treated everyone like crap."

"Sometimes it's necessary to be selfish to understand unselfishness."

"Like my brother, Eric," said Terry as he fell asleep. "He's unselfish."

"Yes," said Stan. He smiled, stood up and seemed to pray over the sleeping boy. Then he left the room to talk to Mike Armstrong.

Mike was standing at the door of his office. "Hey, Stan, come in. Sit down."

"Thanks," said Stan. "I actually feel like I need to sit down. This work becomes more complex the longer I do it."

"That's just like medicine," said Mike. "We advance, disease and illness catch up. We discover a cure for one disease and a new one appears."

"Right." said Stan. "It's good and evil of another sort. It's hard to watch goodness destroyed even although in the end it prevails."

"You think so?"

"I do. Christ died on the cross and Christianity was born. The death of Jacques Molay, the Grand Master of the Templar, led to the creation of the Freemasons. The death of the Rosenkreutz family left their only survivor to become one of the purest men to ever live and create Rosicrucianism with a view to advance man through knowledge and goodness."

"I watched you pray over Terry," said Mike.

"I'm a priest. I also pray for you."

"You are a strange and very interesting man," said Mike. "I don't know that I can believe what you believe, but it's fascinating."

"Oh, it's much more than that, Mike. What you have is that syndrome that almost all doctors have. You are so close to life and death on a daily basis you develop a God complex. Don't take it as an insult. It isn't meant that way. It's a fact of life that you make decisions every day that most people may only have to make once or twice in their lives. As a result, you cease to believe, if you ever did."

"I'm not insulted, Stan. The God complex is hardly a new idea and to tell you the truth, the pain of watching and waiting to see if a patient will live or die does erode faith. Some days I think God exists, most other days, if He does, then He is elsewhere and the decisions are left up to me."

"I understand," said Stan.

"I wonder," said Mike. "Will you see Mrs. Shepard?"

"I will."

"Good. Tell her things look quite good. His white count is up. I have to lie down for an hour. See you later."

"Okay," said Stan.

Chapter Fifteen

Anna opened the door to Stan. "I'm sorry to drop by so late," he said. "I just left Mike Armstrong. He wanted me to tell you things look quite good. Terry's white blood cell count is up."

"Oh, come in. That's good news. I went by his office but he wasn't there and I waited as long as I could. I'm so glad you are here helping us. I was feeling anxious and was about to call, but as always when I need an answer you appear."

Stan laughed, "Just another aspect of being a magician."

"If only you were," said Anna. "I have three wishes you could grant immediately."

"Have a little faith. We have a Master Magician on our side. The plan is unfolding."

"I wish I believed as you do."

"Now that one I can help you with," he said as he sat down.

"Is there anything I can get you?"

"No, thanks" said Stan. "I'd just like to see Eric if I may before I go home."

"Of course, he's in his room. I'm sure he was hoping you would come."

Stan entered Eric's bedroom. He seemed to be studying something but he closed what he was looking at before Stan could see what it was. "Studying," said Stan.

"Not really," replied the screen.

"Terry seems to be improving. How do you feel?"

"Useless, imprisoned," came the answer.

"Medicine is advancing at an incredible rate and you're young. I'm sure we'll be able to change your life drastically in the next few years."

"I have no wish to be imprisoned for the next few years."

"It wouldn't be my choice either," said Grimm. "At least you're conscious now."

"Barely," said Eric, "and my head hurts."

"You're lucky it's still on your shoulders," said his friend.

"Where are we?"

"I don't know, but it stinks and we haven't eaten in days."

Both men were chained hand and foot to the walls of their prison. The floor was covered in damp earth and straw. Eric winced as a rat bit his leg then he crushed it between his knees. "Breakfast," said Grimm.

Just then the door opened and an old man placed two bowls of weak porridge next to them, kicking them as he left. Grimm lifted his chained legs and kicked the old man hard enough to send him to his knees.

"Enjoy your breakfast," said the old man. "It will be the last you get from me."

"I'd rather eat the rats," said Grimm.

The old man picked himself up and left, bolting the door behind him. Eric shouted, "How long have we been here?" No one answered. Grimm said he thought it might be one or two weeks. They managed to pick up the bowls and swallow the distasteful gruel.

Eric opened his eyes as Anna fed him some type of baby food. It tasted like mashed peas. The helmet was on his desk and Anna was oblivious to anything but feeding him, so he swallowed the mush as quickly as he could so that he might get back to his only form of communication.

"I'm taking you to Doctor Kissen today," said Anna. "Then afterwards we'll go upstairs to see Terry."

Eric sat in his chair motionless and Anna took the dishes back into the kitchen. She passed through the living room and noticed Sid in his chair in front of the T.V. pressing the remote while the chair rose and fell rhythmically and the T.V. remained a blank screen.

"Okay, Dad?"

"Hello, dear," he said and returned to the finger rolling action that controlled the remote.

E.J. Kissen was just entering the hospital as Anna pulled up in her van. "Good morning," he said as he stopped to help Anna get Eric out of the van and up the ramp.

"Good morning," said Anna looking at him for the first time as a man rather than a doctor. He smiled at her realizing that something different had just passed between them.

"It seems we've been seeing a lot of each other lately," he said.

"You certainly seem to spend much of your time here," said Anna. "Maybe you should have a hobby."

"I have a vacation coming in a couple of weeks. That's always a good time to regroup."

"Any plans?" asked Anna.

"Not really. I'm not much of a planner in that way. I usually wait till the last minute, mostly because I really need to be here until the last minute and sometimes beyond that. Let me take my jacket off and I'll check Eric. I'll meet you in his computer room. I'm sure he'll have something to add to the conversation."

"Oh yes, E.J., he is always enthusiastic about coming to visit with you."

They went into the computer room to wait for E.J. Anna put Eric's cap on his head and the screen immediately came to life. "He likes you," crossed the screen.

"I like him, too," said Anna.

Kissen entered the room and said, "That's good because I like you, too. Actually, I am fond of the whole family, Grandpa included. Alright, now that we have that out of the way let's check you out, Eric, and see if there are any positive changes."

"The only positive change that would make any difference would be the one that allowed me to walk out of here."

"I don't think that is going to happen," said Kissen.

"No," flashed on the screen, a pause and then, "what will happen will be my death so I can be free."

"Eric," said Anna, "please don't say that. Dying is not the answer to your problems."

"Neither is living in this body, in this time," walked across the screen.

"I don't understand you," said Anna.

"I know," said the computer. "How could you? You've only known me for a few months."

E.J. Kissen sat on the desk and said, "Let's get the tests done and then I have a suggestion, if you'd like to change the direction of our conversation."

"Alright," said Kissen, "everything looks good. Blood pressure normal, reflexes are the same, no significant changes."

"On the outside at least," flashed the computer.

"That's right," he said. "Okay, Anna, in two weeks I'm on vacation. I've decided I am going to Stamford. My father lives there and Stan is curious as to why such a small town has so many churches. I'm going to ask him to come with me. I thought we could talk to Mike Armstrong and if it seems Terry is in good enough shape to come we might all go, you, Stan, Terry, and Eric. I, of course, would be the tour guide."

"Oh," said Anna. "I thought you weren't a planner. I mean, that sounds wonderful. Is your father a man of the cloth?"

"No, he's an English professor at Oxford with an interest in history, particularly Stamford's. He has a cottage there, actually. It's called the Manse. It used to be the minister's house for one of the more famous churches. Even in Medieval times there were fourteen churches and a couple of monasteries and, I believe, four priories. Anyway, there are more now. I think in excess of a hundred, but I'm not sure. Dad will be able to give you more exact information and delight in the fact that someone is interested in his ramblings of ancient Britain."

The computer flashed, "I want to go."

"Right O then. That's the plan. Now we just have to execute it. Why not nip upstairs and see how Terry is and we'll discuss the details once we're sure he is okay to go."

Mike Armstrong came out of Terry's room just as Anna was about to enter it. "Mask, Anna," he said. "He has a fungal infection in his lungs but the count is up so it's good news and not so good news. A couple of days and we'll have a clearer picture. How's Eric?"

"Rebellious, I think, would describe how he is at the moment."

"Yes, I think I can see his point of view. A mind that is running and leaping and a body that can't. I can only imagine how that must be."

"I know, Mike, I wish something could be done to help him, but I don't see that happening in the near future."

"Well, let's get this one stable first," he said as Terry smiled across the room at them. "Get your scrubs and mask on and meet me at the soccer player's tent."

As she looked at Terry she said, "Mike? We were invited on a mini vacation with E.J. and Stan to visit Stamford. What do you think?"

"When?" he said.

"In about two weeks."

"Maybe. It's too soon to say. I'll let you know. If Terry can't make it, I still think you and Eric should go. I'll be here for Terry. Anyway, let's go in and see him. Don't mention the vacation just yet."

"He will get better, won't he?"

"He's improving in some ways, but he has a fight on his hands, Anna, and I promise I'll do all that I can and Stan Wolf has many contacts in the world of science and medicine and he is a relentless crusader."

"That sounds like you said 'no.'"

"What I'm saying is I don't know. Let's go in now because a conversation that lasts this long gets him anxious. He's been waiting for you all morning."

Terry waved and mouthed, "Hi mom."

"You look better, dear, a little thinner but better."

"He's starving me," said Terry. "I think he's being paid by St. Ninians soccer team to keep me out for the season.

Chapter Sixteen

"What month is it?" said Eric.

"I think it is August," said Grimm.

"We've been here at least three months," said Eric.

The sound of the bolt on the door being opened sharpened their senses. "It's September you turds. I've carried you for four months," said the old man.

"You can barely carry yourself," said Eric. "Go away and die."

"Aha," said the old man. "So the Viking spirit still lives in one of you at least."

Grimm reached out and grabbed his ankle. As the old man fell he said, "All right. You'll both die in here."

"So will you, old man," said Grimm as he sunk his teeth into his Achilles tendon. "You will not walk out of here."

"Wait!" said the old man. "I have a hammer that you may release yourself. Unhand me."

"The hammer first," said Eric.

"Take it," said the old man. "You'll need it. Hardrada has come and he will not take or keep prisoners. A Viking's death awaits you both."

Grimm released him as he took the hammer from him. "Get out now," he yelled, "or you will be the first to die."

The old man took off at a run leaving the cell door ajar. The sound of carts, animals and people running in panic filled their ears. "The King has left us to die," said Grimm.

"Pick up the hammer and break the chains from the wall," said Eric. "The King does not know where we are but I know where he is."

"Where?" said Grimm.

Eric pulled the coin that hung around his neck. "He is here, close to my heart. I will never desert him and he will never desert me, or you my friend. He gave you the spear that his father carried so complain no more and tear those chains from the wall. We have a king to protect and at least one war to fight."

"You're right but I fear that, knowing Godwinson, one war will not be enough."

"What became of Tostig, I wonder," said Eric.

"He may be dead," said Grimm.

"Enough talk, hammer at the chains until we break free of this wall."

Grimm hammered at the wall. When he tired Eric took over. Their strength seemed to have deserted them. After two hours of hammering and pulling the chains broke free. Eric stood up and pulled Grimm with him. They went outside into the deserted village.

Grimm said, "Where are we?"

"Look," said Eric as they watched the dragon ships sail up the river Humber.

"It's Hardrada," said Grimm.

"No," said Eric. "I think it's Tostig, but we are close to York. We must find the men of Wallingford and the king, otherwise this will be a fight that will not be fought by us."

"Look," said Eric, "the Blacksmith shop. Come with me and I'll remove our chains."

"Who taught you to Blacksmith, farm boy?" said Grimm.

"Wulfstan," said Eric.

"It sounds like you saying my name. Are you?"

Eric opened his eyes. Stan Wolf stood before him and Eric wrote, "Wulfstan. It is kind of your name I suppose."

"Yes," said Stan, "but you said it before you wrote it. I heard you say it."

"That's funny," wrote Eric, "because as I understand it my vocal chords don't work."

"I know. I must have imagined it. Anyway, it sounded real. I imagine in my mind what I want more than anything is to have you speak to me. It's an embarrassing kind of arrogance, but I can't help it. I feel I know you and in my mind I can hear your voice."

The computer answered him. "We know each other in another place and time as you have already said. I believe it, and don't know how to tell you except by saying I want to be there, not here."

"Maybe if we take this trip to Stamford you'll feel better," said Stan. "I have always wanted to visit. It is such a quaint town with lots of history. It was one of the five boroughs of an area known as the Danelaw."

"I hope Terry can go," the computer screen said.

"Well, in a couple of weeks we'll know, how about if I read to you for awhile?"

"No thanks. I'm tired," crossed the screen and it went blank.

The wind whipped and cracked the banner and it opened up to reveal the black raven of Harold Hardrada. "This is an invading army," said Eric. "The old man told the truth. Hardrada has joined Tostig. Look. The Icelandic and Scottish pennants are there, too. Malcom, the Scots King, has joined the Viking and the Traitor. All we need now is William landing in the South and we'll have what you predicted, two wars for Godwinson. I wonder if he knows."

"He knows. It's not him who was imprisoned. It was us. We must follow the Humber until we find him or death finds us." The Viking Armada continued past them up the Humber. "There must be five hundred dragon ships," said Grimm.

"They will put York to the sword long before we reach it," said Eric.

"York will know by now that they are coming and so, God willing, will the King and his army. I pray we get there before the battle is over. We deserve one before the raven tears our flesh from our bones."

"I just want to live long enough to kill Tostig," said Eric. As the night descended on them, they lay down exhausted in the shadow of a great oak. "I wish I had the strength to go on," said Eric.

"Sleep now. There will still be miles to travel in the morning."

Chapter Seventeen

"Good morning," said Jennifer. Eric opened his eyes. "So you're off to visit Stamford," she said. "Let's wash your face and tidy you up. Terry will be home later this morning and Granddad will be staying with me for a few days. It should be fun for all of you, even with the renegade priest."

Put the helmet on thought Eric, although not loud enough for his aunt to hear as she left the room saying, "C'mon, Dad, let's get you packed for your holiday with me. I'll show you the classier spots of York."

Sid was sitting in his chair oblivious to all that was happening around him. Eric looked at him as Jennifer bustled around getting his bag packed for his long weekend with her. I'm just the same as my granddad he thought, sitting in a chair watching the world and time pass. At least he lived, even if he can't remember it. I haven't lived and I can remember it. If this is a dream I never want to sleep again. If my other life is a dream, I want to sleep forever.

The front door opened and a much thinner Terry and happier Anna walked through it. "Hi," said Terry as he walked over to Eric and put the cap on his head.

"Hi, yourself," the computer answered.

"Oh, I'm sorry," said Jennifer. "I forgot all about the headgear."

"You wouldn't forget if you were the one that needed it," sped across the screen.

"Eric, you seem angry with me. Are you?"

"With so much to be grateful for why should I be angry? Besides, that's an emotion like jealousy, hatred and the other one, love. As I heard you tell Wulfstan these are feelings I couldn't possibly know or understand as I can't interact with the world."

The screen went blank and Anna said, "Eric, calm down. Your aunt only said that because you are confined to a wheel chair."

Anna paused and Eric said, "I understand that for all of my life you spoke for me, but I've never heard you speak for her before today. I suppose that now that you know I can think for myself, you can go back to thinking for my thoughtless aunt."

"Eric, please," said Anna.

"Why do you call him Wulfstan instead of Stan or the Reverend Wolf?" said Terry.

"Oh, just another one of their little secrets," said Jennifer.

"We all have secrets," clicked across the screen.

Jennifer looked at Anna who mouthed 'no' in reply to the unasked question. "C'mon, Dad," said Jennifer. "Let's begin our vacation. See you in four days, Anna." She kissed Terry and leaned over Eric and whispered, "Don't get up."

The screen buzzed, "I'll tell Stan you said hello."

"Stan knows how to reach me if he wants to."

"And he hasn't?" crossed the screen. "Maybe hello isn't the right word."

"Eric, I don't know what's gotten into you," said Anna. "Apologize to your aunt, please."

"I'm sorry, Aunt Jennifer. My words were unkind. I don't have any excuse. I'll give Stan any message you'd like. I wish I could be kind and patient like you are. I suppose it's because you work with people like me that you handle my acting out so well."

Jennifer embraced Anna and said, "See you when you get back. We'll have a nice time. It's been ages since I've spent time with Dad. It will probably be refreshing for both of us," she smiled and left Anna with Terry and Eric.

"Well, the adventure begins. I have us packed and ready. All we need now is our tour guide. I'll get the van ready. You boys catch up. I'll be back in five minutes."

"A life threatening disease and a mind imprisoned for life. Not much to catch up on."

"I think you should stop feeling sorry for yourself. Your mind was imprisoned. It isn't any more."

"You're right, Terry. I'm sorry. I'm grumpy. I'm just keen to get to Stamford."

"Why?"

"I'll tell you once we get there."

"By the way, why are you mad at Aunt Jennifer?"

"She's changed towards me," typed Eric. "Maybe because she knows I'm in here. I don't know."

Chapter Eighteen

As the van drove into Stamford both boys were silent. Anna was enchanted by the picturesque village, all stone churches, Queen Ann houses and Georgian architecture. They drove down the High Street past Red Lion square and on to the edge of the old walled town to Bath Row where the Manse that E.J.'s father occupied sat quaintly in the shadow of a small church.

"It's actually a priory," said E.J. "St. Leonard's built a few years after the Battle of Hastings."

They pulled into the driveway and a tall, elderly man stood waiting for them. E.J. got out and shook hands in a very formal manner. "Dad, this in Anna Shepard and her sons, Terry and Eric, and my friend Stan Wolf."

He shook hands with Anna, said, "Hello boys," and looked at Stan, held out his hand and said, "I've been looking forward to this for two weeks. How nice of you all to come. Please call me Eli. My son, Emmanuel, gets a little stuffy about our biblical names so we both use the shortened versions. Come away in."

The cottage was comfortable in an old world way, just like the town. There were books everywhere it seemed, along the walls, on the coffee table and especially on Eli's desk which had so many different sized piles it resembled the Manhattan Skyline.

"I have a housekeeper, believe it or not," he said. "Anyway, for four days we'll explore Stamford. Emmanuel will be our tour guide. I'll give the background historical information. I'm sure that Stan and I will have a spirited discourse on why Stamford has so many churches. There are not quite the hundreds my son imagines, but we have more than our fair share.

"Terry, I've heard a lot about you and you probably know nothing of me. So, we'll have lots to discuss. I always admired warriors and E.J. tells me that you are a powerful fighter." He walked over to Eric who sat in his wheelchair his head at an angle with his cap on his head and his computer in his lap. "Eric, my son talks about you constantly, but in the last few months all I hear about is you and Reverend Wolf. I can only hope four days will be enough. I've never heard a story like yours and I hope you'll like and trust me enough to share it with me. So let's begin with some refreshments. What would you like?"

"Tea, please," flashed the computer.

"Right! Emmanuel, in the kitchen. You're in charge of tea. I am going to have a port. How about you, Anna?"

"Yes, please."

"Stan?"

"Thank you, yes."

"Alright, E.J. I know needs some of that port wood Glenmorangie, which leaves Terry."

"Tea, please."

"Right, two teas, my lad. Anna, come with me to the bar. Stan, have a seat with the boys."

E.J. stuck his head out of the kitchen door. "He was a captain in the household cavalry. Can you tell?"

"Actually, I was a major when I retired, Doctor Kissen."

"Oh, yes, sorry. I forgot about that."

"That's alright. It's just what I'd expect from a Cambridge man."

"He's never quite forgiven me for choosing Cambridge over Oxford."

"It's the one decision that I find questionable."

The afternoon passed pleasantly and quickly as E.J.'s charismatic father held court with his new found audience. "I thought for dinner I'd take everyone to the Crown Hotel and we can finish getting acquainted and get down to the business of enjoying the town."

"Great idea," said Stan. "I'd like to be your co-host if you don't mind."

"No, no" said Eli, "You're my guests".

"Okay," said E.J. to Anna and the boys. "Just let them fight it out. This promises to be a lively weekend."

"The Crown Hotel is situated in All Saints Place. There are many small streets named for churches or priories. St. Mary's Church, for example, is on St. Mary's Hill. We are very much a town of Church and State," said Eli.

"I see what you mean," said Stan. "It's very beautiful. It feels like one has stepped back a few hundred years."

"Indeed," said Eli. "Medieval Stamford was known throughout Europe as a center for religious studies, and many of the Monastic buildings remain as they were then."

Chapter Nineteen

The Crown Hotel was beautiful and very old. The conversation was lively except for Eric, of course, for whom it was one sided. He got to listen and, at Eli's insistence, brought his laptop and headgear so that his comments flew across the screen, responding to everyone in the group with Eli eventually catching on to the fact that even although he didn't look like it, he was very much interested in conversation and indeed the history of Stamford. There was a lull in the conversation when Eric asked Eli if they could visit Stamford Bridge. It was Terry that answered.

"Stamford Bridge is up where we live, we can go there anytime. It's the name of a football stadium as well. It's been shortened to The Bridge."

"It's historical, though," said Eli. "Harold Godwinson fought a great battle there, actually about this time of the year in 1066. It was his first year as king and his last year of life." The screen went blank and Eric opened his eyes.

Grimm was already awake. "Look north," he said, "a battle is about to take place."

"I know," said Eric.

Eric and Grimm forced themselves up to continue their march towards York. A horseman, scarred and ancient, came out of the mist as they stumbled towards York on the Old Roman Road the Legions had used centuries before.

"Who are you?" said the warrior.

Eric smiled. "Wulfstan, its Eric and Grimm."

Wulfstan looked at the tired, emaciated housecarls. "It seems I found you in time for your first real battle."

As he spoke the mist blew away and Eric and Grimm found themselves surrounded by housecarls, an army of warriors as far as the eye could see. Godwinson appeared as if by magic. His banner, The Dragon of Wessex, snapped in the breeze behind him. He looked at them with his cold, blue eyes and said to Wulfstan, "Which direction were they heading?"

"North," said Wulfstan.

"You intended to visit with the Great Hardrada?"

Both men dropped to their knees. Eric said, "Yes, Sire, we knew you would all be tired, but still hoped you might catch up to join us in the fight."

Godwinson roared with laughter which rippled backwards through five thousand men who laughed because the men in front did. "Feed them," he said to Thorkill who had ridden out to see his men he had long thought dead. "You can bathe tonight. We won't fight before tomorrow. And get them some clothes before they freeze to death."

The army rested at Tadcaster ten miles from York. At dawn the next morning Eric and Grimm felt much better. They had bathed, eaten warm food and drank mulled wine. They were dressed for battle. Eric carried a battleaxe that he said felt unwieldy. Wulfstan rode up and withdrew Eric's axe from his saddle.

"This is yours. I believe it was a gift from the King. You should know where you leave it, unless you are dead." Before Eric could answer, Wulfstan threw Grimm Godwin's giant spear. "This is yours because no one else can carry it. Do not leave it unattended." He rode away to the forefront of the army.

They entered York to the astounded looks of the Yorkshiremen. "The King has come!" someone yelled. The brother earls, Edwin and Morcar, rode to meet the King.

"Sire," said Morcar, "we did not expect you."

"I am a little late," said Godwinson. "I see Hardrada stopped before he reached York."

"He stopped," said Morcar, "because my men that didn't drown in the Ouse lie dead at Fulford Gate. We are preparing gifts and hostages for him now before he marches into the city. You are more than a little late."

Wulfstan and Thorkill moved forward as the King raised his hand. "Wait! As I said, a little late for York, not for England. The gifts he receives we carry with us on our backs and by our sides. As for hostages they will be the men who lie on the battle field with the men of Norway that we kill."

The sound of the housecarls' roar and the steel against the shields was deafening. Morcar visibly shook as the shockwave almost lifted him from his horse.

"Tonight sleep well," said Harold, "for tomorrow we have the pleasure of doing battle with one of the finest warriors who has ever lived. Harold Hadrada wishes to test English mettle." Again the men cheered, then dispersed to eat, prepare their weapons and sleep.

Eric, Grimm, Thorkill and Wulfstan were together in a room behind where they had stabled their horses. The four men sat together and Wulfstan said to Eric, "Remember all you have learned. Stay with your axe friend. Tomorrow we go against men like ourselves."

"Who will cover your back?" said Grimm.

"I will," said Thorkill, "and he will cover mine as we have done since we were boys. Now go to sleep. At dawn we must be ready."

Eric's eyes opened and he reached for his axe but his arms wouldn't move and he was being pushed along the cobbled streets of Stamford while Eli rambled on to everyone about the historical architecture of the churches, in particular St. Mary's Church which he was saying occupies a prominent position on St. Mary's Hill and is built around a thirteenth century tower with a one hundred and sixty three foot high spire that was added a century later. Eric's body suddenly went into muscular spasms.

"Get him back to the van. Let's get him home," said E.J. "I'll stretch his muscles and see if he can get some relief."

Getting Eric into the van caused quite a commotion. Stan Wolf and E.J. lifted him. He still managed to kick Terry in a massive involuntary movement from his hip. Terry collapsed and Anna picked him up and helped him to the front seat.

E.J. injected Eric with a sedative and said to Anna, "I'm sorry. I don't like to do that but he is in some sort of distress. Dad, will you drive? Take us to All Saints Hospital. It's the closest I think."

As the van drove in to All Saints Hospital, a doctor and two nurses stood outside. They eased Eric onto a gurney and pushed him into the emergency room. Anna and Terry followed. Terry did not seem to be doing very well. Eric lay sedated in the little hospital ward.

E.J. came out of the ward and said, "He's resting right now. It's difficult to know what's going on in his brain. He seems to be having changes, how constant or how positive or negative they are I can't tell. Let's see how he is tomorrow and we'll decide whether we should stay on for two more days or return to York."

"How are you, Terry?" said Eli.

"I'm okay, my stomach hurts."

"Show me," said E.J. He lifted Terry's T-shirt and saw that he had a massive bruise on his abdomen.

"Oh," said Anna, "you're hurt."

E.J. felt around his abdomen and said, "Let's keep you in here for one night, too."

As they gathered around his bed E.J. pulled Anna aside. "I think his liver is bleeding." He turned back to Terry and said, "I want to have your injury checked out."

"Okay," said Terry. "Can I be beside Eric?"

"I'm sure we can arrange that," said Eli.

"I don't suppose I'll be able to talk to him," said Terry.

"You will," said E.J., "but not till tomorrow."

The boys lay side by side in the small hospital ward. Terry looked across at Eric whose body seemed tense even in unconsciousness. "Are you okay?" said Terry. Eric visibly relaxed and Terry smiled and said, "I'm glad you've calmed down. You fought like you were going into battle."

Eric opened his eyes, "What did you say?"

Grimm laughed, "I said I feel calm going into battle and I'm glad you are my brother."

"And I'm glad you're mine," said Eric as he placed his axe across his saddle.

Godwinson and the earls, Morcar and Edwin, rode to pray for victory. Godwinson had married their sister, Aldyth, as a strategic move to keep them aligned with him. However, by the dark and brooding looks on their faces it would seem to have been a futile gesture. The three men entered the church while the army stood ready. Half an hour passed and they came out followed by Aldred, the Archbishop of York, who blessed the mighty host. Harold took his place at the head of his housecarls with his brothers Leofwine and Gyrth by his side.

Grimm said to Eric, "It takes a brave man to marry the widow of a man he has killed."

"What are you saying?"

"I'm saying Aldyth, the sister of the poisoned Earls here, Morcar and Edwin, was married to Griffith of Llewelyn. Harold beheaded him."

"That's right," said Eric. "He beheaded him, but he was already dead. His own men killed him to save themselves. He was to be executed by the order of King Edward."

"Godwinson killed him none the less. I would not want his wife in my bed," said Grimm.

"What about Edith of the Swan neck?"

"Don't mention her. No one speaks her name, but if you ask me that's his real wife."

"No one asked you," said Wulfstan. "Remember yourselves. You are housecarls, not housewives. No more gossip." With that he rode away.

Godwinson turned to face his army. He smiled and said, "We are not expected, so I imagine the Norwegians are having a restful day by the river. Let's proceed carefully and see if we can interest them in a little exercise."

Chapter Twenty

The Viking forces sat around on the meadows by the River Derwent. They were expecting gifts and hostages from the defeated Northumbrian Earls. It was almost a holiday atmosphere. Men were wrestling and talking. The early morning mist was burning off as the sun rose. Godwinson's army got closer and they could see Hardrada's banner, Landwaster, its black raven lifting in the breeze. Next to it Tostig's banner hung limp, the Dragon of Wessex with the Northumbrian cross behind it, seemed to be ignored by the morning breeze.

Suddenly Harold Godwinson reached over and took Grimm's cloak and wrapped it round his body saying, "You and one other follow me. Wulfstan, stay, if they take me destroy them all."

Eric spurred his horse and rode forward with Harold and Grimm. As they neared the Vikings, Harold waved a white makeshift flag to show he had come as a messenger. The Vikings stood up and watched as the unexpected trio approached. Hardrada came forward as the riders reined in their horses. Eric was shocked at the sheer size of him. He must be seven feet tall he thought as he measured him in his mind against Tostig whom he knew to be six feet tall, and there beside him was Copsi, the Scottish pirate, his discerning one eye looking at Eric. He leaned over to speak to Tostig just as Harold spoke.

"I bring a message from the King to Tostig Godwinson."

"What message from my brother?" replied Tostig.

"He offers you one third of England if you return to him now."

"What does he offer the Norwegian King, Harold Hardrada?"

"As he has come so far to take a piece of the English Kingdom he shall have it. The King offers him seven feet of English soil as he is taller than most men."

The Vikings rose up like a surging sea monster. Tostig held up his hand for silence and said to Harold, "Tell the King his offer comes too late."

"As you wish," replied Harold. He took one last look at his brother, then turned and said to Eric, "The price of the crown is higher than I wish to pay, but the die is cast and destiny will rule this day." They spurred their horses and rode back to the English line.

"I think we'll take the boys back to York, Dad," said E.J. "Most of the weekend is over anyway and I'd like to get Terry back to see Doctor Armstrong. Apparently his liver is badly bruised and Mike thinks we should return as soon as he is discharged, which will be tomorrow about 11:00 a.m."

"Alright," said Eli. "That sounds like the thing to do. I wanted to suggest that if you can get Terry out earlier it might be best for you to rent a car and take him straight to see Mike, and the Reverend Wolf can take Anna and Eric in the van later in the afternoon."

E.J. looked at Anna and said, "I want to get Terry back as soon as possible. I think Eric should stay one more day and I would be happy to return and bring him back tomorrow. I don't think the problem he has is serious. I think it relates to him being locked in. That is to say, the incident yesterday was essentially caused by frustration."

Anna said, "I'm coming with you and I'll return with you to bring Eric home."

Stan Wolf interjected and said, "If it would make it easier, why don't I bring him home by way of Stamford Bridge? It would save both you and Anna an extra journey which is unnecessary. He's settled at the moment. It seems the fact that he couldn't find Stamford Bridge is what created the problem, or rather the fact that it isn't in Stamford."

"That's certainly possible. How do you feel about Stan bringing Eric home?"

Anna said, "If you think it's okay and Stan doesn't mind."

E.J. said to Stan, "Keep me informed if there are any changes." He laid his hand on Eric's shoulder.

Eric turned and looked at the Viking army.

Chapter Twenty One

Godwinson's army surged forward and the Vikings withdrew across the small bridge that crossed the River Derwent. The meadows on the other side would allow them a stronger position to stand their ground. The bridge was narrow so the mighty Norwegian army was streaming across two men abreast. Standing in the center of the bridge was the Norwegian King yelling at his men to get across the bridge while he carelessly stood with his mighty war axe across his shoulder. As his army began forming up on the other side of the bridge, his archers sent a hail of arrows across the river and into the English army. The English drew back and reformed up out of bow shot as the rest of Hardrada's army crossed the Derwent. There was a lull as the two armies faced each other. Hardrada stood in the center of the bridge swinging his axe. From the ranks of his warriors walked a giant as tall as Hardrada, but much broader. He spoke to the King who laughed and clapped him on the back, giving up the bridge to him.

Grimm called out to the warrior, "It's good you sent the King away, but you didn't send him far enough."

The warrior looked back at Grimm and yelled, "I asked that I might hold this bridge until the fighting Saxons arrived! The King gave me the bridge and said, 'I don't think they will get here in your lifetime, but I give you the bridge.' Try and cross it and you will understand why he gave it to me."

"You will soon learn, my friend, that your King cannot give what he does not own," said Grimm. "As to your lifetime, enjoy this day because you will not see the sun set."

Grimm and Eric charged at the great Northman who held the bridge. Eric was there first. As their war axes clashed Eric was stunned by the force of the giant's strength. As Grimm tried to close in on him from the other side, the Viking changed his axe to his other hand hitting Grimm with the flat of the blade and knocking him off the bridge into the river. Eric swung at the Northman, dropping his blade for a belly cut.

The Northman stepped back laughing, "Nice try, little man," he said as he reached over and gripped Eric by his sword belt and threw him into the river. As Eric surfaced Grimm pulled him to the river bank with his spear.

"Keep him busy," said Grimm. "I'll get him off the bridge." Grimm slid into the water carrying the mighty spear of Godwin. Eric tried to reach the forefront of the fight but Godwinson himself had engaged the Colossus on the bridge.

"You are holding up the battle, my friend," said Godwinson.

"This may be all the battle you get, My Lord," he replied.

Godwinson feinted and attacked. The Northman parried his blows with ease. "If that is the force of your attack you should go home before you get tired or die," said the Viking.

"You're a brave warrior, but careless," said Godwinson.

The Northman laughed and once more attacked the King with ferocity. Godwinson ducked under the strokes easily and came up fast and furious cutting to his chest and then his head as he laid open the giant's cheek to the bone. The Northman just laughed. "A kiss from a King," he said as his huge axe was raised and descended on

156

the King's head. Then his chest burst open as Grimm's spear came from beneath the bridge and drove through his back and chest. As the axe spun from his lifeless fingers he pitched forward and Godwinson's cheek was sliced cleanly by the spear point as the giant was held fast on his knees by the spear whose shaft was impaled in the bridge planks and its point through his body.

"I know who did this," said the King. "He killed a hero like a coward." As he turned he saw Eric. "Bring him to me when this day is done."

"Sire," began Eric but Godwinson had already crossed the bridge and the housecarls were streaming over behind him. Eric, caught up in the tide of battle, fought with a feeling of foreboding.

The battle waged for six hours. The Vikings stood behind their shield walls as the English advanced. Eric was behind his shield next to Thorkill and Wulfstan but as the battle began his thoughts were concerned with the more immediate problem of staying alive. As the shield walls crashed together men were cutting with axes and swords. Eric had a sword across his back and an axe by his side. Godwinson's gift axe was in his belt, but in his right hand he used a saxe, a short powerful sword for stabbing and slashing at the groin and legs of the enemy. There were agonized screams of men dying as the shield walls surged together. Suddenly he was looking into the one angry eye of Copsi, the pirate. His red hair was loose and slicked with blood which obviously was not his.

The boss on Copsi's shield was the same one that he had worn on his arm and it was almost as vicious as the axe that was fast demolishing Eric's shield. The blade was a two hand span arc with a one hand span powerful spike on the back of the blade so that as he smashed down on Eric's shield the axe, after several blows, went through it and he pulled the spike upwards which split the shield as it raked across his chest. Eric felt the chain mail ripple against him. He threw his axe into his left hand and withdrew his long sword from his back in one motion. He drove the short stabbing sword through Copsi's axe arm and as the weapon fell from his nerveless hand, Eric cut him from shoulder to hip. He stepped across his lifeless body as Wulfstan and Thorkill called to tighten the line. He picked up Copsi's shield and got back behind the shield wall. They surged forward again and the Norwegian shield wall broke and that was when he saw Grimm standing behind the King guarding his back.

As Eric fought his way toward his axe friend, Grimm looked at Eric and smiled. Hardrada stepped in front of Grimm as he turned back to protect the King. The Norwegian King was magnificent in his mail shirt which all knew he had named Emma. His axe was bloody and as Grimm faced him he smiled with joy. They circled on that bloody meadow and traded blow for blow. They seemed well matched as they fought. A Viking warrior had reached Godwinson and was about to strike. Grimm threw his axe which tore through the warrior's chest. He turned back into the arc of Hardrada's axe. He ducked under it and withdrew his short stabbing sword just as Hardrada changed direction in mid swing, embedding the axe in Grimm's chest. Hardrada reached forward to pull out the axe and Grimm drove his short sword into his neck. Hardrada dropped to his knees. The dying men faced each other on their knees.

Hardrada looked at Grimm and said, "I've traveled far for this moment," and he fell forward against Grimm dead.

When Eric reached them they lay side by side like lovers in a last embrace. Eric could not hold back the tears. "Grimm," he said. "I never believed this moment would come."

"Don't cry little brother. I knew this would happen as it did. The runes foretold it when I was a boy. Better a warrior's death than a King's displeasure," he said and closed his eyes.

Eric fought his way forward with his sword and Copsi's shield. His axe and short sword lay on the battlefield or embedded in some enemy. He could not remember which. He reached the King at the same moment that Harold reached Tostig. As the brothers faced each other Eric tried to step between them.

"No," said Godwinson. "This is my brother. Stand back."

Eric felt time slow down as Harold said to Tostig, "Brother come back to me and I give you my oath that we will rule England together."

"It's too late for that," said Tostig. "I'll rule with Hardrada, a brotherhood of true warrior kings."

"Hardrada is dead," said Godwinson.

With that Tostig was silent. He attacked his brother ferociously. Harold had no choice but to defend himself as they clashed back and forth as they must have done many times as boys. Harold swung his axe low then changed direction, cutting upwards and across Tostig's neck.

Tostig looked at his brother and made no attempt to defend himself. It was too late for Harold to stop the blow. As Tostig fell Harold dropped his axe and ran forward to hold the body of his dying brother. Eric stood back as the King's anguish poured over his brother's body.

"You have made me Cain, brother. Forgive me, for God surely won't."

159

"The King is dead!" screamed a Viking warrior and the battle slowly came to a standstill. Men stood in silence as Harold Godwinson rose from the body of his dead brother.

"It's over," he said in a loud, clear voice.

Olaf, Harald Hardrada's son, and the Vikings were given leave to transport the body of Hardrada from the battlefield. The three hundred ships that sailed up the Humber remained there. Only twenty four ships were needed to carry away the survivors of the battle at Stamford Bridge. Eric rode to York with Wulfstan and Thorkill. They stabled their horses. As Eric was brushing down Midnight he heard the footsteps of Wulfstan as he came out from the stall and over to Eric.

"I'm sorry about your brother," he said.

Eric turned but found that once more he could not move or speak and was in the accursed metal chair again. Stan Wolf was driving the van and they were just pulling into Stamford Bridge. Stan parked the van and came back to get Eric out.

"I'm sorry I don't have your lap top or helmet. There was some problem with the computer. However, E.J. has taken it to be repaired and Sir Charles is here to see me, actually, to see you. I suppose you're quite famous in the world of electronics. Anyway, this is Stamford Bridge. Let's look it over and if you have any questions you'll have to remember them when we get back to the house or York General, whichever comes first.

"Terry is back in the hospital. It seems he has not quite recovered from his accident and Mike wants to check his white cell count so I thought we would take a little tour of Stamford Bridge and then head for home. This is the famous bridge. It's a little better built than when Harold Godwinson fought here but the River Derwent I'm sure hasn't changed that much."

It's changed alright, thought Eric, and I need to get out of here and see Terry.

Chapter Twenty Two

So, thought Eric, I'm getting history lessons and geography lessons and a fictional account of why I can't have my computer. He really must think I'm stupid to swallow that rubbish.

"Well," said Stan, "I don't think we'll tarry here much longer. Let's get home and catch up with the news on Terry and your grandfather."

Eric sat in his seat behind Stan thinking. He knows I can think and he also knows I can't answer so why doesn't he just shut up and drive.

"I know it will be tough for a couple of days without the computer but I promise I'll get it back to you as soon as possible. I'd like Sir Charles to check it out as he will be here, and E.J. will give you a complete work up as soon as we can see him. Then we can check on Terry, your mother, and perhaps see your Aunt Jennifer. We're going to be busy for the next few days so don't make any plans. Ha Ha."

Eric kept his eyes closed and hoped that when he opened them he'd be back with Grimm and his comrades in arms. Then his mind flashed on Grimm lying dead near the bridge they were fast leaving behind. He opened his eyes and could see only the dull skies of Yorkshire and the impending rain storm. In the back of his mind he could hear Stan Wolf chatting away about Terry, Jennifer, Anna and everyone else in this unfulfilling life he was stuck in. God must be real, he thought, and this is my punishment for the battles I fought in my other life. I had no choice. If I ask Him a question in my mind I wonder if He'll hear it, if He'll answer. "I want to go back," he said in the silence of his head. "Can I?" The question hung in the empty cavern of his mind which held all his thoughts and dreams and plans, but no voice.

"You'll be home soon," said Stan.

Eric was startled by the broken silence. It resounded in his head as if Stan had answered his question and he suddenly knew he was going back. He didn't know when, just that he was. He closed his eyes and said, "Thank you, God."

They arrived at the house and Stan brought Eric in. Jennifer stood by the door and said to Stan, "Anna's still at the hospital with Terry. Doctor Armstrong wants to run more tests."

"Yes, I thought that might be the case. Eric is probably tired so I'll leave him with you for now and go to the hospital. I have several people to see in regard to both boys."

"Fine," answered Jennifer. "That should cheer Eric up."

"Maybe it would if you gave him a chance."

"We never did have our dinner and discussion, Stan, did we?"

"No, perhaps one of these days. Time seems to be moving faster then my ability to keep up," he answered.

Jennifer looked at him and instinctively knew he no longer wished to share anything with her, especially time. As she watched him drive away she thought how interesting that he had become more a part of her family than she had ever wished to be.

"Alright, Eric, into your room, nap time," she said. "I like you better like this. The hat and computer just confuse you and make you imagine you are something that you are not."

Eric smiled in his mind and thought no, it shows you what you are not and if I were you I wouldn't want to see that either. She put him in his room and closed the door. I wonder how Granddad is he thought. The door to the bedroom opened and there he stood.

"Hello, my brave boy. How are you? Let's have tea." Oh, oh thought Eric. He's lucid. "Jennifer, make some tea, dear, will you?"

"Dad, I put Eric in his room for a nap."

"He doesn't need a nap, dear, he needs tea, so hop to it, girl. Kettle on, please."
Jennifer went into the kitchen and Sid wheeled Eric into the living room. "Haven't talked to you in ages," said Sid. "Where have you been, or it might be where have I been? I was away for a weekend trip with Jennifer. She said we had a wonderful time. Can't remember a damn thing about it."

A few minutes later Jennifer brought in the tea, Sid's in a mug and Eric's in his special cup with the straw. "What makes you think he wants tea?" she said.

"I want tea," said Sid, "and his company."

The front door closed and Anna came in and said, "Tea. Oh, good, me too. Thanks, Jennifer, you've been like an angel to me."

"It's no problem. It's what I do," she said. "So how's Terry?"

"He's resting right now. Mike said they will begin testing him tomorrow after he's had a night's sleep." She went over to Eric and kissed his head. "So how are you feeling? I know you need your computer to answer. Stan and E.J. were having a debate when I left the hospital. Mike told me they seem to think the computer and the helmet are functioning normally. However, it still may be the problem in terms of how it is affecting your brain, Eric.

So tomorrow you'll have a Cat Scan just to make sure everything is okay."

"I think that's a good idea," said Jennifer. "He hasn't been himself since he started using that device."

Anna looked at her sister and said, "Hasn't been himself? It's the only time he's been himself. If not for Stan Wolf and his incredible thinking cap I would not have known my son."

"Your son," Jennifer said quizzically.

"Yes," said Anna. "He is a bright, thinking human being and no one knew except him."

"That's not exactly what I meant," said Jennifer. "I sense and, in fact, have experienced a meanness in him."

"I can't think where he would get that," said Anna. "I think we are all a little tired It's frustrating and challenging for all of us and you deal with it at work and at home. I appreciate all you've done for us, but you probably need a rest as much as anyone else, so why not go home and I'll call you tomorrow and give you an update."

Jennifer put her coat on. "See you tomorrow then." With that she was gone.

Anna sat down with her tea and held Eric's hand. Sid clicked the remote as he sat on his favorite chair and it began its slow rhythmic ascent and descent. Anna was about to change the remote but seeing her dad's peaceful smile and her son sitting with her silent and relaxed she held his hand and enjoyed her tea as Sid moved up and down rhythmically in front of the blank T.V. screen.

Chapter Twenty Three

"Tell me something about Sir Charles Paul," said Anna.

E.J. paused for a moment then he said, "It's a long story, but I can give you a condensed version. Sir Charles Paul was knighted by the Queen for his contribution to science and, as a result, to medicine and almost every other area of human endeavor from video games that can be used therapeutically to sophisticated cameras for use in the medical field and, indeed, many other areas, even an electronic ear that almost cures deafness. He became the Bill Gates of spirituality and science, spirituality because he believed in God before he believed in science and has since found that he believes science exists because of God.

"Both he and Stan Wolf attended Oxford thirty five years ago intent on the priesthood and finding God. Somewhere along the way he decided to find God through science rather than the church. Stan, on the other hand, stayed with the priesthood. As a priest he was outspoken and controversial. Sir Charles, as a scientist, was the same, but it can be argued that both found God; Sir Charles through science, the universe and the significance of mankind as part of it. Wolf, his best friend, found it in an obscure and ancient order known as Rosicrucianism whose ideas and philosophy shook the Vatican.

"The theory being, I believe, that through the ages there will always be eight good men, not just good, but good as Christ, Gandhi and Mother Teresa were good. I don't imagine it's just men. Anyway, that's Sir Charles and Stan. I am just a physician, but knowing them has affected the way I see medicine and indeed the world." E.J. took a

166

deep breath and said, "So now we can go in and talk to them. I just wanted you to know the kind of men they are. Mike will be in on the meeting because, as you may know, Stan came to York General at his request for funding for the oncology department. We've since discovered that both men are interested in all aspects of medicine, illness and the human condition and, in regards to Terry and Eric, I think we need all the help we can get."

Anna looked at E.J. and said, "You have changed. You're much more human than you used to be."

He smiled, "I think that's called evolution. Come on in and meet Sir Charles and our team. Eric's scan is in one hour."

Sir Charles looked to be in his sixties like Stan, erudite and sophisticated. He stood conversing with Stan and Mike Armstrong as E.J. and Anna entered the conference room.

"Good morning, Gentlemen," said E.J. "This is Anna Shepard, Sir Charles, mother of Terry and Eric. Everyone else you've met."

Sir Charles smiled, "I'd like to begin by asking that we all drop the 'Sir.' It makes for clumsy conversation. Stan has called me Chuck since we were seventeen and I'm comfortable with that. It may not fit with a knighthood, but then I'm not here as a knight, I'm here as you all are, to find solutions. So, that said, E.J. begin."

"Alright," said E.J. "While we were in Stamford Eric, while wearing the helmet, became very fractious; lots of involuntary movement, eyes rolling, almost the same symptoms as an epileptic fit. Now this hasn't happened before, however, over the last few months since he had the helmet and computer he has had some unusual behaviors. It's almost like he leaves. He goes somewhere else. It's only been a couple of times that I've noticed it, but I'm still concerned as to the cause. Could the helmet be affecting his brain waves?"

"The short answer to that question is no. However, let me give you a little more detail," said Sir Charles. "First of all, the helmet is harnessing the electrical echoes of Eric's brain waves. So, in effect, the only electricity is being created by Eric. The software used was designed to adapt to the patient's increasing ability to move the cursor."

"I understood that when it was explained and shown to me months ago, but something is different and I was hoping you could help explain it."

"Remember the key words are 'increasing ability.' Think about it, a boy 'locked in' for twelve years suddenly is given a window to the world and it is open."

"I was used to test it, E.J." said Stan. "In fact, both Chuck and I tried the helmet on Eric's computer and it is working very well."

"Then the problem may be with Eric. He will have his CAT scan in about half an hour and I'll have the pictures in about one hour," replied E.J.

"Right, then," said Mike Armstrong, "keep me posted. I have to get up stairs and see Terry; the kick did severely bruise his liver. He seems to be feeling better today. However, I want to keep him in this week for observation. He has improved since the stem cell transplantation, but his white cell count has dropped and we just need to keep an eye on him. He's been asking for Eric so I said if it was alright with you, Anna, he could drop by later."

"I think once we've seen the CAT scan," said E.J.

"Alright," said Sir Charles, "let's deal with the CAT scan first. Then, Mike and Anna, we should sit down with Terry's records and progress reports and see what tack we need to take with him."

"He was improving," said Mike, "but you know this monster. It sleeps, feeds on you in silence, then rages back to life to devour you. It will need vigilance and all of your weapons, Sir Knight, to slay this dragon."

"I've made a life of slaying dragons. I don't intend to sleep now," said Sir Charles.

Anna sat tearfully looking round the room at the four men. "I can't thank you enough," she said.

"The thanks is in winning," said Stan, "and the sure knowledge that we are not fighting alone."

Chapter Twenty Four

Eric was wheeled into the room for his CAT scan. He looked at the massive doughnut shaped machine and thought, 'another cell, double claustrophobia, too bad I can't scream. I suppose I could go mad, but what good would that do. I'd be the only one that knew'. He was wheeled forward and lifted into the machine. Nurse Scott and someone else lifted him. As he lay there his legs began to spasm involuntarily.

"Try and relax," said Anna.

Eric thought, 'I am relaxed. It's my body that's a little out of control'. The stranger that had helped Nurse Scott slowly stretched Eric's legs until they relaxed and he lay quietly on the machine.

"I'm the radiologist," said the voice. "This will feel a little strange, like being stuck in a doughnut. Try and stay still. It will take about half an hour because I'm going to take lots of pictures of your brain."

'It's my best feature' thought Eric. 'Stay still, he must think I'm in control of this body. It's kind of funny, I'm locked in and he's locked out with no way of communicating, only he doesn't know it'. All of a sudden he was disappearing into the massive doughnut. As it began to spin around him the voice continued to speak. "Just be calm." Oh, just shut up", thought Eric.

Eric lay in the machine as it spun around him with the ever present monotonous voice of the radiologist giving him instructions he couldn't follow. He felt as he did when he was chained to the wall with Grimm, only Grimm was gone and he was trapped alone in a prison within a prison. Suddenly his mother's voice cut clearly through his reverie.

"He can't follow any of your instructions so would you discontinue your monologue, please?"

"I do it with all my patients," said the radiologist. "I find it relaxes them."

"He hasn't been relaxed since the day he was born so I don't think listening to you for half an hour is going to do it."

"Alright," he said and the room became silent except for the click and whirr of the machine.

"Well done, Mum", thought Eric. "I've never heard you tell anyone off like that before. I prefer the silence to his 'stay calm, start by relaxing your eyes, your face, chest, arms, legs all the way to your toes. If I could do that I would have been gone ten minutes ago and he could have continued to listen to the sound of his own voice which is, unfortunately, very annoying".

As the silence enveloped him he began to think about Grimm. "I have to get back to bury him. The crows and kites will be tearing his flesh". If I close my eyes I might make it back. He closed his eyes and listened, but all he could hear was the click and whirr of the machine and the rustle of the clothing of the nurse as she moved around the room, that and the sounds of his mother and the radiologist as they coughed or moved. "I think I've been back for three days. I need my computer to talk to Terry and I must get back because war is once more coming to England and I must be with the King. Grimm and I swore to each other to protect the King unto death. He has fulfilled his promise and now it is my turn and I won't be here while he is dying somewhere else".

Eric's body went into spasms and the radiologist said, "I'll relax him. I think you had better get Doctor Kissen and probably Sir Charles in here now."

"Why? What's wrong?" said Anna.

"I don't know what's wrong. That's the problem. This is not what I would expect in the brain of a person in Eric's condition."

Doctor Kissen, Sir Charles and Stan Wolf came into the room. The radiologist led the way to show the images of Eric's brain. "The brain looks almost normal. The anatomy doesn't fit the condition. It simply doesn't look like one would expect in a patient with Eric's level of C.P. For example, the language center looks normal. This area here, responsible for his motor skills, also has no signs of abnormality."

"Alright," said Sir Charles. "I want a P.E.T. scan and a D.T.I. so we can accurately describe what is going on in Eric's brain."

"Wait!" said Anna. "Is it necessary that he go through all of this?"

Sir Charles looked at her and said, "It won't hurt him, Anna, and it may give us an opportunity to help him."

"How?" she said.

"I don't really know. That's why I think we should do the P.E.T. scan."

"What is that?"

"It is helpful to use in conjunction with a CAT scan. It's a short lived radioactive tracer isotope, which decays by emitting a positron, and which has been chemically incorporated into a metabolically active molecule."

"Hang on," said Anna. "Simplify, please."

"Oh, of course. We inject him with a chemical. It concentrates in areas of the brain we wish to examine. He is placed in the scanner and we get the pictures, so to speak."

"Alright, and the other test, the DT whatever you said?"

172

"Ah, yes, that's the diffusion tensor imaging. It measures the restricted diffusion of water in tissue. Basically, Eric's brain looks like it has created new pathways for the nerve fibers or axons that transmit messages between neurons."

"What are you saying? That he'll be able to walk, talk, what?"

"I don't know the answer to those questions. What I do know is that his brain is changing in a positive way. The test will let us see more clearly what the changes are. They may or may not tell us why. It appears his brain has been building new pathways to reestablish connections to the areas involved with speech and motor control to compensate for those areas damaged. How functional they will be I can't say, but it is unusual to say the least and if there is a down side I don't know what it is. We initially wanted to check him out because E.J. saw some unusual behaviors that he thought might be caused by the cap and computer. I tell you again, that is not the case.

"The changes in Eric's brain are being brought about by the brain itself. Statistically it's probably one in several hundred millions where something like this happens but it is happening. Therefore, I would like you to authorize the tests for Eric which we, of course, will pay for. If we can improve the quality of his life we will, Anna. It also may give us information to do the same for thousands of other people who are 'locked in' just like Eric."

E.J. came over and stood beside Anna and said, "Well as the problem isn't the cap and computer let's give them back to Eric and ask him what he thinks."

"That's a splendid idea," said Sir Charles.

"Let's get him in his chair and give him a break from this machine. Then we can brainstorm, so to speak."

Eric was lifted back into his chair. 'Brainstorm, funny,' he thought. 'It sounds like that's what may be going on in my head. I can't wait to get my cap and computer back'. As the cap was placed on his head, and the computer came to life, so did his thoughts. "I want to see Terry before I discuss anything, please."

"Right," said Anna. That's a good idea. Besides, we need a rest from CATs, PETs and MRIs."

'We do,' thought Eric

Terry sat up in bed and watched as Eric and his chair were moved into position by Anna who then stood outside the window to his room putting on masks and gloves. He was in a protective environment, a room with a visitation room attached. The room had an intercom system so communication could be conducted through the glass partition. Eric wrote, "This is a different room."

"It's a Laminar air flow room," said Mike Armstrong. "Terry has to be protected from germs as his blood count has dropped and this affects his immune system. So for a few days you'll talk through the intercom. You'll be able to use your computer and cap at the window. If you need help Stan or your mother can relay anything you write."

"Is he going to be alright?" said Anna.

"As I said, his white blood cell count is down so he will be prone to infection until we stabilize that."

"Is this because of me?" typed Eric.

"No," said Mike. "This was probably happening anyway. The bruising is a minor problem. The larger issue is regarding the bone marrow transplant."

"Meaning what?" said Anna.

"I think we may have to repeat it."

Anna sat down and fought back the tears. "Come into the office," said Mike.

"I'll stay here," flashed across the screen.

"He'll be okay," said Mike.

Anna looked at Terry who waved weakly. "Turn my back to him so he can see what I say," clicked the computer.

Mike turned Eric and said to Terry, "I'll put the intercom on for you as only you will be speaking. Can you see Eric's screen?"

"Yes," said Terry.

"Alright, Anna, I think they'll be okay. Come on."

"How do you feel?"

"I'm fine," said Terry "I'd rather you were facing me. I feel like I'm talking to a computer."

"Me, too. At least I can hear you."

"You never did tell me why you wanted to go to Stamford so desperately."

"It was Stamford Bridge I wanted to go to."

"Why?" said Terry. "Was it the soccer club?"

"No," flashed across the screen.

"What then?" said Terry.

"It'll sound like a strange idea, but I wanted to be at the battleground." The computer clicked away and the word 'battleground' seemed to be jumping off the screen.

"There's nothing to see is there?"

"Not anymore. Anyway, I'm sorry I kicked you. My body sometimes just does that."

"Well, if you think you know when it's going to happen I can probably get you on the soccer team."

"Very funny," clicked the computer. "I'm surprised you can still remember how to play soccer."

Terry began to laugh at the banter he was having with the boy in the wheelchair, his brother who had become his best friend. His laughter turned into a cough which caused him to vomit. Eric could hear the noise

Terry was making but could not see him. His body went into spasms as he moaned, knocking over his laptop, his body half turned in the chair and he saw Terry vomit blood. He heard his mother scream as he fell from the chair.

He opened his eyes and looked into the doleful eyes of Midnight who licked his face into consciousness. "You fainted," said Wulfstan, "but I sewed you up anyway. Go and bury your friend. You don't have much time."

"Loss of blood, my Lord. I don't faint." He swung into the saddle and winced as he realized the skin on his chest fitted a little tighter thanks to the needlework of Wulfstan. He rode back to the battlefield. He knew exactly where Grimm had fallen. The mist rose like a specter of death over the bloody field and thousands of men were held in its deadly embrace. Even the giant Norsemen hung like a puppet from Grimm's mighty spear. Midnight twisted and turned in agitation from the gruesome sights and smells. As the wind whipped up and dragged the mists across the battlefield the smell of death, decay and the souls of men seemed to follow.

Eric stood over Grimm. Tears ran down his face. The ravens were circling and landing wherever they chose. They had already pulled at the massive wound in Grimm's chest. Eric covered him with a cloak and put his sword belt around him, set him across Midnight's saddle and rode out behind the mists in the company of heroes being carried to Valhalla. He rode southeast into Lincolnshire to Grimm's village which was on the banks of the River Haven which in turn flowed into the Humber. He did not know the name of the village or the old priest who came from the tiny church to greet him.

"His name is Grimm Havelok," he said. "Have him buried in a place of honor and his name written on stone above his grave." He carried his friend into the church and gave the old man a pouch of silver coins. The priest bowed. As he raised his head Eric pulled his Saxe and placed it under his throat. "I ride to join the King. I will be back. If he's not where he's supposed to be when I return you will be buried on that day."

"I have known Grimm since he was a boy," said the priest. "I give you my word as a man of God he will be properly cleaned and prepared before his family sees him. Come, I will show you where he will rest."

"No," said Eric. "I must go. Tell his family he died saving the King and he was killed by a king." Eric mounted Midnight. As he was about to ride away he turned in the saddle. "How old was he?"

The priest looked at Eric and said, "He would have been twenty-five on September twenty-fifth I believe."

"The day he died," said Eric as he turned and rode south. 'I'll be in London before the King' he thought. Just outside of Leicester he encountered a horseman on the road heading north. As they drew closer the horseman drew his sword and pitched forward, falling from the saddle. Eric dismounted cautiously. As he drew nearer he saw the rider was mortally wounded. Eric gave him some water and his eyes opened.

"Where is the King?" he asked Eric.

"He is still in York, friend. We defeated Hardrada's army only yesterday."

"The council sent me to get him. William of Normandy has landed at Pevensey and is pillaging the country."

"Who attacked you?" asked Eric.

The wounded courier lifted his arm as if to protect himself. Eric turned too late as the quarter staff crashed down on his head.

Chapter Twenty Five

Eric opened his eyes slowly. Stan Wolf and Anna stood by his bed. His chest felt tight and he had a headache. 'What happened to Terry', he thought. "You fell out of your chair, and that's a first I might add," said Anna. Eric began to moan softly. "Terry's alright," said Stan. "Mike Armstrong is in with him now. You can't have the cap right now because, as you can probably feel, you've got quite a bump on your head and besides the computer is broken." He reached for the intercom and spoke into it. "Terry, Eric is awake and seems to be okay."

Mike Armstrong's voice came from Terry's room. "Tell him I'll be out in a few minutes."

Eric had gone quiet and Stan replied, "He heard you."

"Good," said Mike. He came out of the room and removed his paper cap, gloves, mask and coat. He came over to Anna, Stan and Eric and said, "Where's the computer?"

"Broken I'm afraid," said Stan. "Don't worry. Chuck has it and it will be repaired before the end of the day."

"Well, I don't suppose you need to talk right now," said Mike. "But I know you can listen," he said to Eric. "As you know your brother has a rare combination of two different types of Leukemia and as a result is affected with two different sets of problems. The one that caused the bleeding is a result of a drop in Terry's blood platelet count. These cells help prevent and control bleeding by making blood clot. A.M.L., or Acute Myelogenous Leukemia, can also cause bleeding gums and enlargement of certain organs; the liver, for example. It can also cause vomiting. So what happened is a result of the disease. He had blood from a nose bleed go into his stomach while he was laughing, threw up and there was a lot of blood. So he will be resting here and being treated for a few weeks. I know you will be undergoing some tests so I don't expect you boys will be getting together before Monday or Tuesday of next week.

"You're at a disadvantage because you don't have your computer or cap. That can't be helped. I have work to do to help Terry and you have work to do to help you. So let's get on with it and we'll see you next week. Rest assured it looked worse than it was."

'Rest assured', thought Eric. 'That sounds like bullshit. He's talking to my mother and Stan. I'm just the veggie in the wheelchair. I need the cap and computer to communicate. I must help Terry and then get back. The King will have the news by now and I must be with him when he faces Duke William and the Norman army'.

Stan Wolf suddenly walked away from Anna and Mike Armstrong. He placed his hand on Eric who heard him say, even though he did not speak, "You will."

Eric calmed down and thought, 'did I really hear you say that'?

"No," came the reply, "you heard me think it. There is more to Rosicrucianism than science, my friend, and you will fulfill your destiny. I am not yet sure what that is, but it is becoming clearer that it is somewhere other than here. So rest for the moment and the cap, computer, and tests that await you downstairs may provide us with some clues as to where and what that is. Tomorrow we'll talk more."

Anna's voice broke through his reverie, "Are you okay, Stan?"

"I'm fine," he replied, "just a little tired, we all are. Mike thanks for explaining everything to Eric. It was good for me to hear. It reminds me why I came to York General. It renews my commitment just listening to you. Of course, young Eric Shepard was an added surprise as I'm sure we were for him."

Mike Armstrong actually laughed, "There have certainly been a few surprises since you walked through that door. We're working harder, learning more, getting more help financially than we've ever had. I feel better about what I do. The whole hospital feels good about what we're doing. Your energy and drive are contagious and although you've explained it to me, a Rosicrucian is still a mystery to me."

"Think of me as a priest."

'Think of me as someone who needs to understand', thought Eric.

'Tomorrow' came the reply.

Eric closed his eyes and slept for the first time he could remember in a long time. His eyes shot open and standing beside his bed was his granddad. He looked at Eric and smiled.

"Well, my brave boy, how are you?"

"What's wrong?" said Eric surprised by his own voice. "I spoke," he said.

"Yes," said Sid. "It's a special occasion."

"Oh!" said Eric as he got out of his bed and stood next to his grandfather, surprised again by how tall he had become and how fit and healthy his granddad looked. "So what's the occasion?"

"I'm leaving," said Sid.

"Where are you going?" said Eric.

"I'm going to see some old friends and maybe some new ones."

"When will you be back?" asked Eric.

"I won't be back, my brave boy."

"I don't understand," said Eric.

"I know," said Sid, "but you will soon so go back to bed and sleep. I wanted you to know you brought great joy to my life."

Eric found himself back in bed drifting off to sleep wondering where his grandfather was going when Anna screamed. His eyes opened and once again he could not move or speak, but he could hear the gentle rhythmic sound of his grandfather's chair moving back and forth. No one came for awhile, then the door opened and Stan lifted him into his chair. 'What happened', thought Eric.

Again the unspoken reply, 'your grandfather has passed.'

Stan pushed him into the living room. Sid still looked like he was asleep in the slow moving chair. Stan wheeled Eric over to Anna who said, "I couldn't find the remote." He gently reached over and switched off the chair. "Sit down. I'll make tea."

Anna burst forth with a torrent of tears and all she could say was, "Tea, yes, he'd like that."

Eric sat in his chair feeling lonelier than he'd ever felt. Then suddenly he thought about Grimm and in his mind he smiled. 'He'll meet Grimm', he thought. 'They'll like each other'. Then he heard Stan thinking, 'Grimm?'

'My axe friend, brother in arms: our conversation, remember'.

'It may have to wait until tomorrow.'

'Till tomorrow, then', he thought.

Chapter Twenty Six

It was wet and windy. The service was brief and Sid was laid to rest. Terry was in the hospital. No one had thought to give Eric his cap and computer. So here he was again, trapped in his head at the whim of external forces.

"It's smaller and lighter," said Stan as he placed the new lap top in the special holder that had been made for Eric's wheelchair. "The cap is also more efficient than the last one so tomorrow we would like to continue with the tests. There may be more changes in your brain activity now that you can communicate. You can let us know what you think or if you feel any changes."

"There are many changes I'm sure you can't see, but I'll have the tests anyway. I want you to make time for our talk. I have many questions and I don't have much time."

"I see," said Stan. "I'll ask your mother if you can spend the day with me on Thursday."

"Fine, till Thursday then," flashed the computer then clicked off.

Eric was wheeled into the room where he was to have the second of the three scans that had been planned for him. This time the radiologist was a woman. She said to Anna, "I don't know what Doctor Kissen has told you about this test or how it is conducted, so I'll briefly explain. It is similar to an M.R.I. It allows us to measure restricted diffusion of water tissue, hence the name D.T.I. The principle application is in measuring the white matter. Stop me if this is over your head," she said.

Anna smiled, "It is over my head, but keep going anyway."

"White matter is one of the two main solid components of the central nervous system. It is composed of nerve cells, or axons, which connect various grey matter areas of the brain to each other and carry nerve impulses between neurons. White matter is the part of the brain and spinal cord responsible for information transmission. The grey matter is responsible for information processing. What we are looking for is any kind of change, positive or negative. Although from what I've seen of the CAT scan, the changes all seem positive."

Once more Eric was lifted into the machine, only this time the radiologist was very quiet and Eric lay in the silence as his brain was viewed from six directions. It took almost two hours and Eric was exhausted by the tension of wondering how long he would be alone.

The radiologist came out of the room carrying the photos of Eric's brain. "Well," she said, "let's get you up and back in your chair." Nurse Scott helped lift Eric into the wheelchair.

"How does it look?" said Anna.

"I'll show you," said the radiologist. "Let's go to Doctor Kissen's office. He'll be waiting to see what we have here."

"Does anything seem wrong?" asked Anna.

"No, actually everything seems fine."

They walked to the elevator and took it up one level to Doctor Kissen's office. He opened the door waiting anxiously for them to arrive. "Come in," he smiled. "Well, Doctor Brown, let's see what we have."

Doctor Brown passed the envelope with the images to him and said, "I think you'll find it interesting."

E.J. Kissen opened the pictures and set them up on the screen in his office. "This can't be right," he said.

"If you come to the radiology department I'll show you the whole 3-D picture on the computer," said Doctor Brown, "but as you can see here this is a normal brain. There is evidence of newly formed axons. Sir Charles is right. Eric's brain has created new pathways."

E.J. looked at Doctor Brown and Anna and said, "The changes are quite literally unbelievable. He has reversed damage in the white matter, but it looks like there has been regeneration in the grey matter. Let's get Sir Charles up here. This is strange."

Eric watched and listened to every one discuss his brain. He heard his mother say, "Will he get movement in his limbs?"

"I don't know," said E.J.

Doctor Brown said, "As far as I can see from the CAT scan and the D.T.I., there is no reason why he isn't standing here discussing this with us."

Eric moaned gently and Anna put his cap on his head. The computer flashed, "There's one reason. I can't!"

Sir Charles breezed into the room. "So what's all the commotion then?"

"These pictures, Sir Charles," said Doctor Brown.

"Chuck, please," he said. He looked at the pictures and said, "P.E.T scan, then we'll discuss. How are you, my boy?"

"I think I'm ill. Doctor Brown said there's no reason why I shouldn't be standing up discussing this with you but I can't seem to move," said the computer.

"One more photo session in the doughnut and we'll decide what's to do."

"There is no obvious reason according to the scan why he is even in a wheelchair," said Doctor Brown.

"Doctor Brown, isn't it?" he said.

"Yes," she replied.

"Well, Doctor Brown, look at Eric and not your images of his brain and you'll see the reasons he is in a wheelchair are obvious. Alright, then, I think rest is in order for you Eric. Anna, may Eric spend the rest of the day with my good friend, Stan, and we'll do the final scan tomorrow? Is that alright with you, Eric?"

"Yes," said the computer.

Anna said, "I'm worried by all these tests."

"Don't be," said Sir Charles, "we don't have any bad news. It all looks very positive. We just need some more information."

"What more will the P.E.T. scan tell you?"

"The CAT, D.T.I. and P.E.T. scans will be read in combination. It will give us anatomic and metabolic information. It is useful to do them one after the other but in Eric's case we could not do that as the hospital did not have a P.E.T. scanner. However, we've purchased one on behalf of the hospital, a donation from Stan and myself, and although it is preferable to do those types of scans back to back, I think we all agree that Eric needs a break from the discomfort it causes him.

"You look exhausted, Anna. I'm about ready to leave," said E.J. "If you like I'll take you home. Stan said he'd be here in about fifteen minutes."

"Eric, would you like to spend the rest of the day with Stan," said Anna.

"Yes, yes and yes," danced across the screen.

"Okay," said Anna, "but I'll wait until he gets here."

"He's here," clicked the computer. "Listen."

The crisp, sharp click of Stan Wolf's military style walk could be heard reverberating down the hospital hallway. Sir Charles smiled, "Good ears. Alright, then, until tomorrow."

Chapter Twenty Seven

Stan wheeled Eric into the living room of the small cottage he lived in on the outskirts of York. "I'll make us some tea," he said.

Eric thought, 'why don't you just speak to me telepathically'?

"It's much harder to do that than simply just to speak," said Stan. "I think you have a fair idea of what the Rosicrucians are. However, I'll answer any questions you have and I think perhaps you can do the same for me."

"Alright," clicked the computer.

"Suppose we start with Grimm," said Stan.

"Grimm was my axe friend. He died at the battle of Stamford Bridge," clicked across the screen.

Stan was quiet for a moment and then said, "What about you?"

"I'm a housecarl, like he was, in the service of Harold Godwinson, the King of England, in the year 1066."

"This is a dream you've been having for some time?" said Stan.

"I think you of all people know better than that. I need answers as to why I'm here and how I get back to where I want to be," the words pulsed on the screen as Stan watched Eric for any sign of movement other than the words his thoughts sent across the screen. "Am I right about Horace, the boy from the soccer team?"

"Yes," Stan replied. "He has been chosen as one of the eight." He paused then said, "So has Terry."

"What do you mean?"

"May I explain?" said Horace as he entered the room

"Your chance will come" said Stan. "Right now I'd like you to listen and just be with Eric".

Stan stood for a moment and then he said, "I've chosen Terry. Each one of us, that is to say each one of the eight, must choose someone to carry on. As our tenure ends we must select the next eight to carry on our work."

"When does your tenure end?" clicked the computer.

"When we die," said Stan.

"Why Terry?" clicked the computer.

"Although we choose the next eight it isn't random any more than the universe is random. We are guided in our choice."

"What if Terry dies?" clicked Eric.

"He won't," said Stan. "I thought that myself. I actually thought it might be you I must choose when we first met. However, it has become very clear that it is Terry who will follow me."

"Does he know this?"

"No, not yet," said Stan.

"When will you tell him?" clicked the computer.

"When he is ready."

"That doesn't make sense. "He may never be ready."

"He will be ready," said Stan. "Does fighting for Harold Godwinson in a battle that cannot be won make sense?"

"It makes more sense than being fed by a straw and lifted back and forth between a wheelchair and a machine which tells us what we already know; my brain works and my body doesn't. Do you know why I am here? My purpose, I mean?"

"No, I don't, but it is of great importance and will become clear I promise you. So, tea?" said Stan

"I've changed my mind," said Eric. "Water, please."

As Stan brought Eric water he said, "We still have much to talk about," stumbled and threw the water in Eric's face.

"Get up," said a harsh voice. Eric opened his eyes and wiped the water from his face. Standing before him was a tall Viking warrior. Eric got to his feet as the warrior placed his sword at his throat. "You would already be dead but for your horse," he said. "He chased me into the trees and the other horse he savaged till it ran away. Who are you?"

"I am a housecarl of Godwinson, and you?"

"I'm an Icelander. I escaped from Stamford Bridge once I saw the way the battle was going. I put my axe into the back of the Saxon, but he refused to fall from his horse till he saw you. So call your horse. I need him."

"Take your sword from my throat or it won't be me he comes to when I call."

As the Northman lowered his sword, Eric whistled quietly and Midnight came racing from the forest. The Icelander moved back nervously and Eric saw the quarter staff that had felled him lying at his feet. He kicked it up into his hands. As the Icelander raised his sword he hit him in the throat with the staff and Midnight was on him with savage fury. Eric stepped away as his warhorse killed the warrior. Midnight did not stop his attack until there was nothing to fight but the bloody earth.

"Come," said Eric, "we must ride north and find the King. I no longer know how old the news is but we have only been here a few hours. The sun has barely set. So William has come at last. I must also tell Grimm. He would not forgive me if he entered Valhalla not knowing."

Eric rode into York at sunrise and Godwinson, talking to Wulfstan, turned and was the first to see him. "He has come then," said the King.

"Aye, Sire, they landed at Penvensey two days ago and are pillaging the countryside."

Godwinson called the earls, Morcar and Edwin, and asked if they would ride south with him to face William of Normandy. The earls claimed their armies were too fatigued, but would join the King in two days. Wulfstan called the men of Wallingford and London together.

"We must now face Duke William. He pillages our southern coast. Who will ride with the King?"

The carls roared their acceptance of the task at hand. By noon the armies were riding south. Eric sat on Midnight like a man in a trance. His shirt was soaked with blood.

"Your wound has opened," said Wulfstan.

"It's not serious," said Eric as he slipped from the saddle unconscious into the arms of the ancient warrior.

"Take him to the village where he buried Grimm," he said. "It's close on the banks of the River Haven. Have him stitched up and tell him to join us in the South when he can." With that Wulfstan rode back to the head of the army and the King.

Thorkill entered the village with Eric behind him tied onto Midnight. He stopped in front of the church. The elderly priest came out and said, "I suppose he's here for the burial of his friend. It takes place tomorrow."

Thorkill looked at the priest through eyes of exhaustion and weariness that comes with a life of war and killing. "He is wounded. It needs to be stitched. Find someone to do it. When he awakes he will want to ride south. Keep him here. It is already too late." The warrior took out a pouch of silver coins.

"I have been paid," said the priest.

"Your name," said Thorkill.

"Christian, Sire."

"Proper for a priest I suppose. I've never known an honest one." He threw the coins to him. "I won't need this where I'm going. Take care of him." As he turned his horse he said, "What do you call this place?"

"We renamed it Grimsby, Lord."

"Not Lord, priest. Warrior, like him and the one you bury tomorrow." He wheeled his horse and was gone.

Eric was taken to the home of Grimm's mother. His father had gone to join Godwinson. She bathed and stitched his wounds and he fell into a deep exhausted sleep. He dreamed he was walking in the little churchyard. He entered the church and there, in front of the alter, lay Grimm, his wounds stitched and his body oiled and clean. He wore his finest breeches and a soft leather shirt. His axe was by his side and a crimson cloak fell from his shoulders half covering the stone slab on which he lay. Eric looked at his face which had turned pale beneath the weathered and tattooed skin. He knelt beside him and felt a great sadness overcome him. He touched Grimm's face and tears blurred his eyes.

Grimm's eyes opened and he said to Eric, "Stand vigil with me, brother, so I may enter Valhalla knowing you cover my back."

"William has come. I'd hoped we would fight him together," said Eric.

"Take my axe. Leave yours. We will always be together."

A burst of light blinded him. He awoke as the sunrise burst through the windows and the shadow of his axe joined with the shadow of the cross above the altar. Eric looked up into the sad eyes of the man on the cross

191

who stood vigil with him. The old priest stood behind him and said, "Grimm is in the hands of our Lord and so are you my son."

Eric turned and Stan said, "Sorry about that. I'm never that clumsy."

Eric sat in the chair unable to move and confused. The computer began to click away. "I understand what you've told me about the Rosicrucians. I don't understand how I fit into the picture. My brother is chosen. I am not. That makes sense to me. However, you have given me a more detailed explanation of what the Rosicrucians are. Why? If he is to be one of the eight and is going to live, why explain it to me. I don't need to know."

"I think you do," said Stan. "You have a purpose in two separate lives across time. Perhaps if you understand your purpose in this life, you will understand your purpose in the other."

"I am moving to an ending in both lives. The purpose I think is to be at the right place at the right time."

"Perhaps it is a beginning."

"And this life?"

"I'm not the one to ask"

"I did ask," clicked the computer.

"Did you get an answer?"

There was a long silence then Eric wrote, "Yes I did."

"Then you'll be at the right time and place in both lives" said Stan.

The computer was silent and Eric lay having his wounds sewn up a thousand years before "computer" was a word.

Chapter Twenty Eight

Terry opened his eyes and standing by his bed was Stan Wolf. "You have a fight ahead of you. Not a fight, a battle, and there will be casualties but you must not falter or give in because this is your true path and I am here to guide you."

Terry smiled weakly, "I am very tired and it sounds like you're telling me I'm going to die. I want to see Eric before I do."

"You will not die, but you must fight to live."

"Where's Eric?"

"He's in the process of having what is called a P.E.T. scan. It's a sophisticated X-ray or CAT scan. He will see you as soon as it is done. You'll probably see Mike Armstrong first." He paused, then continued, "The Leukemia is back and it's likely you will need a bone marrow transplant and Eric is too weak so we must find another donor."

"Is Eric going to be alright? Is there something wrong with his brain?"

"No, quite the opposite. His brain seems to be very much improved, but his body is not responding as it should with such improvement."

Eric lay in the doughnut and the process began again. This time he had an audience; Sir Charles, Doctor Brown, the other nameless, talkative technician and E.J. Kissen. Mike Armstrong, his mom, and Stan Wolf were not there and that worried him because if not with him they were with Terry, and if they were with Terry something was wrong. Sir Charles' voice broke into his thoughts.

"This is the last test, Eric. It's called Positron Emission Tomography. The injection you had about an hour ago allows us to follow what is called a positron. The scanner takes us on a three dimensional tour of your brain. It's a pretty sophisticated scan and much more involved than my explanation. The end result is we get information we can compare with the other tests you've had and perhaps get an understanding of some of the changes going on in your brain which, by the way, are all good."

'If they are all good', thought Eric, 'why am I still in a useless body'? Eric was lifted back into his chair by the now silent, talkative technician. He sat in silence as he listened to the buzz of voices discussing the scan of his brain. About half an hour passed, then the buzzing stopped and everyone came out of the room where the scan had been viewed. They all stood looking at him like they expected him to pick up his chair and walk. If he could have laughed, he would have.

He closed his eyes and heard the old Priest say the final prayer over Grimm. The day was bright and sunny as they filled in the grave that entombed his friend. "Is it still September?" said Eric.

"No," said the priest. "It's October."

"I must leave," he said. "My horse, where is he?"

"Your friend said you were not to go south, that it is already too late."

"My horse, bring him to me now." He turned to walk away but exhaustion and battle fatigue once more took over as he pitched forward and fell face down on the damp, autumn earth.

Jennifer, Stan and Anna were all in the adjoining room to Terry's. Inside, Mike Armstrong looked like he was about to step onto the moon. His head was covered; he wore a protective suit over his clothes and had on his mask and gloves.

Terry had become increasingly weak. He opened his eyes and smiled, "Nice disguise, but I recognize the blue eyes. How are you, Doc?"

"I'm fine," said Mike, "just dealing with the challenges that you're throwing at me."

"Wrong word. I'm too tired to throw anything," said Terry. "How about presenting you with?"

"Okay, presenting me with. You have some visitors. I'll turn the intercom on."

Anna spoke first. "Hello, Love, I know you don't feel great, but we're on track for a new donor."

Terry smiled. "Okay," he said.

Jennifer came to the intercom and said, "I was tested but am not a match, but we'll keep looking."

"Good," said Terry.

Stan said, "Remember our little pep talk."

"Eric," said Terry.

"This afternoon," said Stan.

"Okay, then let me rest till then. Sorry I'm so tired."

Anna, tearful and exhausted, left with Jennifer.

Eric was back in his chair with his computer. Stan, Sir Charles and E.J. sat around the desk facing him. Sir Charles spoke first, "Well, Eric, it's interesting. Having reviewed all the scans your brain has changed in several very positive ways and your body obviously hasn't and we, and several other experts, have no idea why the brain is repairing itself and your body is not."

Eric's computer began to click as the words poured across the screen. "So really things haven't changed. My brain works and my body doesn't. You didn't understand it before and you don't understand it now."

"The brain you have should allow you to do everything that we do and there is no rational explanation why it doesn't," said E.J.

There was silence then the computer began to click once more. "Actually," said Eric, "my brain does allow me to do everything that you do and more. The problem is your need for a rational explanation. Perhaps Stan can help you with that, but I have a need to see my brother and I'd like that to happen before you start your explanation, Stan, rational or otherwise."

The three men all looked at Eric without saying anything. Stan stood up and said, "I'll take him to see Terry and we can discuss this when I return."

They went into the visitors' room with Mike Armstrong. Terry's illness and treatment had visibly weakened him. He looked at his brother in the wheelchair and said into the intercom, "How are you? Tired from carrying all that extra brain around?" He tried to laugh but ended up coughing so that Mike had to get changed and go into his room, raise him on his pillows and make sure his intravenous medicines and nutrition were all still connected.

Eric's computer began throwing words across the screen. "Stan, tell my mother we can't waste any more time looking for another donor. Ask Mike how soon we can do it."

"I'll do my best," said Stan, "but your mother is already concerned about you."

Eric's computer flashed back, "I think the purpose of my life is to save Terry's life so he can carry on the work that I have begun."

"How long have you known?" said Stan.

"Not long, a few seconds, it's just now beginning to make sense to me."

Stan called Mike through the intercom, "I think we must talk with Anna," he said.

Mike came into the room and looked from Stan to the computer and then to Eric. "Okay, I'll call Anna. I think she is downstairs with E.J." Mike left the room and Eric's cursor began to spit words across the screen.

"Stan, I don't have much time. Tell me what you know."

"What I know is what I've already told you. Sometime late in the Eleventh Century there was a monk who some say was originally a Benedictine from the Monastery of Saint Albans. He had outrun a great evil which pursued him. Twelve knights, Normans in the service of William the Conqueror, sought the body of Harold Godwinson which could not be found on the battlefield of Hastings. William had guessed that someone had lived through the butchery of the battle to spirit away the body of the King. The last Saxon King of England. The fact that there was no body started a firestorm which created a legend around Godwinson. "The King lives" was whispered the length and breadth of the country. Ahead of his pursuers and the fire ignited by the legend, rode the monk and his followers carrying "The Rule of St. Benedict" in its original scroll and a silver casket carrying the heart of Harold Godwinson. William knew that someone had taken Godwinson's body from the battlefield. His spies told him that a group of monks were traveling north fast on horseback with some kind of casket attached to its own horse. There were whispers that the monk had been a warrior on the battlefield of Hastings who had sworn that he would never kill again and extinguish the light that God had given to man. As God's man he swore to protect that light against the darkness of evil, an evil reflected in the butchery he had witnessed at Hastings in the name of William, England's new King.

A hundred years later a monk led the council held in Saint Felix Lavragais in the year 1167. He was a Cathar. The name Cathar is Greek. It means "pure ones". Catharism proclaimed that there exists a spark of divine light, given by God to man. The spark had to be nurtured to ensure that it would never go out. A Cathar monk rescued Christian Rosenkreutz from the Catholic Inquisition. The spark within Rosenkreutz began the Rosicrucian Order. The order was cloaked in secrecy to protect the concept of pure goodness. The reason for this was that evil is attracted to the light to extinguish it. The guardians of the light became the Knights Templar and the Freemasons."

"Are you saying you think I'm a Rosicrucian?" clicked the computer.

"I believe that "The Guardians of the Light" are sentinels of good over evil that have been nurtured from century to century to ensure that the light is never extinguished. It began in the Dark Ages, and I believe that you are the bridge that connects the beginning to the present time. Reincarnation is an idea as old as time and you are moving through time to be sure that we don't lose our way."

"Like the Olympic Torch?"

"Exactly"

Anna came into the room like a hurricane. "Eric, you are too weak to give Terry another bone marrow transplant."

"I'm stronger than him," clicked the computer, "and if somebody doesn't give him a transplant soon there won't be any need. He's dying."

Mike Armstrong came in behind Anna. She turned to him and said, "That's not true, is it?"

"He's very ill. We can't wait much longer."

"Alright," said Anna, "but if anything happens to you I'll never forgive you."

"Even if I pick up my chair and walk?" clicked the screen.

Mike Armstrong intervened, "Okay, this time we'll do the stem cell transplant. That means we'll be taking blood from you, Eric, and giving it to Terry."

"Oh, great," tapped out the computer. "Will we be using the suicide pilots?"

"The 'suicide' gene therapy will be used for the same reasons as before."

"I know," clicked Eric, "graft versus host rejection. I should have had that when he was well. I could have rejected his wheelchair driving technique. Just kidding, Terry, let's get you up and running." Then he clicked off.

Chapter Twenty Nine

The procedure was set up as before. Eric was in the room close to Terry. This time it was a little different. For the previous five days Eric had been given medication to increase the number of stem cells released into his blood stream. The process is called Apheresis and the medication, Filgrastim, caused him to feel a little achy in his bones.

Mike came into the room and said, "Okay, Eric, this should be easy. What happens is this. We take your blood out of a vein in your chest. It goes through a centrifuge which will remove the stem cells. The blood is then returned to you and, of course, you will make more stem cells and your brother will have healthy stem cells which should put him in remission and back on the soccer team, eventually. Any questions?"

The computer clicked three words, "No, get started."

"Okay," said Mike as the nurses prepared Eric for the venous catheter, the flexible tube that was to be placed in his chest to remove the stem cells. As the catheter was inserted in his chest Eric closed his eyes.

Grimm's mother said, "You must rest. You have opened the wound in your chest again. No more walking in your sleep. You stood vigil with my son, now he is at rest in the arms of God and you must rest or you will join him before your time."

Eric tried to rise but the priest made him drink a thick mead that sent him into oblivion as Grimm's mother said, "Three times I've sewn this wound. I hope you gave him enough to keep him asleep until tomorrow at least."

"He will sleep for three days with what I have given him," smiled the priest.

"I have a feeling it may not meet with his vision of where he should be. When he awakens he will ride south. Perhaps we could keep him asleep long enough that he might want to stay," said the old woman. "I think God wished to replace the son I lost."

"He may," said the priest, "but not with this one. Look at the scars and tattoos. He is closer in blood to Grimm than you are. This youth seeks death in the service of Godwinson, as did your son. They are brothers in war."

Eric's dreams were a mass of contradictions. He stood by his hospital bed and looked at the boy who was sick. Terry looked weak. As he turned away he saw his face in the mirror tattooed with strange symbols and the scar on his forehead where Grimm had knocked him down. He wanted away from this place, but when he tried to leave he found once more that he could not move as he lay trapped in a bed next to his brother. He could see movement from the corner of his eye. He tried to twist to see what was moving, but could not move. Then it crossed his vision and turned towards him.

Midnight, covered in blood and flecked with foam and sweat, came thundering towards him. He tried to call him, but his voice would not come. The fiery stallion came on, tramping all in its path. 'He doesn't know me', thought Eric as he tried to scream. He closed his eyes as Midnight was almost upon him. Then silence enveloped him, but he could still feel Midnight's breath and the sound of him snorting.

He opened his eyes to look into the massive mouth of Midnight as his huge pink tongue slobbered him into consciousness. He had a headache and the fire in the cottage had died down. Midnight took up almost the whole room, but still Grimm's mother slept on. Eric backed his horse out of the cottage and left his gold inlaid armband on the table. As he rode out of the village the priest stood by the road.

"What is the date?" said Eric.

"It is the twelfth of October, my son."

"It's my birthday," replied Eric. "I'm nineteen years old."

"Not very old, my son."

"It may be as old as I'll ever be," he said as he gently squeezed Midnight with his thighs and the horse broke into a trot which cleared them of Grimsby as they headed south to join the King. 'I'll come back after we've beaten William', thought Eric, but he knew regardless of the outcome he would never return to this place if he could avoid it. His path and purpose left no room to return. He pulled his cloak around him and rode south.

Chapter Thirty

Eric rode through the night exhausted but determined to join the housecarls in the defense of England. As dawn broke he could see the road blocked by hundreds of peasants, all heading south to meet William in battle. As he passed through Stamford he thought, 'It'll be Christmas before I join Harold if I travel with this mass'. He turned Midnight off the rode and traveled through the countryside to the east of Stamford heading for Penvesey where he knew the Norman army would be waiting for them. As he rode through Andredsweald Forest there were strange sounds which reminded him of Stamford Bridge, the clank of swords and armor, but he saw no one. He stopped Midnight and brushed him and cleaned the sweat from his coat. He held his reins and leaned his saddle against an oak tree. He closed his eyes for a moment and the sounds of fierce fighting pulled him awake.

Mike Armstrong, E.J. and his mother were all round his bed along with several nurses and a lot of strange equipment. Anna looked like she had seen a ghost and Mike held two flat, square objects in his hand attached to a machine by wires. It took him a minute to realize what was happening. He couldn't speak and he was glad about that.

"He's back," said E.J.

Mike looked at Eric and sat down on the bed. "It's a defibrillator," he said. "Your heart stopped and, just in case you're interested, so did mine. E.J., Nurse Scott, take over. I need a drink." Everyone looked at him. "Water," he said.

"I need some water, although something stronger might be in order later."

Eric thought about his cap and computer but could see that was the last thing on anyone's mind except his own, so he just lay there and listened. They were all talking to each other at the same time. It was rather amusing. Then he noticed Stan Wolf who had been beside his bed and he hadn't seen him, but his hand was on his arm.

"You'll be alright, Eric, and so will Terry," said Stan. He said it quietly but everyone stopped talking and he smiled.

Mike Armstrong smiled back. "The stem cell transplant will take place tomorrow. Terry is resting. I'll explain the process to you when you've had some rest, but I want to explain what happened to you. Five hours into the procedure your heart stopped. It's not clear why. However, things look like they are back to normal. Your resting heart rate and blood pressure are good. I'm keeping you up here with me, and E.J. will be keeping a close watch on you. Quite frankly, you scared the living daylights out of us.

"We got the stem cells we need. They will be stored in a refrigerator until tomorrow when the transplant procedure will take place. Terry is tired from the drugs and radiation we gave him so he's resting. You are tired, as you should be after what you've gone through. I'm suggesting you have your cap and computer for ten minutes. Then I'd also like you to rest. Both Doctor Kissen and I will be monitoring you for the next twenty four hours. As for Terry, you'll have to wait to talk to him. He's very weak."

Eric was given his computer. It began to click. "I am tired. I don't need to talk to Terry. I just want to know when it's done and if he improves. Hi, Mom. I need to rest." The computer clicked off and he heard Stan say telepathically, "You'll be where you are supposed to be and so will I. Terry will have questions by next week".

Eric replied telepathically, "I don't have a week. I have two days".

Stan answered, "Rest, you have more than two days in this life".

"How?" came the response.

Stan placed his hand on his head and thought, "Rest", and Eric passed into oblivion. He was dreaming of x-ray machines and the large donut spun around his head and he could hear voices, the technician talking to Doctor Brown. Sir Charles said, "We'll find an explanation. The changes in this boy are very important to science." Then everyone went silent and Wulfstan spoke, "There will be no more tests," he said.
Eric sat up and Doctor Brown screamed as the scarred, tattooed warrior leapt to the floor to stand beside Earl Wulfstan.

Sir Charles was about to respond. Eric's eyes opened and there talking quietly together was Sir Charles, Anna, Stan Wolf, Mike Armstrong and E.J. Kissen. The only one who did not look worried was Stan Wolf.

Anna said, "Oh, you're awake. You look much better and I'm sure you must be hungry."

'They all talk to me like I can answer', thought Eric. 'That computer did come in useful. Unfortunately, I'm still useless without it'.

Stan placed his cap on his head and his computer in front of him as he and E.J. propped him up in bed supported by pillows. The computer came to life. "How's Terry? It's today. The transplant is today, isn't it?"

"In about an hour," said Mike Armstrong, "and Terry is okay. He had a good night. In a few days we'll be able to tell how well it has gone, but I'm confident it will be just what the doctor ordered."

"A funny line, doc, but hardly original."

"Being original was never my strong point although it seems to be yours," he said with a smile.

"Thanks," said the computer. "Did someone mention food, I mean mush?"

"He's back," said Anna.

Chapter Thirty One

Terry lay in bed looking up at the I.V. "I've had his bone marrow, now his stem cells. We'll be like twins," he said weakly.

Mike Armstrong said, "Not exactly, but you have much of the same genetic material. The transplant in your case is called Allogeneic because it came from your brother and he is compatible with you. If it had been from an identical twin it would be Syngeneic. Anyway, I don't imagine we need to discuss the differences in names. It looks good and I'm convinced you'll be feeling much better very soon."

"How long?' said Terry.

"Well, you'll be here for a few weeks. It takes time for the stem cells to travel to the bone marrow and produce new white blood cells, red blood cells and platelets. This is called engraftment. It usually takes two to four weeks after transplantation. I'll be sticking you with needles frequently to test your blood count."

"How long before we know it's in remission?" said Anna who had been sitting quietly listening.

"It will take one or two years for complete immune function recovery. We'll be testing his blood and bone marrow to make sure the new marrow is doing its job. Terry, you'll be in this protected environment room probably for a month. The risks during this time include infection and/or bleeding. You will be on antibiotics and possibly have a transfusion of platelets to prevent bleeding and red blood cells to treat anemia. Short term you'll have nausea, fatigue, loss of appetite and you may lose more hair than you already have. However, as I say, that's short term and we'll be here to make sure you come through it okay."

"What about Eric?" said Terry.

"He's fine," said Mike. "He even gave some extra blood in case you need the transfusions I just mentioned."

"He's tough, my little brother," said Terry.

Anna looked at Mike who said, "Yes, he is, but he'll be here for a few days after the procedure and you'll probably be able to see him in two or three days."

"Oh, good," said Terry. "By the way, how is Aunt Jennifer?"

"She's been busy, but I'm sure she'll be in to visit when she can," replied Anna.

She waited outside the room for Mike Armstrong.

He came out and said to her,

"What I said about the transplant being Allogeneic is true. Both you and Jennifer have the same genetic information which makes them cousins. I didn't tell him Eric is not his brother. He has enough to contend with and so does everyone else."

Anna answered, "I agree," and left.

The next few weeks were traumatic for Terry. He was so sick he could not see Eric or even Anna. His days were filled with nausea and vomiting and he did need the transfusions for anemia and bleeding. His head was as smooth as a billiard ball and almost as white. Eric had recovered but had little to say on his computer. He ate and slept and Anna asked E.J. and Sir Charles if he was suffering from some malady they had missed.

"It seems he is depressed," said E.J. "His brain function is normal. We'd still like to continue with our observations to try and find the reason that his brain is developing new neurological pathways while his body continues to deteriorate."

"Deteriorate?" said Anna.

"Well he has lost a little weight," said E.J., "and his muscles spasm more often. Then there was that moment during the Apheresis when his heart stopped. These are all reasons for concern."

"So what is happening to him?"

"We don't know," said Sir Charles. "We're reviewing all the scans and quite honestly it's baffling."

"Why don't you go home and rest," said E.J. "This has been tough for you having both boys going through life threatening situations. Eric is resting and a few days of rest will probably be just what he needs, and you certainly could use some. I'll call you this evening and keep you updated."

"He's been here for three weeks," said Anna.

"If he can see Terry in the next couple of days I'm sure that will cheer him up," said Sir Charles.

"Alright," said Anna. "I'll go home. Call me if the boys ask for me. Otherwise I'll be back tomorrow. I should go and see Jennifer. I haven't seen her in weeks and I didn't think about it until Terry asked for her."

She got up and left the office and was about to look in on Eric when E.J. said, "He's asleep. Let him rest and you do the same."

"Alright," she said and walked out through the doors like a woman in a trance. E.J. was about to walk into his office when behind him he heard the foot falls of Stan Wolf. "Stan," said E.J. "I wondered where you had got to."

"Oh, I had some things to do at home, catch up on my life and meet with old friends. You know that sort of thing."

"I understand," smiled E.J. "These past few weeks have been time consuming for all of us."

"Almost all of us," said Stan. "I stopped by to visit Jennifer Shepard and I think she was at home but she didn't answer the door. It may be because she finds me a bothersome old cleric, but I think it is something else."

"What do you mean exactly?"

"I'm not sure," said Stan, "but she seems to have become more distant in the past weeks. I don't mean with me. I was thinking of her sister and those two young boys. She seems to have no interest in the outcome."

"That's quite common with certain family members," said E.J. "Mike and I come across that very thing quite often. There are people who just can't cope with the relentlessness of certain conditions, so they don't. They find a way to exit gracefully or otherwise. They disconnect. Come into my office. Eric is asleep anyway."

"Actually, I came to see Terry. The soccer coach, Bob Anderson, and young Horace Rose are going to meet me here."

"Terry has been sleeping a lot but Mike says he has improved and holds high hopes for his recovery."

"That's encouraging," said Stan.

"I'll call up if you like and see if he's awake.

"No, don't do that. Let's talk a little."

"About what?"

"That subject that you couldn't face. How you lost your faith."

"Oh, that. I wouldn't know where to begin."

"Try."

E.J. paused then began. "My father was a major in the Household Cavalry, as you know. In July 1982 he lost four of his men and seven horses in an I.R.A. bombing. He was wounded and hospitalized for a month. During that month I had a particularly hard time at my hospital. A little boy like Eric choked to death while his father sat next to him reading a book. He had a cold and the mucus just blocked his esophagus and he died quietly alone next to his father. I was also planning to get married in October and that didn't work out so you might say July through September 1982 was when I decided God did not know or care about my existence."

"It is fascinating to me that both you and Mike work in such difficult fields and neither believes in the power you need the most, the divine power of God."

"I haven't seen much of Him in my work."

"Perhaps you should look a little more closely. I don't think God left, you did."

"Religion and politics are bad subjects to discuss, Stan."

"It's neither politics nor religion we're discussing. It's your faith, or lack of it."

"Oh, come on, Stan. You yourself considered leaving the church."

"That's true, but I didn't consider leaving God and what's more important, He didn't leave me."

"Stan, you're a man who has spent his life in pursuit of spiritual understanding. I've spent mine trying to find ways to repair broken bodies that can't be repaired."

"Then how do you explain what is happening to Eric's brain?"

"I can't, but neither can you or Sir Charles or anyone else in the medical or scientific field."

"Okay, so that leaves God I think."

"If God is fixing his brain, why doesn't he fix his body?"

"I'm not saying I understand the ways in which God works. However, maybe he doesn't want to put you out of a job."

"Funny. That's funny."

"Not really."

"Alright, we're having this debate. Tell me why in God's name would He let one boy, Nathan, who was like Eric, die and let Eric live?"

"I can't really answer that, but here's what I think. God took Nathan back simply because Nathan could not continue alone."

"Meaning?"

"Meaning Anna Shepard is constantly caring for and protecting both her boys. Nathan's father sat with him. As his son suffocated he read a book."

"So God is responsible for the good stuff and we're responsible for the bad?"

"There, you see that wasn't such a stretch. Now you're beginning to understand."

"I didn't say I agreed with you."

"I didn't say that you had to. Anyway, it's good to see that the spark still burns. How about calling Mike now so that I might see Terry?"

"Okay," said E.J. "I'll be here for a while so if you need me later just come back down."

"May I ask you one more question?"

"Why not?"

"What did you do when you thought your father might have been killed?"

E.J. stared at him silently then said, "I asked God not to let him die."

"Did you do the same for Nathan?"

"No, it was too late. That's not true. I was consumed by fear and self-pity. Nathan died. My father stood in Death's shadow, and my fiance fell in love with someone else."

"Ah, you came face to face with your own mortality. That can be frightening."

"I couldn't save Nathan, my father, or my relationship. I blamed God."

"Do you still?"

"No, I blame fear and self-pity."

"Good, that's the first step to finding your faith."

"What's the second?"

"Be courageous."

"Like Christ?" said E.J.

"If all men could aspire to the courage of Christ, death and darkness would have nowhere to hide."

"And I'd be out of a job," said E.J.

"Me too," said Stan.

Stan stepped into the elevator and ascended to the Oncology Department wondering if Terry would indeed be the next of the young adepts to carry the light and reflect goodness without compromise. "Evil is the absence of God as darkness is the absence of light", he said to himself, "Only when is God ever absent?"

The elevator doors opened and Mike stood there waiting for him. "Are you talking to yourself?" he said.

"Musing," said Stan, "just musing over rhetorical questions."

"Oh, good," said Mike, "I don't want two of us on this floor that are talking to themselves. Terry's already asked me if I'm praying."

"Are you?" said Stan.

"Yes," said Mike. "I think we all are." With that he pushed open the door to the observation room and they went in to see Terry. He was sitting up in bed and Horace and Bob were in the observation room looking through the window.

"How are you feeling?" said Stan through the intercom.

"Not great," replied Terry.

"Things are going to be better very soon," said Horace as he squeezed his face against the intercom.

"Horace," said Terry. "I keep seeing you disappearing and reappearing where Stan was. What's going on? It's creepy."

"I think that's just the drugs and your state of mind right now," said Stan. "But while we are on an unorthodox subject, I thought I might discuss something with you."

"I don't really feel like discussing anything right now," said Terry.

"Remember the secret organization that we talked about?" said Stan.

"Oh, yes," said Terry, "maybe once I see Eric we can talk. I know he's interested."

"That's fine," said Stan. "Let's do that."

Bob looked at Stan then said to Terry, "In a couple of months you'll be back on the soccer team."

"I don't think so," said Terry.

"Why not?" said Horace.

"I don't have any interest. I want to spend more time with my brother now that we can talk. I don't want to waste time."

"What about the team?" asked Horace. "Everyone has been waiting for you to come back."

"I know. I'm sorry, but the truth is by the time I'm fit enough to play everyone would be worried about me getting hurt; my mom, aunt, doctors, my grandpa and my brother. It isn't what I want to do anymore."

Bob Anderson said, "I think you might be right. Maybe you could help me coach."

"Maybe," said Terry, "but I'm anxious to see my brother so could we talk after I've seen him?"

"Of course," said Stan. "He's asleep now but I think Mike said you could see him first thing tomorrow."

"Thanks. That's great. I don't want to be bad mannered but do you think it would be okay if I slept now. I'm kind of tired."

Stan, Bob and Horace got up to leave. "Sleep well," said Stan.

"I will," replied Terry. "I was dreaming of my granddad earlier. He was young like Eric only not in a wheelchair. He was a goalie just like you, Horace." With that he closed his eyes and was asleep.

As Stan and Bob stepped out of the room Bob said, "Should we have told him?"

"No," said Stan. "I think Anna will want to do that."

Anna parked her van on Bellevue Street about half a mile from Jennifer's apartment. She walked along the tree lined street admiring the buildings and thinking how well Jennifer had done with her expensive car and very chic penthouse apartment. Jennifer had an uncanny knack for getting what she wanted and getting rid of what she didn't want.

Anna rang the bell and Jennifer's voice cracked through the intercom. "Come up," she said.

"It's me," said Anna. No answer. The door buzzed and she entered the building. The elevator was slow and smooth. Jennifer stood by the apartment door.

"Come in," she said.

"Thanks," said Anna. "I would have come sooner but with both boys in the hospital the days just seem to disappear."

"I understand," said Jennifer. "I've been busy myself. I've actually met someone who is running a program for the National Health Service. He's rather high up in the government and wants to appoint me as his second in command, so to speak."

"That's wonderful news. The boys will be impressed."

"I'd rather you don't tell anyone right now. We, that is Robert and I, wish to keep things low key at the present time."

"Are you romantically involved?" asked Anna.

"I'm meeting him in half an hour so I must get ready. Give my love to the boys."

"You didn't answer me," said Anna.

"No, I didn't," replied Jennifer.

"Okay," said Anna. "So, do we get to meet him at least?"

Jennifer looked at Anna and replied, "No. You won't ever meet him because he doesn't know you exist. I want my life and your life separate."

"What about the boys?" asked Anna. "Eric is your son."

"No," said Jennifer. "Eric is your son. He was my problem. I asked you to help me solve it, not adopt it." Anna stood speechless. "Listen," said Jennifer. "Dad is dead, our lives are completely different and there is no place in mine for a boy like Eric."

"What about the thousands like him that you will be responsible for?"

"What about them? They are my career, nothing more. Now please excuse me. I'm late."

Anna ran along Bellevue Street till she reached her van. Her heart was thumping, her head was pounding and she had no idea who she had just spoken to. She got into her van and drove home. It was damp, drizzling, misty and depressing. She sat in the van cold and lonely. As the minutes passed she realized there was nothing to come home to so she reversed out of the drive and drove to the hospital.

The air was damp and misty. The sounds that Eric had taken for the sounds of battle were not. They were the sounds of preparation. He crept out of his hiding place and looked down on a city of pavilions. The pennants and colors of William of Normandy and his lords and knights were flapping in the morning breeze; William de Warenne, Hugh de Montford, Odo, Bishop of Bayeux, William's half brother, who with the lords of Normandy led the army that had come to conquer England. His breath caught in his throat. There must be ten thousand men here, Bretons, Mercenaries and Normans at the center, two thousand infantrymen, archers and crossbowmen. His eyes followed the massive Norman army across the valley. His eyes looked to the hill and there behind the shield wall fluttered the Dragon of Wessex and the fighting man, the banners of Godwinson. A tightly packed three thousand men stood in defiance of a giant.

I must join them, thought Eric. He turned to Midnight and gently stroked his muzzle. "This is where we must part," he said. "I can't get over there with you and

217

even if I could I won't have you die at the hands of those Norman butchers." He strapped his axe across his back, cut the girth, removed the saddle and bridle, and brushed him down once more. Then he kissed him as he might kiss a lover, his tears mingled with the sweat of his beloved horse as he turned and stole away in the direction of the Norman encampment. His eyes looked upward to the Saxon army that had begun to chant insults at William the Tanner of Normandy.

As Eric crept up behind the tents he thought, 'The sky is overcast; if only it will rain we'll all have some time'. Before him was the battle tableaux, Saxons and Normans about to fight a battle that would change England forever. Eric stopped outside the pavilion of Ivo de Ponthieu. He could hear the voices of several of the knights who appeared to be having a heated conversation. The language was perhaps Breton or French. Eric could not understand the words but he understood the hatred. One of the men, a big ugly brutish man who constantly spat and picked at his nose and other places, was ranting and raving and punctuating each word with a cut and thrust of his huge sword. Eric slipped past taking in a powerful whiff of sweat and garlic. 'These Normans dress in nice colors', he thought, 'but they don't wash much'.

As he looked across the Senlac Meadow, at the thousands of warriors that had come to take the crown from Harold Godwinson, he had a strong feeling of foreboding. 'After today', he thought, 'the world will not be the same, certainly England would not'. No matter which way the wind blew Eric decided that after today, if he lived, he would be a warrior no more. This would be his final battle, win or lose. He looked across the great expanse of the battlefield which was covered with Norman infantry and cavalry. They seemed to know their business well. Eric was winding his way close to the front line of William's army when suddenly he saw the Duke himself, and his brother Bishop Odo, who Eric knew to be his own age, a bishop at nineteen. They were sitting on horseback surveying the scene and he could hear William's voice being carried on the wind from his position behind the Pavilion.

"We outnumber them and we are better armed. Their only advantage is the high ground. Yet I still have this nagging feeling in my gut."

"That's good," said Odo. "One must never underestimate one's enemy, especially this one."

Eric looked at the men talking and the mile between him and his friends. I could kill them now, thought Eric, and there will be no battle. Before he realized what he was doing he raced out from behind the pavilion and covered the ground in four strides. He pulled his short stabbing sword from his belt as he leapt upon William. The Duke leaned forward as Eric leapt upwards toward him and hit him with a fist encased in chain mail.

As Eric landed hard on his back he heard Bishop Odo say, "Kill him," and William of Normandy say, "I shall personally kill any man who harms him. Take him to my quarters." Eric was pulled roughly from the ground and the Norman Duke looked into his eyes.

"A housecarl," he said, "One of Harold's fighting men. It takes a brave man to attack an enemy knowing that the outcome can only mean his death."

"Or a fool who does not know who he attacked," said Odo.

"He knew," said William. "I have looked into the eyes of many men who wished me dead."

As Eric struggled to get up E.J. Kissen put his hand on his shoulder. "It's alright, Eric. I think you must have been dreaming."

The blood from the wound above his eye blurred his vision. He saw E.J. turn and walk away as Midnight came thundering towards him all bloody and foam flecked. Only this time he didn't flinch or try to call his name. There was no need. The stallion scattered men and horses in every direction. The hands that held Eric released him. Knights scattered in every direction as Midnight reared before William and Odo. The wily bishop was thrown from his horse. William managed to keep himself in the saddle but his horse was on its hind quarters in the mud. Eric leapt on Midnight's back and they galloped through William's army which parted as before a storm. They broke through the front ranks and went racing up the slope towards Harold Godwinson and the Saxon army. Behind him Eric could hear the bowstrings of a thousand archers pulled back in unison.

"Wait!" screamed William as he rode along the line of his archers. His horse was covered in mud. His knight's helmet rested on his saddle so his men could see his face. "Put up your weapons and watch," he said.

Eric and Midnight approached the shield wall and a great cheer went up as the warriors parted the wall for Eric and Midnight. The wall closed immediately. They were inside.

"That," shouted William, "is how I want you to fight today. He came alone to kill me while I was surrounded by ten thousand men, then rode ahead of a thousand bowmen who could have killed him with the weight of their arrows alone so that he might fight and die with his King whose army we outnumber three to one. If there are even a hundred men like him who defend this little island, then this will not be a battle, it will be a war and I do not want a war. I want a decisive battle. Prepare to win or die because the men on that hill are no ordinary men. This is what they were born to. The prizes will be rich and all will receive their share even if it is only a small piece of English soil."

The sound of the housecarls' singing reached his ears. He turned in the saddle and looked at the tattooed warriors who sung:

"William came from France,
He'll learn to dance
A rare thing for a tanner.
We'll teach him steps
That he'll regret
When he falls beneath his banner.
The bastard lord
Who bears a sword
And thinks he has no match,
He'll change his tune
And very soon
When he faces Harold's axe."

There was a loud cheer and axes being beaten against shields. William shivered involuntarily and said to his men, "Ready yourselves, we're about to have a dancing lesson." With that he rode to his pavilion to have his squire help him with his armor and to prepare his plans for the battle.

Meanwhile, Eric stood before Wulfstan. The earl smiled at him, "You've come far from your village, Eric."

"Yes, my Lord, a journey I began with you."

"And will probably end with me," said Wulfstan.

"I didn't think I would get here in time."

"You probably wouldn't have but for Midnight," said Wulfstan.

Thorkill clapped Eric on the back. "You're like a malady that can't be cured. Even the Normans couldn't kill you."

Chapter Thirty Two

It was the fourteenth of October in the year 1066. Eric Shepard had been in his twentieth year for two days. Below where he stood were ten thousand Norman Knights; archers, lords, mercenaries and the Iron Duke who intended to rule Britain. How he had come to this place he could hardly remember. He was a farmer's son who fell under the spell of Harold Godwinson. He was still under it. In his mind Eric knew he would, like the three thousand housecarls he was a part of, die for Godwinson, but somewhere in the dark recesses of his mind he had a brother that was dying and he knew he was meant to save him. 'How do I get there from here', he thought.

Wulfstan came up behind him and laid his hand on his shoulder. "Rest," he said. "The battle won't begin for two hours. If it does, and you still sleep, I will wake you."

Eric turned and Anna smiled at him. "You're awake at last," she said. "I was so worried."

Eric wriggled and E.J. Kissen put the cap on his head while Stan adjusted the computer on his bed. "How's Terry?" clicked his computer.

"Much improved," said Anna. "It was nerve wracking for a while, but he seems to be improving slowly but surely. He is very antisocial and doesn't want to talk to anyone until he has talked to you."

"Well, can I talk to him?"

"Yes," said E.J. "We'll get you up there this afternoon. Let's get you some breakfast and a bath. Terry I'm sure will be doing the same. We'll take you to see Terry about two this afternoon."

"He doesn't know about Granddad," said Anna.

"Let me tell him," clicked the computer.

"Well, I don't know," said Anna. "I think that's a heavy responsibility."

"Let me tell him, please."

"Alright," said Anna. "I suppose you can explain it as well as I could."

"Mum, it's not an explanation. It's the conclusion of a life and man that we all loved."

Anna began to cry. "It was easier to talk to you before you could talk back."

"That's probably true of anyone," clicked the computer. "After breakfast I must see Terry. Will you take me up?"

"After two," said Anna.

"I'm impatient to see him."

"You're impatient period."

After Eric was fed and bathed, the morning passed slowly. Anna finally took him up to see his brother. When they went into the observation room both boys began chatting right away. Terry wrote on his computer and talked at the same time. Eric clicked out his responses.

"How are you?" said Terry.

"Fine," clicked Eric. "That's my question, too."

"I know," laughed Terry. "I'm much better. Your stem cells really worked."

"What are brothers for if not to share stem cells," clicked Eric.

"I'm grateful that you saved my life and glad that you're my brother."

"Me, too," said Eric. "Will you get home soon?"

"Doctor Mike said in a week, possibly two."

"That's great," clicked Eric. "When can we be in the same room?"

"In two days. I have a chest infection which is almost better thanks to you and antibiotics. I'm really beginning to feel like my old self."

"Oh, I hope not," clicked Eric. "I like your new self better."

Terry laughed and said, "Me, too."

"There is something I have to tell you."

"Good or bad?" said Terry.

"It isn't good or bad."

"Is it granddad?"

"Yes, how did you know?"

"I had a dream about him and he was young again. He looked like you."

"How can you tell what I look like? You can't tell from what you see in this chair."

"I could see you. You were, or rather he was a goalie."

"Well at least you know your soccer skill is genetic."

"He looked like you, Eric. It's true, honestly."

"I'll miss him," clicked Eric, "but I had a dream about him, too. In fact, I don't even know if it was a dream. He came to say goodbye to me."

"I wish I had treated him better," said Terry. "I wasn't very nice to him".

"No, you weren't, but at least you were consistent. You weren't very nice to anyone."

"I know, and I regret it. I am going to be a hundred times better when I get out of here."

"That's truer than you know," clicked Eric.

"What do you mean?"

"Let's talk after you talk to Stan Wolf. He can explain it to you."

"He's already tried," said Terry. "It's the secret society stuff, isn't it?"

"Yes, let him explain this time."

Mike Armstrong came in dressed in his space suit and said to Terry, "As long as you're discussing being a hundred times better let me confirm that you are. All your numbers have improved according to the blood work. The stem cell transplant is a hundred percent."

"What does that mean," said Terry.

"It means you have one hundred percent of your brother's bone marrow. It's all healthy. It also means you'll be leaving the hospital a little sooner. I will still want to see you twice a week, probably for the next few months at least. It seems we've cleared up that nasty little chest infection you had and your immune system is on the mend."

"How long before I go home?"

"A week, maybe ten days. Get rested, healthy, and then I'll decide."

Anna smiled and said, "Mike, thank you for everything. I'm sorry I've been so difficult at times."

"Hardly," he said and winked at Terry. "The patient," he said, "now he was difficult."

Terry just smiled and said to Eric, "A couple of weeks pal. Then I'll really get to know what's going on in that ever improving brain of yours."

Eric typed into his computer, "Maybe you could let Doctor Kissen and Sir Charles know as well because so far they just know how to play with the expensive donut machines."

"Alright, that's enough for today," said Anna. "Let's get you back home." Anna said goodbye to Terry through the window. Eric and Terry typed goodbye at the same time.

E.J. Kissen was in his office as Anna passed with Eric. "Hang on, Anna. Where are you taking him?"

226

"Home, of course."

"No, I don't think so. I'd like to keep him at least until Terry is ready to go home."

"Why?"

"I'd like to keep an eye on him. He's losing weight and we don't know why."

"Probably hospital food," clicked the computer.

"Oh, Eric, you're awake. I forget you are computer connected at all times."

"Not really," clicked the computer. "Sometimes there is just no use for it. If I have to stay can I be in the room with Terry? Even if I'm on the opposite side we can still talk."

"I'll talk to Mike," said E.J. "I don't see a problem. Anna, you can go home. Take a break. Both boys are on the mend."

'I'll be on the mend when I see the King', thought Eric.

"Will you be okay?" said Anna.

Eric typed, "Yes, Mom, come in tomorrow and you can watch the dueling computers." She kissed him goodnight and Nurse Scott came round from her desk and wheeled him back to the elevator.

Mike Armstrong met them on the tenth floor. "So you want to spend the night with the big brother. So here's what we'll do. You'll both be in a tent across from each other in the Laminar Air Flow Room. He's pretty much kicked the infection and you seem healthy, if a little leaner than usual. This way we'll all be able to keep both of you in our sights. Either Doctor Kissen or myself will be in to check on you every hour or so. Oh, by the way, I believe Stan will be visiting later. However, he'll be in the visitation room until I'm happy that Terry is completely over the infection."

"Will we be going home together?" asked Eric.

"Most likely," said Mike. "It will be strange not having the Shepard family running all over the hospital."

"Yes," clicked the computer. "It must drive you nuts when I'm running amok."

"You're a very funny guy, Mr. Shepard. Nurse Scott will get you into bed. Please don't resist."

"If I did, how would you know?"

"Good question, touché. Bed, please."

Eric was put to bed across the room from Terry. Both were encased in tents. Eric typed, "Who would have thought our first night camping together would be in an oncology ward ten stories above the earth." There was no response. 'Hmm, sleep', thought Eric, 'what a good idea'. He lay there wishing someone would take the stupid cap off his head and as if by magic Nurse Scott appeared in her space outfit and removed it and the computer.

Eric closed his eyes and somewhere outside he could hear banging. It sounded like a bass drum, but bigger like maybe there was more than one. He could hear the workmen shouting to each other, "Lift up, pull back now." Then he opened his eyes and heard the chant.

"Eadric the warrior
Followed his prince,
His lord, to the fight
Spear to the battle,
His fearless hearth band
Defends Athelred's Land."

The broken sounds of the Battle of Maldon a death chant carried on the wind. He stood up and Thorkill said, "Be calm, man, get up slowly. You will have to move fast soon enough."

228

Eric looked around him. The carls were beating their shields and chanting the epic poem of battle that had taken place almost seventy five years earlier at Maldon where all had died rather than pay the Viking raiders for peace. The carls chanted and moved in a slow rhythmic sway like some primeval animal preparing to kill or be killed. Eric took his place in the shield wall next to Thorkill and a young warrior called Bernoth.

"Just like the hero of Maldon," said Eric.

"We'll see," said the young man. "At the moment I feel like I will empty my bowels and my stomach at the same time."

"Just keep fighting," said Thorkill. "The smell will keep them away from you."

Just then Wulfstan came up behind Eric and Thorkill. "Come," he said. "We three stand with the King."

As Eric approached the King, Harold Godwinson turned and looked at him, "So you have returned. I was thinking of you but not blaming you. I would blame no man for avoiding this fight."

Eric looked at him and replied, "I have been your man since you gave me this coin all these years ago," he said as he lifted the coin he wore at his throat, "and if death comes today he will meet me before I let you die."

"Well spoken, Eric. I will be glad to have you at my side."

'That's the first time I remember him using my name', thought Eric, but his thoughts were shattered by the sound of thundering hooves.

William of Normandy had created a new kind of warfare; not two armies thrashing relentlessly at each other but a disciplined, organized attack sent in waves against a stationary enemy. The initial attack came not from the thundering knights, but from a thousand arrows raining from the sky. The archers retired and next came the men at arms harassing and attacking the shield wall. The young Bernoth fell as a Norman soldier slashed at his arm. Eric ran forward berserk with anger and cleft the Norman in the chest with his axe and cut off his sword arm with Bernoth's sword.

"Get up!" screamed Eric. "Hold the wall. The knights will be on us at any moment."

Just as he spoke two Bretons from the left flank of William's army crashed through the shield wall. Thorkill ran and jumped up on the horse's flank and beheaded one knight. The other cut back with his sword, wounding Thorkill in the side. Thorkill pulled the sword blade from the knight with his bare hands, knocked the knight from the horse and leapt on him, plunging the knight's own sword through his throat. Eric and Wulfstan ran to the breached shield wall to help the men close the gap.

As a housecarl got up dazed and holding his shield Eric screamed, "Close the door!" and the carl immediately got back into place in the shield wall.

He ripped part of the fallen knight's garment to wipe the blood from his eyes. "I can't see for the blood," he said, and Thorkill who stood beside him holding his own wound said, "That should teach you to duck the next time."

The man laughed a grim laugh and said, "If you had ducked you would have no head."

"True," said Thorkill. "Here they come again."

This time it was the men at arms, the infantry men who charged the shield wall but the Saxons repelled them with ease, the fyrd, the least trained of Godwinson's army drawn from the peasantry and farmers threw stones tied to wooden handles, javelins and lances and at such close range many of the Norman attackers fell. This first wave of attacks made it clear to William that the English would not go down without a fight. In fact, the first combined attack could only be called a failure and almost ended the battle there and then.

The fearful squeals of the terrified, dying horses all added to the mayhem of the battle. The Breton division which had been first to come to close combat with the English army got more of a fight than they expected. They were suddenly in a fight for their lives against heavy odds. They broke off fighting and turned tail and ran. There were knights, infantrymen, archers all running downhill as fast as their legs or horses could carry them. The English let out a resounding cheer. It looked like the enemy was on the run. The fyrd, unlike Harold's army, lacked discipline, not really warriors, more like conscripts. They could not contain themselves. They broke through the shield wall and gave chase cutting and gouging the enemy as they retreated in disarray.

William's two other divisions hesitated when they saw this. They pulled back in an orderly fashion in case the English army, deciding to follow the example of their comrades, attacked their now unprotected left flank. It looked like the battle might be over and Harold Godwinson would have a surprise victory in the palm of his hand. This might have been the case had it been anyone other than William of Normandy who commanded the enemy.

William reacted immediately and rode to block the retreat of his brother Odo's knights and those of his childhood friend, Roger de Mongomerie. The Bretons were already dispersed but he ordered the Norman and Flemish knights to cut off the return to the shield wall of Harold's fyrdmen. The knights wheeled behind them and rounded them up like sheep and butchered them.

Eric said, "We must help them."

The King looked at the massacre and said, "We can't help them. It's a trap they set for themselves. Would you have us all die down there?"

Eric closed his eyes and fell to his knees and vomited.

"This is war, Eric. Mistakes are rarely forgiven."

Godwinson climbed onto his horse and addressed his men. "Those men died because they lacked the discipline they needed to live. We must hold the line. If we do not we will die. If we give chase we will lie on yonder hill with the fyrd. We can and will hold the shield wall until they are spent. Then we will route them, otherwise we die here."

There was a brief respite as both armies and commanders repaired the damage each had caused the other, also to absorb the lesson of the first attack which almost ended in defeat for William but for his quick thinking and the carelessness of the English defenders. Eric sat with Thorkill and stitched his wound. There were many such repairs being done before the next attack

"Did you see those black faces?" said Thorkill.

"I did," said Eric.

"Those were the Breton brigands, not really fighting men, robbers. They call them Talebots from the Norman name for lamp black. They hide their faces to hide their identity. They fear being caught. That should tell you how they feel about dying."

Young Bernoth said, "The speed with which they outran their horses tells you how they feel about dying."

"Or perhaps how they feel about horses," said Eric.

They all laughed which brought a group of housecarls around them. The sound of raucous laughter amid battle had a calming effect on the warriors. One of the housecarls sat beside Thorkill.

"My father was a Talebot," he said.

"He was probably the one who crashed through the shield wall," said Eric.

"Aye," said Thorkill. "He left a message for you." He took the sword which gave him his most recent wound and gave it to the housecarl.

Everyone laughed, even Talebot. "He was someone I never knew," he said, "but the thought of him giving me a sword to leap into the void appeals to me. I'll take it."

"Good," said Thorkill. "Just make sure you use it before you leap into the void."

Again everyone laughed. "I'll use it to keep the fyrd on this side of the wall."

"Enough!" said Wulfstan. "To your places. This is not a feast for merriment." "The crows may think so," said Thorkill.

"Your places," Wulfstan said and pulled Thorkill to his feet. "Stand with the King, Eric." He turned to Bernoth, "You see that the dead and wounded are carried to the rear to be ministered to, or not, whichever is necessary."

He then looked at the tall housecarl who claimed that his father was Talebot.

"Your name?"

"Thor, Lord."

"Get the fyrd, what's left of them, to move the dead and dying enemy to the front of the shield wall."

"Dead and dying?"

"You heard me. There is nothing like the anguish of a dying friend to weaken a man's resolve."

"It hasn't weakened mine, Lord."

"You are a housecarl."

With that Wulfstan walked away leaving the men to their tasks. It must have been close to midday when Bernoth came back to stand by Thor who had just led his party in from the front of the shield wall.

"What's that?" he said.

There was a silent rumble as the earth moved beneath their feet. "Archers!" screamed Thor. The wind from a thousand arrows whistled across the sky and darkened it.

"Shields!" screamed Wulfstan and the shields came up as one. The arrows thundered down on Godwinson's army. Eric's shield covered himself and the King but still he was thrown to the earth as his tunic was pierced by an arrow that killed the carl behind him. He broke off the arrow and pulled himself to his feet. As he was about to roll the body away he looked on the face of Thorkill who had been shot cleanly through the heart. The old warrior had a grimace on his face that could, Eric supposed, be mistaken for a smile.

"He smiles in death," said Thor as he began to chant, "Maldon."

"It's a grimace of death," said Eric.

"As I said," replied Thor.

The infantry men marched forward between the archers as they turned and retreated to the rear. They began moving at a slow trot towards the shield wall while the cavalry moved restlessly behind them, horses pawing the earth nervously.

Thor stood in line next to Bernoth on the shield wall. The housecarls, even the fyrd, were chanting, "Maldon."

Eric and Wulfstan stood with the King with six of Harold's chosen men of Wallingford. The sound of the screaming, running infantrymen crashed against the shield wall. Thor and Bernoth were swinging axe and sword side by side when Thor screamed "Odin" so violently the forward surge of the infantry stopped and he ran berserk into the Norman foot soldiers cutting right and left with the sword Thorkill had given him. The Normans turned and ran and he gave chase, raging after them. Too late he realized that they were only in retreat, that the Norman knights and cavalry might do their work. He stood a hundred yards from his comrades, gigantic and bloody, singing with gusto.

Bernoth tried to leave the wall and join him but Eric and Wulfstan called at the same time, "Hold the line!"

Bernoth turned to Eric, "He will die alone."

"We all die alone," said Eric, "and this is the death he has chosen. Watch. He will not go quietly."

The Norman knights had begun their charge towards the shield wall as the infantry poured between them and began forming up behind them. The sound of thunder came galloping towards Thor. He stepped into the path of the knight he had chosen and the knight in turn lowered his lance for the kill. Time stopped, or at least slowed down as all eyes were on the singing warrior and the knight. As the lance was about to pierce Thor's chest he ran on to it, driving his sword before him. The shocked knight lifted his visor in time to see the blade of the sword before the screaming berserker drove it through his mouth. The force threw the knight from his horse and the Normans veered away from the terrifying sight of the massive housecarl impaled on the lance held by the sitting knight, the warrior's sword still in his hand as it had passed through the knight's mouth and out the back of his head. The knights thundered against the shield wall and Eric felt a thud in his chest.

Mike Armstrong was holding him and Doctor Kissen once more had the defibrillator. Eric's vital signs had stabilized but he was weak and unconscious.

"Mike, get Anna, Sir Charles and anyone else up here that can help us figure this out," he said.

The activity around the bed had awakened Terry. "What's happened?" he shouted.

"Calm down," said Mike. "Everything is under control."

"Well, as much as it can be," said a voice next to Terry's bed.

He turned slowly to look at the face of a tattooed youth about his own age covered in blood and dirt with an axe across his back and dressed like he was going to a Halloween party.

"Who are you?"

"I'm him," said Eric.

"What do you mean?"

"I'm Eric," said the youth as he placed his scarred hands on Terry's shoulders.

"No, you can't be," yelled Terry.

"Calm down," said Mike. "What are you shouting for?"

"Is Eric dead?"

"No, he is not, but for some reason he's becoming weaker. We are all doing what we can. You have to stop shouting. Your mother will be here soon."

"I'm sorry. I was dreaming, I think."

"Alright," said Mike. "Now that you're awake would you like something to drink to perhaps calm you down?"

"No, nothing, thanks. I feel fine."

"Good. I'll keep you posted on what's going on."

"Do you know what's going on?" said Terry.

"Not really," said Mike. "Sometimes the best you can do isn't good enough. We'll have to move Eric to intensive care. Nurse Scott will stay with you up here, Terry. You're on the mend, but it will require some effort from you, so don't let your imagination run away with you."

"What does that mean?"

"It means think," said Nurse Scott, "and I'm here to show you how."

"Thanks," said Terry. "Can you ask Stan Wolf to come and see me when he comes in, Mike?"

Mike Armstrong looked at Terry mildly surprised. "I'm glad we're on first name terms at last," he smiled.

"Oh, I never thought about it. I think there is enough between us to be on Christian name terms, don't you?"

"Yes I do. Stan is on his way."

With that Mike and E.J. Kissen left with Eric being pushed by E.J. and a nurse, the cumbersome bed screeching on the floor as they headed for the I.C.U.

Terry looked at Nurse Scott and said, "I'm stuck here in this room while my brother's life hangs in the balance. I feel trapped. I'm beginning to understand what it must feel like for him; like being in this room only worse and it's forever. I wonder why God sent him here like that."

"Perhaps it was to save you," said a voice from above.

Nurse Scott and Terry looked to the window where Stan Wolf was using the intercom system to full effect.

"Maybe, but I think it's cruel to take him back now that I've come to know him."

"Is it cruel to you, or to Eric?" said Stan.

"Both," said Terry.

"Do you know what has kept your brother going and fighting for most of his young life?"

"I haven't thought much about it," said Terry.

"Perhaps you should," said Stan. "I think this is part of a longer discussion we must have. I'm going down to see Eric and to find out when you and I might talk face to face."

"I think I'll be out in a week," said Terry.

"Alright," said Stan. "I'll be back to see you tomorrow, but in a week we'll talk about the more important questions you have. Oh, by the way, you said that now you understand how Eric felt, trapped in his body."

"Yes, I do in a way."

"If you knew you could never leave this room would you fight to live?"

"No! I don't know, really."

"He did in a space a thousand times smaller than this." Stan switched off the intercom, winked at Terry and headed downstairs.

Chapter Thirty Three

The I.C.U. was a hub of activity and strange smells. Eric opened his eyes thinking there's that feeling again. Sitting by his bed was his mother and Aunt Jennifer.

"I'm surprised to see you," said Anna.

"I'm surprised I came," replied Jennifer.

"They've taken his computer away," said Anna. "He's too weak to use it."

"It's probably for the best," said Jennifer.

"What is?" said Anna.

"Let him go peacefully."

"He isn't going anywhere," said Anna. "Why are you like this?"

"I work with children like Eric. It's pointless to get attached to them. They're unpredictable. What they know, what they understand, or how long they'll live, unpredictable."

"We are all unpredictable, Jennifer. What we know, what we understand or how long we live."

"You know what I mean."

"Yes, I do, but I can't believe you said it. Is that why you never married, because life is unpredictable? Go home, Jen. I can't have you here while Eric is ill."

"No, Eric is why I never married."

"Go home. I'm trying to be nice."

Jennifer got up and took one last look at Eric. "Don't," said Anna and Jennifer turned and left. The feeling of panic Eric felt left with her. "So that's why she doesn't like me. She thought she might have one of her own like me. I wonder if I'll ever see Edith again?"

Stan walked into Eric's room just as Jennifer was leaving. He said hello and she swept out towards the street as if she hadn't heard. "Anna, how are you holding up?"

"Fine, tired, stressed, frustrated, but fine. Thanks for asking."

"Eric, my boy, how are you?"

Eric was in his head. His body was frail, but in his mind he sat in a cavern awaiting the next twist or turn of destiny. Sir Charles Paul came in with E.J. Kissen and they checked Eric's vital signs.

"He is breathing normally, but his blood pressure and heart rate are up," said E.J. "I just don't understand it."

"He looks like he might have run a marathon with those numbers," said Sir Charles.

'Close', thought Stan and Eric heard him.

'I have to get out of here', Eric thought.

"I think I'm going to sedate him until we get control of his heart rate."

Anna stood beside E.J. and he carefully injected the sedative.

Eric's head twisted once and the Norman knight crashed through the shield-wall, his sword and face bloody. The heavily armored horse had knocked Bernoth to the ground. Trapped and broken beneath the powerful animal he drove his sword upward and eviscerated the horse. Its entrails spilled out as it collapsed on his body.

The knight rolled from the dying horse to his feet. His shield carried the insignia of Roger de Montgomerie, William's right hand man and friend from childhood, a crouching leopard ready to pounce. Gyrth, Harold's brother, leapt forward to engage him, but the knight was faster. He smashed Gyrth with his shield and cut upwards with his sword. Gyrth died without striking a blow.

240

Wulfstan attacked the Norman with his axe. The knight raised his shield and Wulfstan drove his short stabbing sword into his groin and beheaded him as his shield fell.

The Norman knights had struck deep into the English ranks. Harold's other brother, Leofwin, was struck by the lance of a Norman knight. As he fell he cut the knight's leg off from the knee. The knight, still on horse back, crashed through the shield wall and rode down the hill screaming. Leofwin stumbled to the shield wall and watched the Norman fall from his horse dying. He pushed himself away from the wall and looked once at his brother, the King, then sat down on the sticky earth and died.

Eric and Harold had been fighting back to back as this happened. When Harold turned and saw his brother sitting in death, and Bernoth crushed beneath the mighty Norman warhorse, he asked Eric to have them removed.

"A moment, Sire," said Wulfstan. "Listen." The sounds of chaos and yelling from the Normans had caught his attention.

"What are they saying?" said Harold.

"They are saying William is dead," said Eric.

He raced to the shield wall and the knights were milling around. The whole army looked like it was on the verge of running away. William was far from dead, but it looked like it was about to happen. He had joined the knights in attacking the shield wall and one of the housecarls, a surly scar faced man called Ulef, short stocky and powerful, not unlike William himself, had grabbed the Duke's horse by the bridle and literally thrown him off in front of the shield wall.

William and Ulef traded blow for blow as both sides watched, the Normans in panic and the English cheering on the fearless little housecarl. Ulef swung his axe against William's shield and lifted him off his feet and he rolled down the hill and lay still. There was silence as Ulef walked calmly back to the shield wall. Several of the Norman knights rode to surround the body of William. The Norman army began to surge backwards like a tree being felled. Suddenly William was up. He leapt onto the horse that had been brought to carry his body away. He removed his helmet and rode towards his army. He threw the helmet to one of his knights, Eustace of Boulogne. He rode along the line of his army yelling, blood running from a gash in his cheek He reached into the hearts of his men and pulled them back from the abyss of fear, and drew himself one step closer to the crown of England.

The afternoon wore on. Both sides became exhausted. The Normans kept up the barrage; the archers, then the men at arms and finally the knights. With each assault the knights breached the shield wall. Harold could only hope that his men would last until nightfall. William and Harold faced each other, both fighting a battle that was to be the blueprint for battlefield tactics for almost the next thousand years, from Agincourt to El Alamein. However, the man controlling the battle was William.

Harold knew he must hold the high ground or lose the battle and William used his archers and knights to soften up and wear down the English. William knew he must win before sunset so Harold would have no respite and no time to gather reinforcements. As his knights rode back from the shield wall, William went to speak to one of his oldest archers, a grisly old man of about fifty years of age named Ralph de Falconer.

"Master archer I have a question for you," he said.

"Yes, My Lord."

"Could you place an arrow in the center of the English army, clear of the shield wall?"

"I could, My Lord."

242

"Regarde!" shouted William and the word passed along the ranks of archers who awaited orders.

Thirteen thousand men watched as the lone archer took his place on the meadow. The silence was palpable as he knocked his arrow to his bow. It was almost like hearing his breath as he pulled the bow string taut and released the arrow. It whistled upwards and across Senlac Meadow and landed cleanly in the center of Harold's troops.

"Bastard!" screamed an English defender.

William looked at Ralph as he walked back across the meadow. He clapped him on the back and said, "A hit I think."

The army cheered and laughed even though they were close to exhaustion. William mounted his horse and rode along the line of his archers. "I want a thousand hits just like that one. Aim high. Archers forward."

A thousand men followed the example of Ralph de Faulkner and the sky above Godwinson's army turned black as death rained down on the last Saxon army to defend England.

As the Norman knights shattered the shield wall, Eric turned to Wulfstan who was pulling Harold to the rear. "Let him go and stand beside me," said Eric. Wulfstan had too many wounds to survive much longer. He was bleeding to death, but still trying to protect the King.

"My days of standing are over," said Wulfstan. "Protect the King, then God has other work for you." He then fell forward to his knees.

"Yes, Lad, let me go," said Harold.

"Nay, My Lord, that's not my meaning. I do not want the Normans to get you alone and I won't have us stabbed in the back. We'll die going forward, not backwards."

Eric looked once more at Wulfstan as he knelt by Harold. In death he appeared as in life, dedicated to the King. The tears were streaming down Eric's face as he watched Harold try to rise, an arrow protruding from his shoulder which he broke off. Eric pulled him up and stood with the King, swinging Grimm's axe in one hand and Wulfstan's sword in the other. Harold looked at Eric and laughed.

"God may have given the work to another," said Eric.

"When I chose you I chose better than the crown," said the King.

Eric and Harold Godwinson stood together, the King and the last of his housecarls cutting and stabbing as the Norman knights poured through the shield wall. As the knights wheeled, cutting left and right, there were about twenty fighting their way towards Godwinson.

Eric severed the jugular vein of the lead horse, decapitating the knight as he fell. Harold's left arm hung useless with an arrow embedded in his shoulder, but his right arm cut down two knights side by side. Eric swung Wulfstan's sword and cleft the helm of one knight and his short scramsaxe drove under the breast plate of another. They cut and thrust together like men working their craft. Eric was bloody and exhilarated. Suddenly Godwinson was down, a javelin in his chest.

Eric turned to look at the knights. There were four of them. The one he had seen in William's camp spitting and picking his nose, Ivo de Ponthieu. With him were Eustace of Boulogne and Odo of Bayeux, William's half brother, and one other, Clifford de Mountfort. Eric stood astride Harold's body, his axe in one hand, a sword in the other. Then he froze. As the flat of Ivo's blade came towards him he saw in its reflection a boy in a chair who drooled and jerked like his body was broken. Then the flat of the blade hit him and lifted him off his feet.

Eric tried to get to his feet but he had blood running into his eyes and a pounding headache. Through the bloody haze he saw Ivo, Odo, and Eustace hack at Harold as he tried to lift his axe. Ivo cut off Harold's head and proceeded to hack off his limbs. Eric threw himself at Ivo and fell between him and the King. Ivo raised his sword and a voice bellowed, "No more! Leave this place now."

As the bloodied knights turned to face the duke his brother, Odo, came forward. William struck him across the face and screamed, "Go now! You have shamed me in the eyes of God and England."

William rode across Senlac Meadow with tears streaming down his face. He entered his pavilion and lay prostrate before the cross and begged God's forgiveness. The four knights came to his quarters and he stepped outside to look at them. To Eustace he said, "Take men and cut off their retreat."

"Sire," replied Eustace, "it already grows dark. Pursuit will be impossible."

"Use the darkness to hide. For this day's work you will live in infamy. You are cowards and liars, swine who took greatness and shamed it and me."

"But, Sire," said Ivo.

"Why are you still here?" said William.

"I don't understand."

"I told you to leave this place."

"You wish me to leave the battlefield, Sire?"

"I wish you to leave England!" screamed William, "And do it now or you will die here."

The fourth knight stood in silence. "Mountfort," said William. "I had hopes for you. No more. Go with de Ponthieu. I have no need of men with the courage to butcher a dead King."

"But, Sire."

"Go. I saw what you did and will never look upon you as one of my men. If you are in England after tomorrow you are outlaws."

Eustace took his knights in pursuit of the English. Ivo de Ponthieu and Clifford de Mountfort left for Normandy in disgrace. Bishop Odo, his brother, stood alone, his nose bloody where William had struck him.

"Odo, my brother, like me a bastard, but you are a bastard without shame."

"We came to defeat him and we did," said Odo.

"Defeat him?" said William. "You took his defeat and turned it into a victory. Who will history remember, the Saxon King who stood his ground fighting till the end or the four butchers who stabbed and severed his limbs after he was dead? You are a bishop, a man of the church. Do you think God will watch such villainy and forgive it because you claim to be His man?"

"I will ask forgiveness for all of us."

"Not for me," he hissed. "Do not include me in your prayers for butchery."

"I ask that you forgive me, Brother."

"Never," said William. "I will not. Now go."

Odo bowed and left. William sat alone in his pavilion drinking wine and reflecting on the path that he had set himself. A commotion outside his tent brought Odo back in.

"Sire, Eustace is back. The English set a trap for them."

William got up and went outside. Standing in the torchlight was Eustace of Boulogne covered in mud or something similar. The smell implied something similar.

"They trapped us," said Eustace.

"They were running away," said William. "It looks more like you fell among pigs. How fitting. Go," said William, "the battle is over. I don't image you were pursued by Englishmen, or pigs for that matter. Leave England." He turned and went back inside his pavilion.

As the sun rose on October fifteenth the battle field came alive with carrion crows and people in search of loved ones that had not returned and the inevitable looters of the dead. An elderly monk led an entourage, a woman in a heavy wool cloak and two younger monks from the Monastery at Saint Albans. The woman was Edith, Godwinson's sister. She had come to identify the body of Harold. One of the young monks dismounted and the body closest to him moved. He screamed and jumped back.

The elder monk said, "Be still."

He turned the body over and Edith from her horse said, "I know him. He is a housecarl in the service of my brother."

"What lies beneath him?" said the monk.

Tears ran freely down her cheeks as she looked on the brutality that had been used on the body of her brother. "Bring them both," said Edith. "We may yet save him and the King must be buried before the Normans find him."

"This boy is the chosen of God," said the old monk. "He lay across the King with no armor and has only minor wounds."

"Let us get away from this place," said Edith. "Death and destruction leave no place here for God."

Eric awoke to the sound of the monks chanting. He opened his eyes and looked into the face of the old abbot. "Where am I?"

"St. Albans," replied the old man. Eric tried to get up. "Don't move just yet. It took three of the good sisters from the convent almost two hours to sew you up and clean your wounds."

"Is the Lady Edith still here?"

"She is and I am asked to inform her as soon as you are awake. You have been asleep for two days. Your wounds are beginning to heal, but I imagine feel a little stiff. Within the hour I will have one of the brothers come and help you bathe and dress. I know you are impatient, but it will not serve you. God has you here for a reason and rushing the questions will not get you the answers you seek."

"I know that, Father. I do not seek to find God. I merely await His pleasure knowing He will find me."

Later, when Eric had been bathed and his body treated with ointments, he sat in his cell in the Monastery of St. Albans and prayed. The door opened and Edith entered alone. He opened his eyes and said, "I was praying, Your Majesty, but I did not think I would have an answer so quickly."

She smiled fleetingly and said, "The King has been buried in a secret place. The Normans will take England quickly. We must decide what to do with you."

"I already know what I must do, Your Majesty."

"I am no longer a queen," said Edith.

"As I said once before, to me you will always be a queen."

"I am a nun in the service of our Lord God."

"That will change nothing that I have to say to you, My Lady."

"Then speak, Eric, for we must make plans."

"I have loved you since first I saw you. I'd hoped somehow to win you. God, I think has other plans for both of us. I intend to take holy orders. Before I do I wanted to say to you face to face that I will love you for all of my life, and though it will never again be as it was on that night so long ago, to have loved you once will carry me to the end of my days."

Edith stood with tears running down her face. "I have sometimes wished that I had been born in another time and place."

"Don't," said Eric. "Such wishes may be granted. It is enough to have known you. True love is a diamond polished by eternity. It need only touch us once."

Edith fell into his arms and he held her until her sobbing had calmed and she looked into his eyes and quickly left him. That was the last time he saw her and that look would haunt his dreams for the rest of his life.

Chapter Thirty Four

The rain had been lashing down non stop for twenty four hours. The old Abbot and another monk stood with a horse already saddled. Eric looked into the eyes of Midnight stunned.

"Where did you find him?"

"He found us. He followed us from Senlac Meadow."

"I thought he had surely died."

"Well, he certainly is old, but far from dead."

"He isn't that old, just battle scarred like me."

"I remember when last I saw you," said the Abbot. "You were running to or from something."

Eric smiled, "Yes, Father Abbot, it takes time to realize that there is no need to race towards destiny, or away from it."

"That's true, my son, but you must leave here now. You are the last of Harold's housecarls. Already the Norman conqueror searches for the body of Godwinson. By sunrise he will know who you are. The might of the Norman army will pursue you because it must. Godwinson is not dead as long as you live. You must go to Andechs in Bavaria. There you will stay with our brothers in the monastery, Benedictines of course, until such times as God reveals your true destiny."

"I think the truth is simpler than that, Father," said Eric as he swung into the saddle. "The Norman wishes to deny the shame of how Godwinson died on the bloody ridge above Senlac Meadow. That he can never do as long as I live."

"Wait," said the old man. "I have something for you." He scurried back inside the monastery and came out with a bag of coins, a package of food, and a sealed parchment.

"I have no need of money, Father. I am a rich man."

"Twice as rich as you were since we found you thanks to the Queen. However, your wealth is a day ahead of you in the care of ten of the most unlikely monks you will ever meet, four Scots, four Irishmen, an Englishman and their leader, Francis, who is Italian, also Benedictines of course."

"Heading where, may I ask?"

"Scotland. There is a ship that will take you, your treasure and your entourage to Norway, then to Bavaria and my friend Hartman. Again...."

Eric smiled, "A Benedictine, of course."

"Of course. The parchment is The Rule of St. Benedict. Keep it safe and dry. It will give you hope, strength and courage in a way you have never known and weapons that have nothing to do with death or war, and everything to do with peace, life and how to love both."

Eric reached down from the saddle. The coins and food he put in Midnight's saddle bags. The parchment he tucked away in the oil cloth beneath his cloak. As he rode out of the monastery he did not look back. He knew there was no part of his past he could take with him. He rode north ahead of William's army and behind the Benedictines who protected his acquired wealth. He rode through the night and caught up with the caravan and the monks at dawn the following day just outside of the town of Grimsby. The Benedictine in charge was a muscular fellow of about forty.

"You traveled fast, My Lord," he said.

"I'm not a lord, Father."

"Francis, Sire, my name is Brother Francis."

"I am Eric Shepard and we'll be Benedictine brothers before I am a lord."

"There are no wealthy Benedictines."

"There will be for it is my intention to make it so. We are close to Grimsby and I have friends there. It's a good place for us to stop and rest."

"I think we should push on," said Brother Francis.

"So do I. I did not think I would see this place again. It is where we will unload the cart. I wish to leave my wealth here in the care of Father Christian and pray over the grave of my brother."

"Alright, Eric Shepard, but the longer we stay here the greater the risk for you."

"After I pray we will all travel much lighter with God speed to Dunedin. I need an hour in prayer alone."

"So be it."

Eric rode into the village church alone. The heavy cart and the Benedictines he sent to the back door. The elderly priest was nowhere to be found. Eric moved through the small church which was cast in shadow. As he stepped into the shaft of sunlight that shone on Christ, he once more came to look into the eyes that would guide his life. A voice said, "I did not think we'd see you again." Grimm's axe was off his back and in his hand in a blur of movement.

The old priest stepped out of the shadows and Eric said, "For a moment I thought Christ had spoken."

"When he does, you will not need the axe. I imagine that is why you are here, to return it."

"No," said Eric. "I am here to leave my wealth with you and in times of need you will use it and when I have need of it you will send what I ask." With that he opened the back door and the Benedictines entered.

Brother Francis bowed and said, "We must hide it now."

"Below in the sarcophagus," said Father Christian.

Within the hour the cart was empty but for a few of the monks' belongings. "Keep the cart. We'll need horses," said Eric.

"There are eleven of you. I think we only have nine horses in the village."

"It will do," said Eric. "The two lightest men will ride together."

"No," said Brother Francis. "We can send half back to St. Albans."

"No one goes back," said Eric. "We leave wealth and secrets behind us. No man will be left for William to extract information from."

"We are men of God and true to our order and you, Sire," said Brother Francis.

"Then find the horses, pay respect to my axe brother's family and come back for me within the hour." As the monks swept out Eric said, "Father Christian, you will take them to Grimm's mother. Have them fed and see that she understands she will have money enough to support herself for as long as she lives."

"I will, my son." He placed his hands on Eric's and said, "You have a new path. God has touched you."

"I need a place to pray alone, Father."

"There is a small room behind the altar where I rest and pray. No one will find you there. I'll be back in an hour."

"Thank you, Father." As the priest was leaving he said, "It was my soul, He touched my soul."

"I have waited all of my life for Him to touch mine," said Father Christian. Then he left closing the doors behind him.

Eric took the parchment containing "The Rule of St. Benedict" and went into the room to read it. The vellum on which it was written was old and the script was colorful and beautifully done. The calligrapher had written with love and commitment. It began;

Listen carefully my son
to the Master's instructions
and attend to them with the ear of your heart.
This is advice from a father
who loves you.
Welcome it and faithfully put it
into practice.
The labor of obedience.
This message of mine is for all,
and armed with the strong
and noble weapons of obedience
to do battle for the true King,
Christ the Lord.

Eric held it tightly in his hand and said as he squeezed his eyes tightly shut, "God, I understand and accept the quest you have given me, but what about Terry?"

Stan Wolf turned to Anna and said, "What did you say?"

"Nothing, I said nothing."

Eric lay still with his vital signs a little below normal but he had been comatose for almost a week. Stan looked at Eric and said , "I thought I heard you ask about Terry." A voice in his head said, 'I did, but stay where you are. I must speak with him first'.

"Stan, are you okay?" said Anna. "You've turned grey."

"I'm fine, Anna, a little tired, but fine. We're all tired I think."

Terry was asleep and seemed to be dreaming. In his dream he was in a cavern and sitting across from him was a youth a little older than himself with his eyes closed; the youth he had dreamed of before.

"How are you?" said Eric as he opened his eyes.

"I'm fine," said Terry. "Where are we?"

"Oh, you're in my head."

"I'm dreaming then?"

"In a way. Do you know me?"

"Eric," said Terry. "You're my brother, but you look different. Is this a dream to tell me you're dying?"

"Not exactly," said Eric.

"You've been in a coma for a week," said Terry. "Will you come out of it?"

"No, I won't."

"You will die then."

"Not really," said Eric. "I'll live in my time and you'll live in yours."

"That's stupid," said Terry.

"Why so?" said Eric.

"What was the point of being born if you're just going to die?" Terry realized his face was wet. He wiped the tears from his face and said, "All that you became once we knew you were in here was just a waste of time."

"I'm not really in here and neither are you. I just wanted to see you and you to see me. Besides, I have something to give you."

"I don't want it," said Terry.

"I know you're sad, but there is good reason for my return to my time. I will begin something that you will continue."

"So you were born so that you could stay with us long enough to make us love you and then you just die."

"No, I was born so that I could live long enough to be with you at the time you needed me most. So you wouldn't die."

"I don't want to be left without you."

"I know. I felt the same way when I thought you might die, but I swear to you, you will not be alone."

"I won't have a brother or a grandfather, just an unhappy mother and a self centered aunt."

"You'll have Wulfstan."

"You mean Stan Wolf?"

"I do."

"Why do you call him Wulfstan?"

"That is who he was."

"Is he still alive in your other life?"

"No, he died at the Battle of Hastings."

"So he's dead in your time and alive in mine and you're dead in my time and alive in yours?"

"Not yet."

"Can't we change it so he lives then and you live now?"

"No."

"Why?"

"I'll tell you. I have work to do and it isn't here with you. It is in another time and you are beginning a similar journey now and Stan Wolf will be your teacher. The longer you are with him the more you will understand."

"Oh, you're back to that Rosicrucian love of goodness and God crap?"

"I understand your anger, but think. If my life can be fulfilling in another place and time would you not want that for me? Or, do you think a life here in a wheelchair in a body that does not function and a mind that does would be a better way for me to live, and if you do would you be willing to try it for even one day? Terry, I came for a reason, you. Your life will be important. You will influence the thinking of men in a positive way"

"You were a warrior and a cripple. I can understand why you would choose the warrior."

"I chose the warrior before I'd been to war. There is no man alive that has lived through a war that would consciously choose it. The same could be said of being a cripple, as you put it. No man that has experienced it would choose it. Harold Godwinson chose me and I chose you, and God, my little brother, has chosen us both."

"I don't want to be chosen."

"That has been said by a better man that you or I and you know how that ended."

"So you're saying I have no choice?"

"No, I'm saying you will eventually make the right choice. I came to say good-bye to you because we are part of the same soul and no matter how you feel now, or even in a year from now, your destiny awaits you, but it will not wait forever and if you decide not to face it, the decision will be made for you."

"What do you mean?"

"I mean if God sends you north and you go south you will find He can turn the world around."

"I think He's already done that."

"That's true, you live."

"Will I see you again?"

"I don't know, but I must go. I will think of you."

Both boys got up and moved towards each other as the walls began to shake and a voice said, "Wake up." Terry looked into the tearful face of Anna.

Eric looked into the face of Father Christian as he said, "The horses are ready. You must leave. The Normans are only a few hours behind you." Eric and the Benedictines rode out of Grimsby within ten minutes. Brother Francis sat behind Eric on Midnight and Midnight was not happy.

Outside the of town of Monkchester near the Roman wall, built to keep the Scots out of England, stood a boy by the crossroads. The monks reined in their mounts as he approached. His horse was standing untied and foam flecked.

"Lord," he said, "I come from Saint Albans. The Father Abbot bade me tell you the men that follow you are knights in the service of Bishop Odo. They are also monks like none we have ever seen in this country."

"They may attack Grimsby," said Eric.

"Nay, Lord," said the boy. "Look to my horse. They close the gap fast."

"How did you get ahead of them?"

"Shortcuts, Sire."

"Well, they must rest. We will push on through Monkchester to Lothian and the ship which awaits us on the Firth of Forth."

"They do not rest, Sire, nor do they speak. They stopped only at Grimsby to read the tracks from the exchange of the wagon to horses. They know eleven men ride ten horses. I think they know their advantage."

"They don't know mine," said Eric. "How many men pursue us?"

"Twelve, Lord."

"Paladins," said Eric. "William's best of the worst."

"What advantage do we have?" asked Francis

"The Scots," replied Eric. "Your name, boy?"

"Harold, Sire."

"A name fit for a king. Go west for thirty miles then turn south. So the Knights are Odo's men. They will know what you've done. Ride with all speed."

"God speed to you, Sire." He mounted his horse and rode west.

Angus, one of the Scottish Benedictines, spoke, "It's about a hundred miles along the coast, Brother. We'll be hard pressed."

"They wear armor and have had no rest," said Eric, "and we are still hours ahead of them."

"We could split up," said Brother Francis.

"No, we stay together. It will be a hard race but we will be on the sea before they reach us."

"Why do they wish to kill you?" asked Brother Francis. "Do they think that will change history?"

"No," said Eric. "Odo will do that anyway. History will record Hastings the way the Normans write it. The past is not what concerns him. It's the future. What he wants to kill is an idea that will live on after we are all dead, and that I cannot let happen. Ride, we must not be taken."

"I have cousins in Dunedin," Colin said. "They are not men of God. Perhaps we can have them delay our pursuers."

"Good, but make sure that is all they do. War and killing are behind us. What lies before us is an unfolding mystery." The horses raced through Monkchester and onto the coast road heading for Dunedin.

Terry looked at Anna and she said, "It's Eric. He's gone." Terry sat up and put his arms around his mother and they both wept.

Mike Armstrong, E.J. and Stan Wolf stood by Eric's bed like knights standing vigil. When Terry came to Eric's bedside he looked taller and stronger. He laid his hands on Eric's head and said, "He looks smaller, my little brother." He looked at Stan Wolf and said, "But we both know how big he really was, don't we? Now I'm ready for that talk whenever you are. Make it soon."

Chapter Thirty Five

Mike Armstrong and Stan Wolf walked into Terry's room. He was sitting by his bed reading. "Good morning," said Stan. "I thought we might begin our talk this week."

"I'd like that," said Terry. "I was thinking after the funeral."

Doctor Armstrong said, "All the tests are good. You can be discharged by tomorrow."

"Why not today?" said Terry.

"We could probably get you out by this afternoon."

E.J. came in and said, "Hi, Terry. I just wanted to let you know that the funeral arrangements have been made. The autopsy was done yesterday and the report said cardiac arrest. Eric apparently had an old heart for such a young man." Stan and Terry looked at each other but said nothing. E.J. went on oblivious, "His body was just very weak and grew weaker since the time he went into a comatose state. His body just shut down."

"Why the autopsy?" said Terry.

"It's the law," said E.J. "It's to make sure that it wasn't anything done while he was in the hospital that was responsible for his death."

"It seems pointless," said Terry. "It won't bring him back."

"No," said Mike, "it won't, but it's done. Now the law is satisfied and we can lay him to rest beside your grandfather."

"What's that you're reading?" said Stan. "It looks rather old."

"I'll talk to you about it later this week," said Terry. "It is very old. It was left to me by Eric."

The funeral, like all funerals, was a somber affair. The day was wet and windy. The casket seemed small and was very light. E.J., Mike, Stan and Terry were the pall bearers. As they laid Eric into the earth, Anna and Jennifer held the cords at each end of the coffin. The men each took one of the other four. Stan, by unanimous agreement, stood by the graveside as Eric's spiritual mentor.

"My friends and family, it seems Eric had a short life but I believe he accomplished more in his fourteen years than many people accomplish in a lifetime. He was a giant locked in a body that couldn't hold him. His spirit had a way of soaring free of the body that was his prison. There was a warrior in that body that somehow came to understand that the concept of good and God were one and the same, inseparable truth.

"He once said he understood why I was still a Catholic priest. I asked him his meaning. He said that while Rome and the popes down through the centuries were scheming and planning to increase their power and wealth, starting Crusades to retake Jerusalem and the wealth from both victim and victor, the Benedictines were copying manuscripts and trying to preserve knowledge and follow the concept of goodness and Godliness. Truth, he said, like God, has no shadow, and a true priest reflects that."

"It was a privilege to know him. I believe we all stand in his light. May he rest in the arms of God."

Terry signaled and they lowered the casket into the ground. After Eric's burial, Anna and the mourners gathered round to thank Stan, except for Jennifer who said, "I didn't understand the eulogy."

"No," said Stan, "I don't imagine you would, but I'm sure Eric was glad you were here."

"Eric is dead," she said.

"Yes," said Stan, "but not his spirit. It has just begun to live." Jennifer shook her head and walked away.

Terry shook Stan's hand and said, "Come over tomorrow. I want to hear what you have to say. Oh, and I think you should read this." He handed Stan the ancient Vellum wrapped in what seemed to be an oilskin.

"What is it?"

"The 'Rule of Saint Benedict,' maybe the original."

"Eric?" said Stan.

"Of course," said Terry. "I was in hospital, digging this up was the last thing on my mind. You're right, though, his spirit lives." Stan looked at him. "In another body, in another time. So you can understand I'm anxious to begin our discussion. My mother will be there because as I'm not eighteen for another six months, I'm sure she'll have something to say about our plans."

"There is no need for you to drop out of school," said Stan.

"Actually, there is no need for me to stay. I'm sure no aspect of my education will be ignored on the path I have chosen. What's more, I have no intention of ignoring it."

"The path you have chosen?"

"Yes, chosen. I'm not exactly sure what that means, but as both you and Eric know it to be the road I will take I'm interested in hearing of the journey as I believe you and I will travel together".

Epilogue
Twenty-Five Years Later

High in the mountains of Bavaria is the ancient and beautiful Monastery of Andechs. The Benedictines who once lived and prayed there are long gone. Sitting in the beautiful mountaintop restaurant alone at a table overlooking the Bavarian Alps is an austere, ascetic, looking man, healthy lean and suntanned with piercing blue eyes. He looks up from his menu as if on cue at the elderly gentleman who is approaching his table with the same silent style of walking he remembered from all those years ago. He stood up and smiled.

"Stan, it's good to see you."

"And you, Imperator," Stan replied.

"Well, now that we have that out of the way call me Terry like you always have," said the younger man. "I much prefer it."

"You are the head of one of the most powerful societies on earth. I think it merits respect."

"I am the man both you and my brother made me. I think that is what merits respect." They looked at each other in silence for a moment. Then Terry said quietly, "Has it escaped you that as head of the Catholic Church you lead the most powerful society on earth?"

They both smiled at this. "That may be what the world believes," said Stan, "but then that is why we exist, to change the world's beliefs."

"It seemed much easier when you first explained it to me," said Terry.

"Well, it was before you were Prime Minister. Running the country does increase the level of difficulty I suppose."

"That's not what increases the difficulty. It's being a politician. Telling the truth becomes an exercise in navigation."

"Not really," replied the Pope. "Telling lies is an exercise in navigation and that is unlikely to change."

"As usual, your wisdom charts my course" said Terry

Stan smiled. "When man realizes that truth and goodness have no compromise he will either embrace that fact, and in so doing contain and control evil or, as I'm sure you've seen many times by now, turn tail and run, to hide in the darkness of deceit and compromise until the darkness envelopes any spark of light within him."

Terry smiled and said, "And that, Holy Father, is why there are only eight of us to guide billions into the light."

A voice filled the momentary silence, "'Feed my sheep' said the Lord."

"Hector!" said Stan as he turned and saw Hector smiling down at them. "How nice to hear you speak the words the Lord gave to St. Peter in his moment of spiritual awakening."

"Thank you, Holy Father. I meant, Imperator, that dinner is about to be served. We are all here."

"Thanks, Hector" said Terry, "I appreciate your biblical 'double entendre'. What news of the Paladins?"

"Nothing since Dubai, Imperator," said Hector

"Darkness follows us like a shadow," said Terry.

"But not tonight," said Stan.

"Right," said Terry. "So let us go in and put the world back on its axis."

The End

Made in the USA
Charleston, SC
03 August 2012